CONTENTS

Chapter 1	7
Chapter 2	14
Chapter 3	21
Chapter 4	30
Chapter 5	35
Chapter 6	39
Chapter 7	44
Chapter 8	52
Chapter 9	56
Chapter 10	62
Chapter 11	67
Chapter 12	75
Chapter 13	81
Chapter 14	86
Chapter 15	92
Chapter 16	99
Chapter 17	108
Chapter 18	114
Chapter 19	119
Chapter 20	125
Chapter 21	133

Chapter 22	136
Chapter 23	142
Chapter 24	147
Chapter 25	154
Chapter 26	159
Chapter 27	170
Chapter 28	177
Chapter 29	183
Chapter 30	195
Chapter 31	202
Chapter 32	210
Chapter 33	216
Chapter 34	222
Chapter 35	227
Chapter 36	231
Chapter 37	238
Chapter 38	245
Chapter 39	249
Chapter 40	256

An Invitation for Revenge

By

A. P. Grozdanovic

A.P. Grozdanovic is the pseudonym of Ian Grozdanovic-Whittle. He lives in England with his wife. He has spent most of his life working in the public sector and is now semi-retired. He enjoys reading, writing, travelling and watching Bolton Wanderers.

His very occasional blog can be found at:
www.apgrozdanovic.com

Other titles by A. P. Grozdanovic
Going Home
Stalag Britain
An Invitation to Kill

Online praise for Going Home
'Great read. I thoroughly enjoyed this love story set in Dubrovnik. It was a well paced entertaining story with interesting characters.' J. P.

Online praise for Stalag Britain
'Stark and worrying book about the fictional effects on Britain's vote to leave the EU. Certainly, gave me things to think about.' J. O-P.

Online praise for An Invitation to Kill
'Fast paced and hard hitting! A gritty cat and mouse thriller penned with panache.' C. M.

This Edition
Text Copyright © 2024 Ian Grozdanovic-Whittle

This is a work of fiction. The characters and incidents are products of the authors imagination. Some places exist. Any resemblance to real persons (living or dead) or events is entirely coincidental.

For June, Gospava and Zinaid.
I miss you every day.

Also, for my wife Ranka, who gives me the time and space.

My thanks to
Ranka Grozdanovic-Whittle
&
Chris Martin
for their invaluable help.

An Invitation for Revenge

By

A. P. Grozdanovic

CHAPTER 1

'Come on!' Nick Mason tried to convince. 'We hardly know each other. This is supposed to be an opportunity for us to catch up. You know? Shoot the breeze, get to know each other.'

'There's nothing for me here,' Ashley, his sister admitted, taking a gulp of strong black coffee. She put the cup back on the bedside table. 'Nick, I'm an investigative reporter. I feed off stories, city life, not deck chairs and idyllic afternoon swims in the Adriatic.'

She stuffed the last of her clothes unceremoniously into the battered suitcase and clipped the latches into place.

Mason sat on the bed next to the case and looked up at his sister. The bright mid-morning light from the window shone on Ashley, her hair slightly shading her face. He held an old polaroid photograph of their mother his sister had given him when they first came out to Dubrovnik. Unlike Nick, his sister was very much like their mother in colouring, blonde and fair. He was dark like their father, William, the petty thief who had brought him up after their parents had separated.

'But I need to know about my mother, our mother. What was she like? What did she do? Did she ever talk about another child? Me?' Mason pleaded.

Ashley unplugged the cell phone from the wall socket, checked it was fully charged, and put the plug and lead into her large handbag, along with Misha Glenny's paperback, 'McMafia', his take on organised crime.

'What can I tell you?' she asked, checking the oversized cell screen for messages from the outside world. 'She was a regular mother. She kept fit; attended yoga classes right up until she was ill.' Her blue eyes glazed over at the memory of her late mother's final days, riven by cancer.

'When did she die?' Mason asked, suddenly feeling the chill from the house air con.

'Why do you want to know all this? It's rough water under the bridge. It's of no use to you now. Look, I'd rather not be the hammer that knocks the nail into that dense head of yours,' she tapped her temple with clenched knuckles, 'but you're forcing my hand. Your mother left you with a career criminal when you were a child. Now, why would you want to know anything about her?'

Mason got up from the bed and walked over to the open second-floor window of the Old Yacht Club that had been converted into a spacious waterfront dwelling. There was a slight, warm salty breeze drifting in from the sea that dissipated once the air-con killed it off. He leaned against the frame, watching the boats coming and going on the choppy waters of the Dubrovnik inlet.

In his grown-up mind he had always known his mother had wanted to take him with her, but in the low moments he searched for the answer as to why she had never come back to rescue him.

Abandoned at five…

'I just do,' he quietly declared with a sad air permeating his response. 'I'd like to know where I came from.'

'Well, since I've found out about my real father, I'd say that delving into one's family history is a vastly overrated pastime,' Ashley reported. 'I don't think I'll be enrolling in any of those ancestry websites. You never know who you might find!'

She picked the suitcase up off the bed, snapped the handle open, and started to wheel it towards the bedroom door.

Mason hurriedly blocked her progress. 'How can you say that? Don't you want to meet your father? Our father?'

His sister shrugged. 'Not particularly. Career criminals definitely interest me, but I prefer to keep them at a safe distance. Preferably in a prison cell.'

There was a momentary stand-off with Mason in the doorway blocking his sister from exiting the bedroom.

'Look, Nick! You're looking for something that I can't give you. I get it; you're lost. But like some sort of jigsaw, the pieces of your life have been thrown on the table and there are bits that have suddenly appeared that aren't on the cover picture.' She put her hand on his shoulder. 'I'm being honest, I can't tell you anything about mum that you don't already know. She was a normal loving mother. That's it! The only mystery that exists is in your head.'

Mason looked down at the floor. He knew he had to settle for the reality of the situation, which was that he was where he was, stuck in Dubrovnik on the Croatian coastline, miles from his English home and estranged from the only life he'd ever known. With a sister he never knew he had. Somehow, he had to get his head around it all.

Ashley gently lifted his chin and asked, 'Now do I get that lift to the airport or do I call an Uber?'

'Come on!' he relented, 'Give me your case. I'll get the car keys.'

Mason carried the case down the staircase and slid it into the boot of the car. He slipped his sunglasses down from the top of his head to shade his eyes from the glaring sun. After Ashley had checked around the house for any stray possessions, and realised there were none, they set out for the airport.

Once they had joined the Magistrala, the Adriatic highway that traces the coast down through Croatia, Bosnia & Herzegovina and Montenegro, the traffic thinned out and Nick began to enjoy the beautiful views the road afforded.

As they passed the vantage point where all the picture-postcards of the Old Town are taken, he asked Ashley, 'Why would you want to leave this place?'

Ashley was peering down at her cell, unaware of the beautiful Dalmatian coastline. 'What?' she asked with little interest.

Nick pulled the car into a layby on the coastal side of the road and parked up.

He half turned towards Ashley.

'Am I missing something here?' Nick pleaded. 'A matter of months ago we were lucky to leave England still breathing.'

Ashley looked up from her phone. 'That's all done and dusted. Finished!'

'Aren't you bothered about Tom Lester at all?'

'Nick he's in jail on remand. He's going to be in jail for a very long time. Drug running, killings, tax evasion. You name it! By the time he's up for parole, they'll have forgotten where they left the keys. Why would I be bothered about him? He's a has-been.' She paused for a moment. 'My advice to you would be to get on with your life and forget about Tom Lester.'

'Put that phone down for a minute, please!' he appealed. Ashley reluctantly killed the phone screen and dropped it into her handbag.

'Tom Lester has a whole army of people that will do his bidding. Don't you remember? He sent his henchman, Kosinski to kill us both. If you think he's going to just forget about what we did, you're living on Planet La-La or somewhere like it.'

'Nick, he thinks we're dead. Bevan promised us he'd tell Lester that Kosinski killed us. He probably hasn't given us a moment's thought since. You're bigging-up the danger posed by Lester. I'm telling you; he's finished!'

'You know as well as I do, these people just don't go away. He has plenty of men just like Kosinski and Bevan still on the payroll.'

'No, I don't! And neither do you. You're letting your imagination run away with you. This isn't some second rate television thriller, Nick. This is real life. I promise you; Lester's influence reaches no further than his very bleak cell wall.'

'For someone who writes about crime you're pretty naïve.' Nick grabbed his cigarettes and lighter and stepped out of the car and immediately felt the morning heat after the vehicle's cool air con. He stood between the vehicle and the safety barrier looking at the ocean. There was a sheer drop beyond the barrier. Having no head for heights, he took a step back. Since he had been in Dubrovnik, he had never tired of seeing the clear waters off the Croatian coast. The water was choppy today, and a slight swell foamed on the shore below.

He lit a cigarette and took a deep drag.

Ashley joined him. 'I think you'll be alright, Nick,' she chivvied. 'You're safe here. Lester's reputation will be shot with all his associates, I'm sure. But if he still has any influence, I'm positive he isn't looking for us. He'll have more pressing matters to engage his brain.'

Nick didn't respond, he just took another deep drag from his cigarette. For a moment, the nicotine cloud lay low in his stomach, then seeped out into his veins and once it reached his brain, he liked it.

'Come on, Nick. Deep down you know I'm right.'

He turned to her. 'You may be right about Lester. But I still think you should hang around here a little longer. I need you,' he begged. 'You're the only person I have in the world.'

'Come on! I always thought you must have had a girlfriend at home waiting for the right moment to come out. Someone special in your life?'

'No.'

'What about your father? You've got him.'

'I'm not sure you've grasped the situation here, Ashley. His two children have run off to another country and left him and everything else behind. It's like being in Witness Protection but without the security! How can I go back to him without alerting Lester's gangsters?'

'Mmm,' she mused. 'Point taken.'

'Thank you for conceding,' he mocked. 'Look, you're the only person I've got.'

'Nick, I'm going and that's final. But listen! I've set up a new email. It's untraceable, at least to anyone looking for us. I'll write it down for you. Memorise it, destroy the paper, and contact me via that. I'll always be on the other end.'

'Wait! How will you know it's me?'

'Easy. You'll be the only one who knows the address. Just remember! Set up a new email and use a burner phone to confirm authenticity. Never use it for anything else and avoid using the same location when signing in. Try and use public computer terminals where you can. No names. No questions. No location. The more information you put in, the more traceable we will be.'

Mason turned fully towards her. 'What happens if I need you to come quick?'

'I won't be coming,' she declared. 'No point putting us both in danger.'

He flicked what remained of the cigarette on the floor and stepped on it. Just before opening the car door, he turned and said, 'Glad to know we're in this together!'

They drove in silence the rest of the way to the airport. Once at the terminal drop-off point, Mason got out and lifted Ashley's suitcase out of the boot, snapped the handle open and passed it to her.

She gave him a piece of folded paper. 'This is my email.'

'It says Julianne Winter. Who's that?'

'Just a cover name for me. Use it sparingly.' She lifted on to her toes and gave him a brief hug. 'Now! Don't get yourself into any trouble when I'm gone.'

'I won't,' he promised.

Mason watched his sister disappear into the airport terminal. Wherever she ends up, Nick thought, she'll never find the sunny weather she was leaving behind. Once the automatic doors had closed behind her, he turned away, got back in his car, and headed back towards Dubrovnik.

Before returning home, he called at the supermarket in Gruž adjacent to where the cruise ships dock. He threw two basic burner cell phones into a basket. He also chucked two sim cards in. Mason then filled the basket with groceries and a pack of four Karlovačko, a local beer. He then drove around the inlet to the Old Yacht Club. Once he'd packed the groceries away, he cracked open a bottle of beer, collected his cigarettes and lighter and then sat at the table in front of the house.

It wasn't quite noon, and he was drinking alcohol. He'd never have done this in England. But there was something timeless about being on the coast in the sun. It relaxes you and the time of day seems irrelevant. Mason lit a cigarette and thanked all the gods everyone else believed in, that he was here, safe and in the most beautiful place on earth.

CHAPTER 2

Two months after Ashley had left Dubrovnik, Mason crossed the Franjo Tuđman suspension bridge and stopped at a red light. Once on green, he'd leave the Magistrala and head down the steep road that would lead him around and past the Cruise terminal. He would then travel through Gruž and on around the inlet back towards Babin Kuk and the Old Yacht Club. A ten-minute journey at most.

He glanced down at the black Messenger bag on the seat next to him. It was zipped closed. Two letters in gold stood out, ZK. They were the initials for Željko Kovačić and they had acted as a passport, getting him over the border from Croatia into Bosnia and back again.

Mason had met Željko at the latter's restaurant when he and Ashley had gone out for the occasional meal. After his sister had left Dubrovnik, Željko had proved to be a good friend. Being the owner and host in his own restaurant, Željko ruled over all he surveyed from a table at the rear of the restaurant. From morning until night, he would sit at his small table welcoming guests, fixing problems, doing deals, entertaining.

The week after Ashley left, Željko had noticed that Mason was sat alone in the open fronted window looking over the new harbour. He invited Mason for a drink at his table. Željko took the cork from a bottle of Plavac, the local red wine, and poured two generous glasses.

'So, how are you doing, Mr. Mason?' Željko asked with genuine concern in strongly accented English. 'I believe your sister has left Dubrovnik.'

Mason wondered how Željko knew that Ashley had left. He

hadn't told anyone.

'Please, call me, Nick.'

'Okay, Nick,' Željko agreed, sweeping his hand through a generous mane of greying hair.

Mason hadn't really thought through what he would say to anyone if they enquired about Ashley's whereabouts. He had assumed that the two of them would be irrelevant to the locals. He went for a simple explanation. 'She had some work to do elsewhere.'

Željko lifted his glass and said, 'Well, here's to absent friends.' The drink just about touched his lips before he returned the glass to the table. 'But may I ask, what kind of work could possibly take her away from our beautiful city?'

Mason looked over his glass at Željko. His host was being very inquisitive. He wasn't about to tell Željko his life story, or Ashley's for that matter. He simply answered, 'She's a writer.'

'A writer?' The words burst out of Željko's mouth a little louder than he might have intended. The couple sitting at the table next to them looked over wondering what was happening. Mason displayed an embarrassed toothy grin towards them. 'What in this crazy world could entice a writer away from our wonderful country, our clear Adriatic waters?'

'She likes to travel,' Mason answered lamely. 'She gets ants in her pants.'

'Not like you then, Nick?'

'No. I'm very happy here,' Mason admitted. 'It's beautiful.'

'I can't disagree, my friend. It's like the Gods have looked down on the people of Dubrovnik, in fact the whole Dalmatian Coast, and blessed them with their own Garden of Eden, with an unabashed dash of Utopia thrown in.' Željko's smile stretched wide across his face, revealing a perfect set of white teeth.

'I'll drink to that,' Mason said and lifted his glass in salute, before taking a drink.

'And how are you spending your time here, Nick? I hope you are taking advantage of the beautiful beaches?'

'I have on occasion. Although I'm not a natural sunbather.'

Željko raised his hand and called the waiter over from the bar, 'Petar, can you arrange for some food, please?'

The young, closely cropped blonde haired, barman said, 'Of course,' before turning away and heading towards the kitchen at the back.

'So, is this a holiday, or are you staying for good? My friend, Luka, says you are a good man and have special skills.'

A couple of days earlier, Luka, the local sea-taxi owner, had invited him around for dinner at his home. His wife, Manuela, had put on a decent spread of food while Luka plied him with alcohol. The wine had flowed freely that night, and Mason had been a little loose with his tongue. With all the alcohol inside him he was sure the only thing he'd said about Ashely was that she'd left to do some work. He now regretted telling Luka about his own past. He decided to play along with Željko to see where the conversation was heading.

'And what would those skills be?'

'Come, come, Nick. We're all friends here in our little town. There are no secrets. We look after each other. Help our neighbours when we can.' Mason knew the proverbial link to family was about to come, and sure enough... 'Nick, we're one big happy family here in Dubrovnik.'

Fortunately, before Željko could continue with his 'all for one and one for all' outlook on life, Petar returned to the table with a platter of meats, cheese and salad. He held a basket of bread in his other hand. He placed all the food and plates in the middle of the table.

'Thank you, Petar,' Željko said. He picked the bottle of wine up and emptied its contents into the two glasses, mostly in Mason's. 'Now before you go back to your other duties, could we have a fresh bottle of wine? This Plavac is exquisite.'

'Of course, I'll be back shortly.' He removed the empty bottle and returned to the bar to get the wine.

'I hope you like our food, Nick?'

'I do.'

'Then please,' Željko opened his palm towards the food, 'be my guest.'

Mason picked a small selection of cured meats and cheese from the platter and began to eat.

Željko lit a cigarette. Mason was tempted to light one himself, but decided he'd eat first.

Petar returned with an uncorked bottle of wine and placed it at his boss's side. Mason saw through the mirror on the wall behind Željko that the young barman then gravitated towards a table where two beautiful young girls sat. One dark, one blonde. Mason guessed that Petar was well-accustomed to ingratiating himself to diners of the opposite sex.

Željko inhaled the smoke deeply, tilted his head back a little and then blew the smoke away from Mason's direction.

'Let's get back to your skills, Nick.'

Mason stopped in mid-bite of the cheese. His stomach turned a little now that Željko was starting to push.

Mason dropped the remainder of his cheese on the plate and wiped his mouth with a napkin. He took a drink from the glass, picked Željko's cigarette pack up and popped one out. He put the cigarette in his mouth as Željko proffered an ignited lighter. Mason leant in and took a deep drag.

'Why do my skills interest you so much?' Mason asked, blowing out a plume of smoke.

Željko flicked ash into the ashtray and smiled.

'I have many people on my payroll, Nick. They all have different talents.' He took a deep drag from his cigarette. The lighted end glowed like a fireball heading in Mason's direction. 'To be honest, I have many different businesses. Some legal, like the restaurant here, and some not so. It's very interesting to have your hands in many different pies, as you Brits like to say. But I must be honest with you, it gives my accountants sleepless nights.'

'And you?' Mason asked flicking some ash into the ashtray.

Željko laughed and answered, 'Me? I sleep like a baby.'

Mason took a drink and asked, 'What do you have in mind, Željko?' He nibbled on a piece of cheese while he waited for his host to answer.

Željko took a sip of wine, the first discernible drink Mason noticed he'd taken. Previously, it appeared he'd just put the glass to his lips.

After giving his answer some thought, the Croat said, 'Nick, I run a small travel firm that takes people from Dubrovnik over the border into Bosnia. Tourists like to visit the beautiful city of Sarajevo and the famous bridge at Mostar. I simply provide that opportunity.'

Mason took a drag from his cigarette and then extinguished it in the ashtray. He immediately lit another, this time from his own pack.

'At a reasonable price, I take it?'

Željko smiled. 'Of course. I provide the best cars for people to travel in and drivers who can get them there safely. I also arrange accommodation in the centre of the city, and tour guides if they wish.'

'This all sounds very good, but where do I come in?'

Željko surveyed the restaurant before answering, careful to make sure he wasn't being overheard.

'Nick, the err, what do you call them? One moment, it will come to me.' He struggled to find the right English word and then like a flash of inspiration, it seemed to swirl down from the ceiling fan that he was looking at, 'Punters! That's it. Yes, the punters need a driver, and I believe from our friend, Luka, you used to be a driver with a special talent. Is this true?'

So, Mason's old life had come back to haunt him. He had hoped that coming here to the Adriatic coast would have helped him put all that behind him. The bank robberies, the drop-offs, the killings. His old life was now front and centre. Was Željko Kovačić Dubrovnik's very own Tom Lester?

Mason decided it would be better to be straight with Željko. He could see underneath that favourite uncle look that Željko projected to his customers, there was steel behind those eyes.

'In a past life I did drive, and for some dubious characters, but I've put all that behind me. I decided jail isn't the place for me.'

His host laughed, 'Who's talking about jail? No, Nick. I'm offering occasional work taking customers to historic cities across the border.'

Mason thought for a moment. He picked a shred of tobacco from his tongue and flicked it to the floor. He turned and beckoned Petar over to their table. The barman didn't look happy as he had been deeply ensconced in smoozing the two girls that had come in earlier.

'Yes, sir?'

'I'd like two large Remy Martin's, please. And put them on my bill.'

Željko interrupted, 'But, Nick, you are my guest.'

'But still! On my bill, please.'

'Yes, sir.' Petar retreated to get the drinks.

Mason leaned forward. 'I'm not a taxi driver, Željko. Neither am I a tour guide. People who hire me, pay for work that's beyond, let's say, lawful. By coming here, I'd hoped to have put that part of my life behind me.'

Petar returned and placed the drinks on the table, then scuttled off to the girls at the other table. Mason couldn't knock him for effort.

'Nick, I will admit to you that this isn't strictly legitimate. That's why I need someone with your talent, your abilities.' Željko stubbed his cigarette out. 'I recently lost a driver. It's a long story, but it's enough to say that the Sarajevo police chief won't let him back into the city.'

'And why is that?' Mason asked taking a drink from the brandy glass. 'If he's stopping your drivers working there, wouldn't I be exposed to the same problems?'

'Are you planning on getting the mayor's seventeen years-old daughter pregnant?'

'I see. No. I think we can rule that one out.'

Željko looked around before he began to speak again, checking no one was listening. 'Good. Now, as I was saying, I've lost a driver. That driver, along with his tour guide duties, would deliver a quantity of cocaine for me to a contact in the Baščaršija, that's the local market in central Sarajevo. You'll love it there. Apart from delivering the tourists and the drugs, there's nothing to do except enjoy yourself.'

Mason lit a fresh cigarette. 'And where are the drugs?'

'Secreted in the car,' Željko revealed. 'Don't worry. If you looked, you'd never find them.'

'And what about Customs?'

Željko took a drink of brandy and confirmed, 'Everything in that respect is sorted.'

And it had been. Mason had transported the cocaine over the border into Bosnia on several occasions since. It was simple work. He'd collect a car, the bag, and the tourists from the restaurant. The bag with Željko's initials contained documents in Croatian explaining the reason for his journey. That Messenger bag was his passport. Once the border guards saw it, they would wave him and his tourist passengers through. From there, he would either go to Mostar or Sarajevo. He'd spend the night in a designated hotel, leaving the car in the car park. He would return the following day, presumably without the drugs. He'd never made such easy money.

Now pulling away from the stop sign, he considered his new life. He'd somehow fallen back into crime but at limited liability to himself. Everyone he encountered on his trips were on Željko's payroll, which meant everything was safe, if not exactly above board.

He'd drop the car off and head back to the Old Yacht Club for a quiet evening with a bottle of wine knowing that, while his life wasn't squeaky clean, there was nothing that could spoil it for him now. His old life was over and in the past.

CHAPTER 3

Mason dragged himself out of bed and sleepily pulled his running gear on. He'd had little too much Badel, the local brandy, the previous night. Whilst this wasn't a regular occurrence, after Ashley had left, he had consumed more alcohol than he was accustomed to. He hadn't been a heavy drinker back in England. In his line of work, a driver for all occasions, it was inadvisable to be *half-cut* behind the wheel of a getaway car. But he had to admit that there was a strange attraction to Željko's restaurant on the harbour road towards Dubrovnik's Old Town.

He stepped out of the front door of the Old Yacht Club. Outside it was warm, in contrast to the air-con cooled house. The cloudless sky was a calming light blue. The sea lapped up onto the low shoreline, wetting parts of the old stone pathway that meandered down and around the inlet. Across the water he could see cars crossing the imposing Franjo Tuđman suspension bridge, named after the first President of modern-day Croatia, high above the water.

Although at home he had always run in the morning, here it was a necessity, as the temperatures rose far too high to run later in the day. Early morning or dusk were the best times for exercise, but as he was usually having his evening meal around dusk, morning it had to be.

Boats came and went as he shook the night's inertia from his body. Slowly his muscles began to relax. He put his headphones on via his cell phone and kick-started a running mix on Spotify. Music filled his ears. Gingerly, he began running along the coastal path in a south easterly direction towards the marina. The path hugged the coastline with occasional houses and restaurants to his right, and the choppy waters of the Adriatic to the left. Boats bobbed up and down as the tidal waters fluctuated. Trees and plant-life sprouted up haphazardly from the arid ground. He felt the salt in the breeze fill his lungs as he breathed heavily with every step.

As the sweat began to darken his shirt, his body and breathing gradually adjusted to the rhythm of his stride. Slowly, but surely, he was starting to feel more like himself.

Within minutes, he'd reached the new marina where larger pleasure craft were docked. Mason didn't like it, just as he detested the influx of Cruise Ships that brought thousands of tourists stomping around the Old Town daily. To Mason this construction blighted the quaint façade of an inlet that must have been unchanged for generations.

He passed Željko's restaurant but saw no one around when he glanced over.

As he reached the outside gym concession on a corner of the inlet, he stopped and began stretching his limbs, releasing his calves and hamstrings from their tightness. The endorphins had begun to release in his body and the feeling of calmness permeated his muscles.

There was no one else using the apparatus so he decided to sit and take a breather. He wiped the sweat from his forehead with the back of his hand. The tranquillity of the scene, the marina full of bobbing boats, the clear Adriatic water, the blue sky, always helped his frame of mind. The terror of the weeks leading up to his escape from the clutches of Tom Lester had taken their toll. He had been at his wits-end when he had found that the very person he had been hired to kill by Tom Lester, was non-other than his own sister, Ashley. Some six months later, with this new life in the sun, he was starting to relax.

Rather than continuing his run to Gruž Market on the other side of the inlet, he decided to walk back to the house for a drink.

Once back, he brought a glass of fresh lemonade out to the front of the house. He set it down on the small circular garden table and sat on a weather-beaten plastic chair looking out towards the harbour. He lit a cigarette and sank back into the chair as the first drag of the day reached his lungs.

The harbour before him was dominated by the Franjo Tuđman Bridge. Small, tethered fishing boats rose and dipped as the water lapped up onto the shore. The sun was rising in the sky and the thermometer had read an impressive twenty-eight degrees. In another hour or so Mason guessed it would be in the crushing late thirties. He had read that the Croatian city didn't normally get this warm. Global warming, or climate change, had certainly met Dubrovnik.

He took a cold gulp of the fresh lemon drink, replaced the glass on the table, and squinted up into the bright blue sky. If he'd consulted a doctor, Mason was certain a rest like this would have been prescribed. He wiped his sunglasses with a handkerchief and placed them across his nose, dimming the bright sun.

As he flicked ash into the ashtray, he spied Luka's small taxi-boat coming towards him. Luka was normally out most summer days, criss-crossing the harbour with foreign tourists and their deep wallets.

Today was a day for the cruise ships. Mason had seen two moored while out on his run. From where he was, they were just out of sight to his right. The blight of historic coastline cities the world over, Mason condemned to himself. He had ventured into the Old Town, some four kilometres away, only once when the ships had been in town. The crowds trampled the old limestone paving stones with impunity. The cafés and restaurants were overrun to the point where getting a table was nigh-on impossible. Good for business. Bad for the environment.

He could now hear the boat's engine chugging as it neared. Mason could see Luka had a paying guest sat behind him.

Mason took another sip of the lemonade, this time swishing the fresh liquid around his mouth, killing the tobacco taste, before swallowing.

Luka sounded the boats tinny horn and waved at Mason. This was his polite way of asking Mason to catch the dock line and tether it to the shore. Mason had helped many times before, not that his friend needed him to. He stood and watched the boat come closer, its engine now idling and the whiff of burning engine oil being carried on the sea air. Luka left the wheel and made his way to the bow. He collected the dock line up and, without dropping any ash from the cigarette drooping from the corner of his mouth, threw it to Mason. Returning to the wheel Luka guided the boat alongside the jetty. Untying his neckerchief expertly with one hand, he wiped his forehead and under his bristling chin, then stuffed it into his jeans pocket.

Mason had grabbed the line immediately and pulled it in, tying it to the wooden jetty in front of the Old Yacht Club. He looked up to speak, to welcome Luka back, but before he could say anything he noticed a familiar face, one he thought he'd never see again.

Bevan, one of Tom Lester's right-hand men sat behind Luka. It was Bevan who had helped Mason and Ashley escape when Lester had ordered their killing.

Luka's passenger rose to his feet in light blue trousers, dark blue deck shoes and a white-linen shirt open at the neck, and called out, 'Nick, how are you?' He staggered unsurely along the short deck while Luka jumped onto the jetty, tethering the stern line up.

'Bevan! What the hell are you doing here?' Mason could not hide his surprise.

Bevan, some 6'2" in height and in his mid-fifties, disembarked gingerly onto the jetty and shook Nick's hand.

'Well, that's a nice welcome?' Bevan said sarcastically. 'Hi to you too! How about a cool drink? This heat's killing me!' He had an overnight bag slung over his right shoulder and a tailored jacket over his left arm.

'Yeah, sure. Err,' Nick hesitated. 'Just a minute.' He joined Luka and asked, 'Anything I can help you with, mate?'

Luka, who had by now killed the engine and was tidying the boats deck up, replied in accented English, 'No, everything is good, Nick.'

'Okay. I might see you later.' Mason gave Luka a wave goodbye as he turned away towards Bevan. 'There's a café on Copacabana Beach. It's just a short walk up the coast. We can have a drink there.'

Bevan turned towards Luka and called out, 'Ciao, my friend.' Luka ignored him.

Mason stowed Bevan's bag and jacket in the house, locked his front door and led his guest the short distance, northwards, up the coast. The path meandered up and down through trees hugging the coastline. Below the path, little pockets of pebble beaches were occupied by sun worshippers seeking more privacy than the main areas afforded.

Within a few minutes the path opened, and Copacabana Beach lay to their right. The beach-side café was sparsely populated, and they selected a wicker-framed, glass-topped table furthest from the other patrons. The white pebbled beach was heavily populated with holidaymakers.

A waiter arrived almost immediately. 'Drinks?'

'*Veliko pivo, molim.*' – Large beer, please, Nick ordered, showing off a little of the Croatian language he had learned.

The waiter looked at Bevan.

'Same.' Bevan said, trusting Mason's judgement. The waiter retreated. 'Nice place you've found here.'

'I think so.'

'Where's Ashley?' Bevan asked.

Nick picked a pack of cardboard coasters from a pile in the middle of the table and dealt one in front of each of them before placing the deck back on the table.

'She took a hike. Suffers from restlessness.'

'Good.'

'Yeah? How come?' asked Mason.

Bevan held his hand up to stop Mason saying any more as the waiter approached with their drinks. The waiter placed two large glasses of beer on the coasters, wedged the paper bill under the ashtray and left without a word.

Bevan took a large draught, then wiped his lips with the back of his hand. 'I needed that,' he admitted. 'It's damn hot out here.'

'It is,' Mason agreed, lighting up a cigarette and taking a drag.

Bevan sank back into his chair and watched the swimmers with envy. He turned back to Mason and said, 'Don't tell me where she's gone. It's best I don't know these details. But I'm curious. Why has she left? I thought you two might have wanted to catch up a little.'

Mason was sitting forward uncomfortably, as if under starter's orders.

'She wanted to go off and write her column for the paper.' He took a deep drag from his cigarette. 'Sitting here in the sun didn't suit her. Writing is all she does. Everything else pales into insignificance.'

'Even above getting to know her long-lost brother,' Bevan asked in mock surprise.

'Afraid so.'

'I hope she's maintaining her anonymity?' Bevan enquired, wiping away the sweat accumulating on his forehead.

Mason nodded. 'Yeah, she's being paid through an international account and writing under an assumed name. You'd have to be Sherlock Holmes to find her.' Nick sat back, took another pull from his cigarette, and said, 'So, let's cut to the chase; how did you find me and what do you want?'

'Nick. Nick. Nick. Can't we just enjoy this sun-drenched setting for a while?' Bevan asked. 'I don't get chance to enjoy such surroundings very often.'

'You told me to lie low. That's what I'm doing.'

Bevan was looking up to the sky, thinking. In his mind, he had practised this conversation with Mason over the last few days. If he was honest with himself, he didn't know why. He liked to say things as they were. Mincing words was not his style.

'Look, Nick, why don't we order some food and then I can appraise you of the situation,' Bevan suggested.

Mason glanced at his watch. It was 11.30am. He didn't normally have lunch until around 1pm. He'd have to make an exception if he was going to find out why Bevan had come all the way to Croatia.

'So, what do they eat out here, Nick?' Bevan asked while perusing the small, laminated lunch-time menu.

Without consulting the menu, Nick said, 'I'm going to have the local meats and a side salad.'

'That sounds good. Think I'll have that too.'

Nick beckoned the waiter back.

'Salad and Prosciutto for two, please,' he ordered.

'Yes, sir.'

Mason waited for the waiter to retreat and then asked, 'Are you going to tell me why you're here?'

Bevan took a drink. He decided honesty was the best policy. It would save time. 'I've come to warn you that you're in grave danger, Nick.'

'From Lester?'

'Yes,' confirmed Bevan.

'What?!' Mason bristled. 'But Lester's in jail, surely? What can he do from there?'

'Lester's not in jail,' Bevan said flatly. 'He's escaped.'

'Shit! Shit! Shit!'

'Look, calm down and just listen for a minute.' Bevan held his hand up and waited for Nick to settle. 'Okay, let me start at the beginning. Kosinski wasn't as stupid as we, or maybe I, had thought. I suspect he tipped Lester off that I may have been the inside source for Ashley's exposé. Lester never asked me outright, but I'd got an inkling. Let's just say I could feel it in my morning piss! Lester had kept me on a pretty tight leash leading up to his arrest. I have a feeling he sent me to kill Kosinski so that he would have something on me afterwards. I reckon he was going to hang me out to dry with the cops.'

Mason stubbed out his cigarette before it's time and immediately lit another. 'So, what's that got to do with me and Ashley?'

'After killing Kosinski I left his body in a place where it could easily be found. Lester wanted to know what had happened to your bodies too. I told him Kosinski had dumped you both in the local reservoir. I hoped that he'd take my word for it.'

'And he didn't?'

'I'm not sure, but he must have got the place checked out. Divers, maybe. I don't know.' He took a draught of his beer. 'Next thing I know, a hitman came calling. Pretty poor example of a killer, if you ask me. Made too many mistakes coming into the house. Had to put a bullet through his head. Ghastly business. Had a lovely, framed picture of the king over my fireplace. Bullet went straight through the hitman's head and ruined the picture. Made a right mess of the house too.

'Anyway, the bottom line is, Lester probably knows you're still alive. I thought it best to come and warn you while I was in the vicinity.'

'But how did you know I was here?'

'Nick, the criminal underworld has its tentacles everywhere. A foreigner can't do drug runs in one country and it not raise suspicion elsewhere.'

'What drug runs?' Mason tried to feign innocence.

'Come on, Nick! Don't take me for a fool. Luka and your friend, Željko the drug-runner. The travel firm he owns is a front, and you know it.'

'But I've only done a few runs for him to Sarajevo and back.'

'Well, once you'd offered your services out here, the feelers were put out back home, as to your trustworthiness and...'

'... Lester found out?' Mason finished Bevan's sentence.

'If I did, he probably did, too.'

'Fuck!' Mason said stubbing his cigarette out. 'That's bad, isn't it?'

'It certainly is my friend.' Bevan looked beyond Mason. 'Now where's that food? I'm starving.'

'It'll be here. They just do things in their own time here.'

'Well, I'm parched. I could do with another drink.' Bevan smiled. 'Ah, good. He's coming.'

The waiter placed the plates of food in the middle of the table. He then put an empty plate in front of both Bevan and Mason. Knives and forks were already wrapped in napkins on the table.

'Another two drinks.' Bevan ordered, sinking the last of his beer and passing the empty glass to the waiter.

'Yes sir.' The waiter answered and then retreated to get the drinks.

Bevan picked a piece of meat up with his hand and stuffed it in his mouth unceremoniously. 'Mmmmm! That's good.'

'Better than anything you'll get in England, I'm sure.' Mason washed his first bite of prosciutto down with the dregs of beer left in the bottom of his glass. 'So, what does Lester think of you being out here?'

'He sent me. Negotiations between Lester and Željko are at an advanced stage. They have a mutual interest in illicit drugs.'

'And me?'

'I don't know if he knows exactly where you are.' He paused and took a drink. 'But I'm sure he'll make some investigations once he arrives.'

Suddenly Nick lost his appetite.

CHAPTER 4

Mason turned over and realised straight away it was a bad move. His head felt like it had been penetrated by several axes and his mouth tasted like the bottom of a cat litter tray. He needed to drink some water, and fast! He dropped his legs over the side of the bed. The instant contact was made with the floor a shock of electric bolted up and split his throbbing brain in two. He grabbed at his head to ease the pain. It was a futile gesture.

The previous evening had been a blur. After lunch with Bevan, they had got a taxi to the Old Town, eaten and consumed more alcohol. Thankfully, for Mason, he had insisted on Bevan checking in at one of the local hotels situated near Copacabana Beach. The last thing he remembered was getting out of the taxi at the hotel door and staggering down the short pathway to his house. How he'd got undressed and into bed, only the Gods knew.

A morning run was out of the question. He stumbled to the bathroom, took a leak, and brushed his teeth; even his teeth ached! He cut a sad figure in the mirror. He had two days of stubble to shave off, and, if he was honest, he needed a haircut too. This easy living was doing him no good; standards were slipping.

He shaved and rinsed the remaining foam from his face, immediately feeling more human. Even in the heat of Dubrovnik, he preferred to start with a warm shower. Then, once he'd washed, he would gradually reduce the temperature of the water. He would then let the cold liquid refresh his whole body for a good five minutes.

Once dried, he dressed in t-shirt, shorts and flip-flops, went downstairs to the kitchen, and made a strong cup of black coffee. The house still felt empty without Ashley. Even though they had only lived together for a short time, and she'd been gone months now, he had got used to his sister being around. It wasn't so lonely living in a foreign country when you had a sibling in situ.

He opened the front door, wedged it ajar with a wooden block and felt the rush of heat from the coastal breeze. Grabbing a packet of cigarettes from the table, he took one out and ignited it with his lighter. This drag was the first of the day, long and deep, a desperate attempt to get the nicotine down into his lungs and coursing through his body. Life always felt better to Nick with nicotine for company.

Placing his coffee cup, a glass of tap water, cigarettes, lighter and an ashtray on a small tray, he took it out to the patio table. He sat down to take in the scene. Like every day out here in the inlet, boats came and went. Nothing got in the way of sea-life. The world always turned. The water splashed up against the quayside as it always did. The flotsam and jetsam rose and fell with the water.

Bevan had told Nick that Lester planned to stay out of Britain for long periods, and, in an effort to extend his business interests, he had contacted Željko about a deal. Željko had the contacts and infrastructure in place across the whole of the former Yugoslavia, not just here in Croatia. If Lester could do a deal with the Croat, he would have access to an unlimited amount of cocaine that he could sell in the UK and elsewhere, raking in vast amounts of cash. He'd become the number one importer of illegal drugs in the UK and possibly the whole of western Europe too. Lester's stay in prison had evidently not dimmed his lofty business plans. To get the deal moving, Lester had sent Bevan to smooth relations with Željko.

Nick couldn't help but see Bevan's unexpected arrival as a sign that he had to get out of Dubrovnik, Croatia even, as fast as possible. He couldn't afford Lester arriving and finding him there. He'd be a dead man for sure. As soon as he'd collected his belongings together and shaken this damn headache off, he would be out of Dubrovnik.

Mason took another deep drag from his cigarette and wondered where his next bolthole should be. He knew little of the continent. Or more importantly, how far Lester's tentacles reached.

As he took a sip of water, he noticed a sheet of paper floating on the water near the jetty. It must have been stuck on a piece of wood jutting out of the sea, as it moved with the lapping of the water, never releasing from its tether.

He took another drink of the strong coffee. It wasn't clearing his head, but it tasted heavenly. You just couldn't get coffee like this in England. The English liked their coffee too wishy-washy for his liking.

The paper in the water intrigued him and he gazed at it idly, half expecting it to be released from its precarious attachment any time. But it never did, and he found his gaze continually being drawn back to it. It wavered, but never escaped from the water's clutches.

Eventually, curiosity got the better of him. He took a last drag from the cigarette, crushed it into the ashtray and rose from his seat. He still couldn't see what the paper was stuck to, so moved closer to the water's edge.

When he finally saw what the paper was attached to, he took an involuntary step backwards and began to wretch. Had he seen what his eyes had just transmitted to his brain? Could it be possible? Was his drunken mind playing tricks?

Mason inched back, closer to the edge of the water, peeking, wishing to God that his eyes were playing tricks on him.

His mind wasn't playing games, he saw that the paper was attached to an outstretched hand, holding it just above the water line. His eyes traced the arm to its body and across its chest and up to its face.

The face, its eyes wide open and the mouth agape, displaying those unmistakeable gleaming white teeth, was none other than Bevan's. He lay just under the surface of the shallow water, as if holding the paper in an offering to Nick. Against all the sickening feelings tearing through his body, Nick reached for the paper and tore it from Bevan's dead hand and jumped back quickly, as if fearing being pulled down into the water along with him.

Nick checked no one was around before opening the folded wet paper out and reading it. It said, 'Someone's been a naughty boy!'

'Shit!' Mason blurted out, a thimble of sick rising in his mouth.

What was he going to do now? How the hell was he going to get out of this? He couldn't have the police coming around asking questions. They would surely link him to Bevan.

He had to do something and fast!

Mason ran back into the house and threw on some tracksuit bottoms and training shoes. Grabbing the keys for his motorboat and a set of dumbbells, he locked the door and made for the jetty. He threw the dumbbells on the boat deck, then collected some brick-sized rocks and quickly threw them on the boat too. Then he uncoiled some rope that had been laying at the back of the boat. Forming a ring at one end, he tied that to the bow. Jumping into the waist-high water, he wrapped the other end of the rope tightly around Bevan's torso, under his arms. Now he cut the line that was holding the corpse in place. Bevan's limp body floated on the water's crest.

Mason jumped back onto the boat and started the engine, slowly moving away from the jetty. He could feel the extra weight of Bevan's corpse dragging on the engine's motor. The rope was just long enough to keep the body away from the turning propeller.

Mason scanned the area to see if anyone could see Bevan's corpse, which was just breaking the water's surface. Thankfully, there were no boats nearby.

He headed out of the inlet towards the open water, the boat rocking back and forth. Fortunately, it was a quiet day on the water. The Cruise Ships weren't due today and there was just a smattering of smaller craft travelling hither and thither. The people travelling over the Franjo Tuđman suspension bridge were too far away to see anything on the water.

Once Mason was sure he was far enough into the ocean, he turned the engine off and moved to the back of the boat. He dragged the rope in, bringing Bevan's body close enough to reach. He wedged the dumbbells into the rope wrapped around Bevan's torso and began to pack the rocks into the dead man's pockets. Using all the rocks he'd brought, he hoped it would be enough to help the body sink down into the sea. Deep down.

Mason looked at Bevan's white face and suddenly felt queasy. He fell back, breathing heavily. Quickly, he turned and leant over the side of the boat, saliva pouring out of his mouth. His stomach heaved and he was sick, emptying all his stomach's contents into the ocean. He sat back and waited a minute to get his breathing back to normal. Occasionally, he retched, but nothing more came up. Eventually, he felt able to return to the task in hand and unhooked the rope. He slowly allowed the laden body to sink lower into the water. Bevan's arms waved a final goodbye as he sank down deeper into the crystal-clear blue water of the Adriatic. Within seconds, Bevan had faded from view. Mason released the rope and then that disappeared along with Bevan.

Mason hurriedly kicked the boat's engine back into life and headed back to the Old Yacht Club at full throttle. Once there, he jumped off the boat. His landing foot slipped a fraction and for an instant he thought he was going to slip off the rickety wooden jetty and into the water. Thankfully, he regained his composure and stance. He grabbed for the landing rope at the bow and tied it loosely onto the jetty.

In the house, Mason ran straight up to the bedroom and packed his suitcase with what little possessions he had. He scanned the room. Nothing left. Then he ran around the ground floor collecting his phone, charger, car keys and cigarette packets. Within minutes he was in the SUV and heading towards Željko's restaurant. Bevan had been killed and placed where Mason would find him. What he needed to know now was: is Lester coming for him next?

CHAPTER 5

The barman, Petar was wiping bottles clean and stocking the shelves when the bar phone rang out and broke the silence. He wiped his hands on a ragged towel before picking the phone from its cradle.

'*Dobar dan.*' – Good day.

After he had listened to the caller, he put the phone down and approached Željko, who was sitting at his usual table reading the morning newspaper, with an espresso and a cigarette for company.

'*Lester, Englez na telefonu!*' – It's the Englishman, Lester, on the phone.

'*U redu, primit ću poziv u kancelariji!*' – Okay, I'll take it in the office.

Željko stubbed his cigarette out into the ashtray and went through the door marked '*Privatno.*' – Private – behind his chair. The office was free of clutter. A small window on the back wall hovered over a chair and desk letting a limited amount of natural light into the room. On the desk sat a phone and an ashtray, nothing more. To Željko's right, as he entered, was a filing cabinet. There were no pictures on the pale green walls. He closed the door behind him.

He opened the desk draw and picked out a fresh pack of cigarettes and a lighter. He lifted the phone up and told Petar to put the call through. While he waited for a response, he lit a cigarette and took a deep drag. As he exhaled, a dense cloud began to fill the room.

'Hello, Željko! Is that you,' a distant English voice echoed in the phone.

'*Da.*' – Yes.

Željko expected to hear the tell-tale click that confirmed Petar had replaced the phone on its cradle in the bar. It didn't come before Lester spoke.

'It's Lester here.'

'Yes. What can I do for you?' He took a drag from his cigarette and wished he'd brought his drink in with him. He looked in the bottom drawer of the desk while Lester was talking and lifted a half bottle of Badel and a glass out.

'I was wondering how our little project is getting along.'

Željko splashed a couple of fingers into the glass and sat behind the desk, 'Fine. All is well.'

'What about our friend?' Željko sensed the anxiety in Lester voice. 'Has he left?'

'Late last night,' the Croat confirmed.

'Good. Good. I'd like to thank you for dealing with that little problem, Željko. It's been a bit of a running sore for a few months now.'

Željko took a drink from the glass.

'I'm just glad I could be of some assistance.' He took a deep drag on his cigarette before adding, 'When do you expect to arrive in Dubrovnik?'

'I have a few loose ends to tie up here and then I will come over. I hope the weather is good. I'm desperate for a little sun. I've been cooped up of late.'

'There are many things we can provide here in Dubrovnik, and the sun is one of them.'

'Good. I like the sound of that.'

Željko lent back and put his feet on the desk. 'How is everything else?'

'Our plans have moved forward considerably. I can confirm that my people are in place in the ports and towns we discussed earlier. All they need is the green light from us and they're ready to move.'

Željko thought for a moment. He still didn't know if he could trust this man. He had never dealt with the English before.

If Lester held his end of the bargain up, they would both be millionaires many times over.

'Have you got the supply chain ready?' Lester asked after a short silence.

Having secured the supply of cocaine for most of the former Yugoslavia for years, Željko was asking his suppliers up the food chain to step up to the mark and provide a much larger amount. The risk would be greater, but then, the rewards would increase immensely.

Željko confirmed, 'Yes. I have secured the merchandise we spoke about. There will be no problems on this side. My suppliers are people who keep their word.'

'I've been let down before. I wouldn't want to be disappointed again.'

Željko could feel the tension in Lester's voice even over the phone. 'Then you have never been in business with a Croat, Mr Lester. Once you shake on a deal, it will be honoured.' He paused for a second, then added, 'As long as this trust works both ways, there won't be an issue.'

'I'm happy to hear that, my friend. Until we meet.'

'Goodbye, Mr Lester.'

Željko put the phone down and took a sip from the glass. He was putting a lot of trust in this Englishman. If things turn sour, it could leave him vulnerable. He had a special place in the grand scheme of things in this part of the world. The production and quality of the drugs he left to others, but distribution was his domain. He had large chunks of the former Yugoslavia sewn up. If anyone attempted to muscle in, he cracked down on them heavily. He had to be aware that there were people in England and western Europe in the same position as him who wouldn't take kindly to a consortium led, in part, by a Croat on their turf. But then all the risks beyond the Adriatic were being taken by Lester. He was the one who would take the merchandise beyond Željko's control. And Željko had bribed everyone through Ljubljana, Zagreb, Beograd, Skopje, Podgorica and back to Dubrovnik. He'd never had any problems with moving his merchandise on. And he didn't envision any on this occasion.

CHAPTER 6

Tom Lester stood in front of the bookshelf adjacent to his large wooden desk. The light streamed in from the office window negating any need for artificial illumination. His suit jacket hung over the chair behind a mahogany desk, his pristine white shirt open at the collar. A recent spell in jail, spending up to 23 hours a day indoors, had lightened his usually tanned face and neck. Lester's lean, toned body, was ramrod straight. His peppered-grey hair, almost flat to his head, had been gelled to within an inch of its life.

He took a sip of whiskey from a gold-rimmed tumbler as he perused the books. The bookshelves reached around the office wall, only stopping for the door and the large bay window. There were so many publications to choose from, he couldn't decide which book he wanted to read next. Soon he would be on a plane, and he didn't want to leave the house without something to read in his carry-on bag.

Thankfully, his foresight in putting his home in the ownership of an offshore company, well out of reach from the British police, had meant his recent incarceration hadn't affected his home or extensive financial interests. He could come and go as he pleased, as long as the Old Bill didn't know, of course.

His escape from prison had been a close call. Calling in debts had been essential. But wasting time in jail, and spending hard-earned cash on his escape, rankled. The reporter, Ashley Clarke, who was at the heart of his uncovering had to be neutralised. The man he'd paid to kill her, Nick Mason, had to die as well. The fact that he'd entrusted the wrong people to carry out the assignment, Bevan and Kosinski, illustrated that a level of complacency had set in, or maybe he was just going soft.

Things had to change.

His latest venture, drug running and distribution through the former Yugoslavia into the European Union and the UK was well on the way to bearing fruit; contracts were all in place. Once the cargo left Croatia, the road was clear all the way to the streets of Marseille, Paris, and Amsterdam, with regular consignments making their way onto UK streets. Even the recent EU/British divorce wouldn't affect shipments. Considering Britain was an island, its border force was as inept as any third world country. Where it wasn't, juicy payments to the right people on the border would oil the wheels for free movement of goods and people.

The money to be made from the coming deal was unimaginable. He'd never dreamed so much cash would become readily available to him. But with the contacts he'd made over the years, it had all become possible. The lynchpin for this operation was Željko Kovačić, a Croatian with contacts throughout the Balkans and beyond. Tapping into Željko's business had been a masterstroke. He had to thank the dearly departed Bevan for that. He'd done all the preparatory work on connections with Željko and his team. It had been a sad decision to cancel him out, but a necessary one. Bevan, or more appropriately Judas, had let him down. Bevan had sold him down the river when he had leaked information to Ashley Clarke. Lester had sent Connelly, a trusted associate, out to neutralise Bevan. Unfortunately, Connelly had been found dead in a skip with half his head missing, so it had been necessary to get the job done by Željko and his men in Dubrovnik. Better in another country anyway, he thought. Less questions to answer.

A tap on the door brought Lester back to the present.

Irwin, the butler, came in and said, 'Mr. Lloyd and Mr Nesby to see you.'

'Show them in.' Lester moved behind his desk and sat down facing the door.

Irwin held the door open as Nesby and Lloyd entered. They both stopped across the desk from Lester.

'Will there be anything else, Mr. Lester?' Irwin asked.

'No, Irwin.' Irwin turned away to leave but then turned back when Lester continued, 'I'm sorry, but can you take the decanter and refill it with the Macallan?'

'Of course, sir.' With that the butler left the room, closing the door behind him.

'Gentlemen,' Lester began, leaning back in his chair, 'I have a little job for the both of you. It has come to my attention that a certain old man lives at the Lynne Residential Care Home. I'm interested in locating his son. I'm not sure the old man will know his son's whereabouts; he's been missing for some time. To be honest, I don't know if the old man still has a full deck, mental-wise. However, the Home must have some contact details regarding the son, maybe even a location.' He emptied the glass of its remaining whiskey, then got up and placed the tumbler on the drinks table in the corner of the room.

Next, he went across to the door and opened it, looking around irritably, and saying to himself, 'Where's Irwin with that drink?' Nesby and Lloyd looked at each other uneasily.

Irwin came into sight with a full decanter, 'Is there anything else I can do for you, sir?'

'Just the drink, Irwin.' He reached out for the decanter. 'I'll take it from here, thank you. You may attend to your other duties now.' Lester took the drink from Irwin and turned back into the office, closing the door.

Irwin stood still for a moment and, as if the instruction took some time to register, turned on his heels and started back towards the kitchen.

Lester poured himself a large whiskey without offering Lloyd or Nesby a glass.

Lloyd was partly thankful. He had been attending AA for some time. He'd almost reached the one hundred-day, drink free marker, a feat he'd never accomplished before.

Nesby, who had no such issue with booze, watched Lester sit

down and take a heavy gulp of the alcohol, disgruntled about not being offered a glass.

'Now, where was I?' He didn't wait for a reply. 'Yes. Of course. I need to focus Nick Mason's mind. Nesby, I want you to frighten his old man. That should do it.'

Nesby bristled. 'Tom, is that necessary? He's an old man after all. Apart from being Mason's father, he's completely innocent.'

Lester sprang to his feet, 'Did I ask you for your opinion, Nesby?'

Nesby fidgeted. 'No Tom. It's just that...'

'Well, just shut the fuck up and listen.' Nesby almost fell back. 'Leave the decisions to me. You're the hired help around here, that's all. The sooner we all understand that the better.' Lester paused for a moment, then asked, 'Have you got that, Nesby?'

'Yes, yes, Tom.' He fidgeted with the knot in his tie. 'I'm sorry. I'll get on with the job.'

'Good.' Lester turned to Lloyd. 'I need you to get as much information as you can from the manager. I believe she was once close to the dearly departed Bevan. If she won't tell you what she knows, go through the files, and find out for yourself. They'll be something in there, for sure.'

'Okay, Tom. Sure thing,' said Lloyd hoping the beads of sweat he felt running down from his temple weren't visible.

'And keep this lunatic in order, will you?'

'No worries, Tom. Will do,' Lloyd confirmed.

Lester sat down and turned his chair away from Nesby and Lloyd and looked out of the bay window. He couldn't see where the land he owned ended. The gardens were immaculate. Just the way he liked them. He decided he'd take a walk later in the day.

Nesby and Lloyd stood, unsure, waiting for further instructions. Lester's back was to them, but neither dared move, in case he wanted to say more.

After what seemed like an eternity to Nesby and Lloyd, Lester asked rhetorically from behind his chair, 'What are you waiting for?'

The hesitant pair took this as their signal to leave.
Now alone in the room, Lester muttered to himself, 'Cretins!'

CHAPTER 7

Mason drove on the top road, *Ul. Iva Dulčića*, at speed. Below, to the left, the cruise ship terminal was empty. Once he had reached *Lapad*, the road was much busier. People were milling around, and the traffic was more congested. He turned left onto *Ul. Od Batale* and down towards the marina, where he ran around during his morning exercise, and left again, turning back on himself onto *Lapadska obala*. He was now back on the coast driving towards the Old Yacht Club. The road was tight and only accessible as a one-way street with the water just feet from his right-hand wheel. How they got the single-decker buses up this road had always amazed Mason.

He stopped abruptly outside Željko's restaurant and jumped out of the SUV, leaving the keys in the ignition, and moved up the steps into the building with ease.

Željko was sat at his usual table furthest from the door. He had a newspaper open and a cup of coffee in front of him. Petar, the young barman, was behind the counter tidying up.

'Nick,' Željko welcomed, rising from the table. 'Come in.'

Mason moved towards the table and shook Željko's hand. 'Hi! How are you doing?'

'Fine, my friend. Please, sit.' Željko gestured towards the chair facing his own. 'Have a drink. Petar, come, take Nick's order.'

Petar came out immediately from behind the bar and asked Mason what he wanted to drink. 'An Americano, please, Petar.' The barman returned to the bar to get Mason's order.

Mason sat down across from Željko.

'So, what can I do for you, my friend? You're not normally here this early in the day.'

Mason sat uneasily in his seat. He knew nothing happened in Dubrovnik without Željko knowing, and that he wasn't a person to make an enemy of. He didn't know whether to tread carefully or just come out with it. He decided on the latter and see how Željko responded. Just as he was about to speak, Petar returned with his coffee and plonked it down on the table in front of him. Mason watched him walk away before beginning to speak.

'I had a visit from a friend, well, an acquaintance, yesterday.'

Željko took a sip of coffee, 'Your acquaintance must have come a long way?'

'He did. All the way from England.' Mason paused for a second, and then continued, 'But he didn't just come to see me.'

'Oh, and who else was he here to visit?'

Mason planted his hands flat on the table in front of him and steadied himself. 'He said he'd come to see you.'

'Me? But why?'

'He said he was here to do a deal with you on behalf of his boss, Tom Lester. Have you heard of him?'

Željko folded his paper up and put it to one side. 'I don't know anything of what you say, Nick. I'm a just a normal restaurant owner with the odd little side-line, as you know. What business would I have with these foreigners?'

Mason looked around to make sure no one could overhear, before continuing. 'Come on, Željko! I'm not a fool.'

The Croat didn't flinch. His eyes were steady and unblinking as Mason spoke. And when he had finished, Željko asked, 'I don't see what this has to do with me.'

'Željko, that man is now dead! I found him outside my house this morning. I want to know what's going on.'

Željko looked up at Petar and clicked his fingers. '*Petar, dvije Šljivovic.*' – Petar, two Šljivovica. He then looked back at Mason as if weighing him up. 'Nick, my friend, business is business. You must understand, nothing is personal.' Petar arrived and placed the drinks, shot-sized glasses of clear alcohol, on the table. 'Take a drink. It's good. Plum brandy, very strong, so sip it. You English have a tendency to gulp alcohol down like it's going out of fashion.'

Mason sipped the clear liquid as he had been instructed. Željko was right. Too much of this stuff would blow your head off.

'So, what was Bevan doing here, Željko?'

Željko put his glass down onto the table before answering. 'Okay. He was sent here by his boss, Tom Lester, as you say. Without going into too many details, I have lots of business acquaintances, not just here but across Europe too. Many of them help me to move cargo around.'

'Drugs?' Mason interrupted.

'Let's just say for your own safety,' Željko paused to find the right words, 'illicit cargo. But it should be of no surprise to you. You have helped me. Anyway, this man Lester wants to get in on the action. He said he could move merchandise around. The deal was to be a very lucrative one for me and my colleagues. Lester's market in Britain and beyond is impressive. If he can get my product out there, I will become a very rich man.'

'So why is Bevan dead? I thought he was here as a go-between.'

Željko downed the remaining Šljivovica and got up. He went around the bar and poured himself another shot. He brought the bottle to the table and raised an eyebrow. Mason nodded. Željko filled his glass and replaced the cork. He then lit two cigarettes and gave one to Mason. They sat for a moment without talking.

Mason broke the silence: 'I could be in big trouble if Lester knows where I am. I need to know what he knows.'

Željko took a drag from his cigarette and blew out a cloud of smoke. 'Nick, this Bevan fellow, had done Tom Lester a disservice. The deal that we have is almost complete. Bevan's trip here had nothing to do with it. Lester sent him here on a, what do you call it? A fool's errand. Yes, that's it. He came here in the belief he was making a deal for Lester, but in actual fact, he came here to die.'

'The bastard!'

Željko shrugged. 'It's business, Nick. Lester needed Bevan out of the way. We helped him. That is all.'

'And will you help him kill me?' Mason asked.

'He has not asked,' Željko assured, tapping ash in the ashtray. 'What has all this to do with you, Nick? You are looking very worried.'

'Let's just say that me and Tom Lester wouldn't see eye to eye if we ever came across each other. In fact, what you did to Bevan would be a merciful death in comparison to what Lester would do to me.'

'Then you should lie low, Nick.'

'I need to know. Are you going to tell him I'm here?'

'If he doesn't ask, why would I?'

'It's just something I needed to know, Željko.'

'Then this is something you need to know, my friend.' Željko took a drag from his cigarette. 'Lester is due to visit soon. I don't know the exact date. When I spoke to him last, he said he had a few loose ends to tie up and then he would come over here in person.'

Mason's face turned ashen.

'Nick be calm. I'm sure you have time to leave before he arrives. He is coming for a simple business transaction and,' he smiled, 'our beautiful Croatian sun, of course. You will be far from his consideration, I'm sure.'

'I hope you're right, Željko. But those loose ends might involve people I know. May I use your phone?'

'Of course. Be my guest.'

*

Nick stood over Željko's desk holding the phone. He dialled the Lynne Residential Home's number from memory. Within a second or two, he heard the dialling tone. 'Come on!' he begged to the other side of the line, not giving a thought to the fact that no one there could hear him. 'For God's sake answer the bloody phone!'

Željko stood in the doorway of his office.

Mason heard a faint click that broke into the ringing on the other side. He immediately blurted, 'Is that Ms Reynolds?'

'Yes,' Charlie Reynolds answered. 'How may I help?'

'It's Nick Mason here. William Mason's son.'

'Yes, Mr Mason. I didn't recognise you. It's been so long. How may I help?'

'Is my father okay?'

'Yes, of course. Why? Is there something wrong?'

Nick didn't want to alarm the staff at his father's home back in England. Exposing them to the news that Tom Lester was on the loose and that his father may be a target, and by association them, Nick felt was something he could spare them. He just needed to get back to England, and quickly.

'I'd like to visit my father soon, Ms Reynolds. I can't tell you exactly when, but it will be soon. Please don't tell him though, I wouldn't want him to get his hopes up.'

Mason could picture her smile from her voice. 'Mum's the word, Mr. Mason.'

'Okay, I'll be there as soon as I can. Bye.'

'Bye, Mr. Mason.' Charlie Reynolds rang off.

Mason took a drag of his cigarette and listened to the phone line go dead. Once he was happy it had, he turned to Željko and asked, 'I need a plane back to England, like yesterday. Where's the best place to get tickets?'

'One moment, I have a friend.' Željko flicked through the address book in his cell. He found Josip Travel and pressed the call button.

'Josip Travel, kako vam možemo pomoći? recepcionarka upita.' – Josip Travel, how can we help?' the receptionist asked.

'Treba mi sljedeći let za..' – I'm ringing about the next flight to,' he broke off, and looked over towards Mason and asked, 'Where in England?

'Manchester,' Mason responded, taking a pull on his cigarette.

'Manchester, Engleska. Da li imate još slobodnih sjedišta na današnjem letu?' – Manchester, England. Are there any seats available today?'

Željko could hear the receptionist tapping on a keyboard. He blew out a cloud of smoke as he waited for the answer.

'Da, imamo slobodna sjedišta na letu u 1-30 poslje podne. Koliko mjesta bi htjeli da rezervirate? – Yes, we have seats available on the 1.30 flight. How many seats did you want to reserve?'

'Samo jedno, hvala.' – Just one, please.

'Jedno sjedište rezervirano , nema problema.' – I can do that for you, sir.'

Željko booked the seat for the flight back to Manchester in Mason's name, then looked across. 'Care to explain?'

'I haven't got time. I'll fill you in when I get back.'

'Okay. I'll text you the ticket information.'

'Cheers!'

Mason drove back to the Old Yacht Club at speed. Once there, he took the stairs two at a time and quickly packed an overnight bag. Since Ashley had left, he had taken over the front-facing bedroom and, with one last look out of the window, shut the wooden blinds. He made sure all the electric sockets were turned off apart from the fridge, locked the downstairs windows and doors and jumped into the SUV. If he was lucky, he'd make the drive to the airport in good time.

As much as he wanted to, he didn't stop to look at the Old Town from the *Magistrala*. Instead, he drove on, pushing the speed limit all the way, cursing the drivers who appeared to hug the middle line. Sunday drivers let loose on a Tuesday. 'God help us,' he thought.

He made it to the Airport in reasonable time, dropping the SUV off at the long stay car park.

Locating the airline desk, he checked in with his passport and the ticket information Željko had forwarded by text. Within a short time, he was through Passport Control and having a coffee and sandwich combo in the café.

Mason saw that there was a couple of computer terminals in the corner for public use. Neither was being used. He finished his sandwich, picked his cup up and sat at the computer station. He thought a Euro per minute was a little excessive, but paid €5 in advance, which was the minimum charge. He then logged in to the email account he'd set up when Ashley had left.

He opened up a new message and addressed it to Ashley's 'Julianne Winter account. In the Subject Line he wrote 'Urgent!' Then in the message, remembering not to use any names, he typed,

Trouble!
TL escaped.
B. erased.
Parent in danger.
On way home.
Where are you? I need help!'

He hoped Ashley would understand that 'TL' was Lester and 'B' was Bevan. He had no time to worry about that now though.

Once he had checked the email had been sent, he signed out of the account and closed the computer down. He returned to the café. This time he bought a large Badel, the local brandy.

While he waited to board, Nick found it hard to concentrate. What had happened to Bevan was terrible. How he had kept his nerve to get rid of his body, he didn't know. Now he was sure his father was in the firing line. He couldn't let Lester and his men get him. He had to beat them to his father, get him out of there and take him somewhere safe. Dubrovnik was probably now out of the question. With Bevan's murder, Nick's safe haven had now been compromised. He would have to find somewhere else. Perhaps the city of Sarajevo would afford him the safety he needed. It wasn't a seaside resort, but it was an anonymous place on the map. From what he had seen on recent trips, he could quite happily settle there.

An announcement over the tannoy system said that his plane was ready for boarding. This brought his mind back to the present. He collected his shoulder bag and headed for the gate. Boarding was quick and efficient. He had a window seat. A young blonde woman sat next to him. He stretched out as much as he could without disturbing her. Although he wanted to rest, sleep proved elusive. His mind just kept going around in circles. The vision of Bevan's face looking at him from underneath the water, almost pleading to be saved, continually flashed up wherever he looked, through the window, across the aisle, through closed eyes.

Just under three hours later, the plane landed at Manchester International Airport without fuss, albeit with a bump and the screech of the engines on touchdown. The usual message of welcome over the public address system confirmed that they'd landed safely at the intended destination.

Once the plane had halted at the Gate, passengers jumped up to retrieve baggage from the overhead lockers. Nick handed the young blonde girl, Taylor, who he had swapped pleasantries with, her small bag from the overhead storage. She gave Mason a smile of thanks. On another day he might have struck up a conversation, but today was different. He had to get back to his father, and fast.

He walked down the airplane's central aisle behind Taylor. As she said, 'thank you', to the stewardess, she looked around at Mason and flashed him a quick smile. He wondered if she had wanted to talk to him more. He smiled back but said nothing as she picked up pace towards 'Baggage Collection'.

He located the Hertz desk and collected the SUV he had booked online before leaving Dubrovnik. The young receptionist insisted on running through the basics, even though Mason told her that he had owned one himself until very recently.

'All in the service, sir!' said the receptionist, with a broad grin as Nick slipped a ten pound tip in her hand.

CHAPTER 8

Mason dumped his travel bag in the boot of the SUV and jumped behind the driver's wheel. A lemon freshener dangled from the central mirror. While he didn't mind the smell, he disliked anything hanging in the windscreen obscuring his view. He snapped it off the mirror and threw it onto the dashboard and kicked up the engine. Before setting off he hooked up his cell to the Bluetooth, enabling him to make calls on the move. Once that was done, he headed straight for the Lynne Residential Home.

The SUV moved effortlessly through the late afternoon traffic. The twenty mile route north would take him on the 602, 60 and 61. If he could get back to town and the Home in time, he'd be able to get his father away before Lester and his men got anywhere near him.

Just beyond the junction Mason was exiting he could see a snarl-up. He breathed a sigh of relief. A delay was the last thing he needed. He took his eyes off the road momentarily, picked up the cell from the passenger seat and swiped the screen into life. He then punched in the Lynne's telephone number from memory. The car speaker woke, and the cell's ringing tone filled the car. He tossed the cell back onto the passenger seat. The ringing went on for what seemed like an eternity, then the sound broke off abruptly and he heard, 'The Lynne Residential Home. Melanie speaking. How may I help you?'

Mason lent forward for some inexplicable reason. 'Hello, my name is Nick Mason. I'm William Mason's son. Is it possible to speak to Ms Reynolds?'

'Of course,' said the friendly voice on the other end of the line.

'I'll just get her.'

Mason heard the phone clunk down onto what he assumed was an office desk. He remembered sitting in the manager's office talking to Ms Reynolds about his father's will. The office was small, but functional with a desk, a couple of guest chairs and filing cabinets, a haven from the stagnant urine smell that had embedded itself into the Home's very structure. He also remembered Bevan saying he'd got friendly with Ms Reynolds. He wondered if he should tell her of Bevan's demise. He decided not to, it would only complicate matters. He just needed to get his father away from there, and quickly.

The silence inside the car was broken by Charlie Reynolds. 'This is Ms Reynolds, Mr Mason. What can I do for you?'

'Ms Reynolds, I'm on my way to the Home now. I'm going to take my father away for a few days.'

'This is a bit sudden, Mr Mason.'

'Yes, I'm afraid it is.' He veered over to the outside lane to overtake a middle-lane tortoise. 'Could you pack a bag and tell him I'm on my way, please? I'll be there within half an hour.'

'Mr Mason, I'm not sure I can get everything organised so quickly. What with his clothes, his medication, and all the necessary paperwork? He's not as agile as he once was. You will need a wheelchair. Have you had experience with wheelchairs, Mr Mason?'

'I'm sure I can manage, Ms Reynolds.' He contemplated warning her that Lester's men might be on their way to mete out the same treatment to his father as they had done to her ex-lover. He decided against it. What good would it do? It would probably just alarm the woman for no reason. His father was safe there for the time-being. 'Can you do your best and have everything in place for when I arrive? I would be very grateful.'

'We'll do my best, Mr Mason.' The click indicated the line was now dead.

Mason hadn't thought through what else he should do except get his father as far away from the Home as possible. As he ruminated on that, he shifted the car onto the slip road off the

61, and on his right, he saw the home of Bolton Wanderers. He forgot the new name for the stadium. It had changed so many times since it was opened in 1997. As he passed the stadium, he recalled visiting once or twice as a teenager. He hadn't quite got the soccer bug. Two left feet his father used to say.

He passed through the Hive roundabout with ease, despite the burgeoning commuter traffic. Within minutes he was turning right into Lynne's car park, facing the local Fire Station. He exited the vehicle and zapped the SUV doors locked with the fob without turning around. Approaching, he could see the main desk through the full glass door. It wasn't manned. Pressing the buzzer repeatedly, he heard the grating noise through the double-glazed entrance.

A young red-haired girl rushed to the desk and reached underneath it, pressing a button. An audible buzz and a click told Mason the door was now unlocked. He pushed it open and let it close behind him.

He approached the desk, stating, 'I've come to pick up William Mason. I spoke to Ms Reynolds earlier.'

The receptionist, now back behind the desk and breathing heavily, leafed through a ledger. Her jacket was draped over her chair, and he could see the name tag, 'Melanie', pinned onto the lapel.

'I'm afraid Mr Mason is out. Do you want to wait?'

'What?' he said, louder than he intended.

The receptionist visibly recoiled. He caught himself. Lowering his voice, he added. 'I'm sorry. Is Ms Reynolds in?'

'Yes, she's in her office. Shall I...'

Before Melanie had chance to finish her sentence, Mason was running down the corridor to Ms Reynolds's office, only just managing to avoid an old lady and her walking frame.

Without knocking, he burst in and demanded, 'Where is he?'

'Mr Mason, I...' Charlie Reynolds started.

'Just tell me where he is? Now! I need to know.'

Charlie Reynolds rose from her chair and began walking around the table in Mason's direction.

'What is it, Mr Mason? You look as white as a sheet.'

'I need to know where my father is. Quickly!' he pleaded. 'He's in grave danger.'

Charlie Reynolds took hold of Mason's elbow and attempted to guide him to the chair, but he resisted.

'It can't be as bad as that, Mr Mason. Your father is an old man. I can assure you, the only danger he's likely to be in is from me if he refuses to take his medication again.'

Her comment didn't lighten Mason's mood. He grabbed her by the shoulders and shouted, 'Tell me where he is, now!'

Charlie Reynolds' eyes glazed over, partly in fear and partly from shock. 'When you called, he'd already gone to the park with Sadie. He should be back soon.'

'That's not good enough! I told you I was taking him away.'

'They were already out Mr Mason. There was nothing I could do.'

'Look, just ring this carer and tell her to bring my father back now… Do it!'

Charlie Reynolds turned and picked up her cell from the desk. She found the name 'Sadie' in the phone book and tapped 'Call'.

Sadie failed to answer.

'She's not answering.'

Mason grabbed the cell from her and listened for himself. No one was answering and the answerphone wasn't kicking in.

He threw the cell onto the desk and turned on his heels.

'Where are you going?'

'To the park. Keep ringing this Sadie person and when she answers, tell her to head back here. And whatever you do, don't tell anyone else where my father is!'

Before Charlie Reynolds had chance to reply, Mason was out of the door and gone.

CHAPTER 9

Station Park was too close to contemplate using the SUV. Coming out of the door and car park, he was immediately on the main road scanning cars. The New Road opening to Station Park lay a short distance on the other side of the Home's walled car park.

As he ran towards the park along the New Road two fire engines opposite rumbled out of the station, stopping the traffic, with their blue lights flashing and piercing sirens drowning out all other noise.

Within moments he turned into the park entrance. The kids play area had a family of four happily climbing on the apparatus. Moving into a jog, he passed the empty caged football pitches to his left. After the enclosure, the park opened into a large bowl area. Scouring the park on the move, straight ahead lay a second playground, sunken at the bottom of the bowl. To his right, a grassy knoll which rose higher than the enclosed play area. To the left he spotted a figure in a wheelchair alongside a bench opposite the grassy knoll. A brown-haired young woman was sitting close by on the bench. It was his father and Sadie, the carer. Apart from the family at the other entrance, they were the only people using the park, which was surprising because the sun was shining brightly down on them.

He approached them at a speed that was quicker than a walk, but not fast enough to cause alarm.

Mason Senior was puffing away contentedly on his favourite curled pipe. Plant a dear stalker on his head and he'd have been a dead ringer for a geriatric Sherlock Holmes, Mason thought. Clouds of smoke rose above his head and then dissipated in the air. When he looked up, he saw his son. 'Now there's a surprise,' he said smiling. 'Hello, son.'

'Hi dad. How are you doing?'

'Okay, son. Okay.' A slight curl at Mason Seniors mouth gave a hint of his contentment.

His father's carer stood up. She was slim and dressed in navy, straight-legged trousers, and a light blue tunic under her tailored jacket, which was open at the front. She was wearing the Home's bland, nondescript, uniform.

She offered Mason her seat, next to his father.

'Thanks.' He sat down and took a pack of cigarettes and a lighter from his jacket pocket. 'I don't suppose Ms Reynolds has spoken to you yet?' Mason cupped his hand around the cigarette, lit it and inhaled deeply. He offered the packet to Sadie as she sat on the bench, but she declined.

"No, she hasn't.' She took her cell out of the jacket pocket and said, 'Damn! The battery has gone again! It's losing power all the time. It's a bit archaic. I'll have to get a new one.' She put it back in her pocket. 'What was it she wanted?'

'She was just letting you know I was coming to the park.' Mason then looked over to his father. 'Dad, I'm going to take you on a little holiday. Ms Reynolds is getting your gear together now.'

Mason Senior took his pipe out of his mouth and declared, 'This is all a bit sudden, isn't it, son? I've not been on holiday for donkeys...'

'It is dad.' Mason looked back at Sadie and then again at his dad, taking another drag from the cigarette. 'Just let me have a quick word with Sadie.' He checked himself. 'Is it okay to call you Sadie? I don't know your surname.'

'Of course. My name's Sadie Kellerman.' She pulled her jacket back to reveal a name tag pinned to her chest with Sadie written on it. 'You can call me Sadie. And you are?'

Mason noticed a glint in her brown eyes as she dragged hair from her face and wedged it behind her ear.

'Mason, Nick Mason. William here is my father.'

Mason Senior stared straight ahead in silence and seemed oblivious to their conversation.

'He used to bring me here when I was a nipper, after my mother left us. It was the only time I remember we ever spent together. I can't say it was quality time to be honest; he always seemed to be meeting someone here. Probably some other crook.'

Mason Senior grunted and moved the pipe around his mouth in displeasure at the younger Mason's recollections.

'I've heard some, let's say unusual stories about your father's past,' Sadie revealed. 'I didn't know whether to believe them or not.'

'Most of what you've heard is probably true. Let's just say the Pope won't be putting his name forward for a Sainthood any time soon.'

'Is anyone's father a saint?' Sadie asked.

Keeping his eyes on her, Mason said, 'Some more than others, I suspect.'

A silence fell over the three of them. The only sound, a slight breeze whispering between them. Mason looked at his father. Sat in the wheelchair, to Mason, his father appeared content. More so than at any time he could ever remember. His recollections were of a father always on the edge of society, looking to make a quick buck, but never quite forming real relationships with anyone, even in the criminal fraternity.

For the first time in his life, Mason was happy for his father. He had finally found peace.

Sadie's Smart watch vibrated a reminder on her wrist. She looked at it and rose from her seat. 'I think it's probably time we got your father back. What time are you leaving?'

Mason turned away from Sadie towards his father, and as he began to answer her, his father's head exploded. In what must have been a millisecond but appeared to happen in excruciatingly painful slow motion, a hail of skin, hair, bone, and brains burst out from the back of his head landing in a gruesome splatter on the grass behind him.

The force of the bullet knocked the wheelchair and Mason Senior's body over backwards. As he landed, his lifeless body remained strapped in a sitting position to the chair, head tilted sideways.

Before any feelings for his father could gather apace, survival mode kicked in. Mason knew what he had to do. Sadie on the other hand stood stock-still in shock, eyes wide looking at nothing, all thoughts frozen in time.

Mason knew instinctively that the bullet had come from the direction of the grassy knoll facing them. He threw the cigarette away, grabbed Sadie unceremoniously and pulled her down behind the bench. Peering over the back of the bench and scanning the knoll, he couldn't locate the sniper's exact position. Mason was sure once he and Sadie moved, more deadly shots would follow.

He looked over to his father. The dead man's hand was still holding on to his favourite pipe in his mouth, a tiny curl of smoke emanating from the bowl. A third, ugly red eye had materialised just above the bridge of Mason Seniors nose.

As he crouched behind the bench, breathing heavily, Mason didn't need to take his father's pulse to confirm he was dead. A twitch here or there didn't constitute life. His lifeless eyes peered in his son's direction. Morbidly, Mason found it hard to avert his gaze from his father.

Sadie was shaking, while holding on to Mason for dear life. Her whole body seemed to be convulsing. He suddenly became aware of her distress and put his arm around her shoulders, pulling her to him.

Fighting back the emotions of seeing his father brutally slain, he half shouted at Sadie, 'Sadie, we must get away from here. And quick!'

'But what about your father? Don't you care?'

'Of course, I do. But he's dead and we're still alive. We have to move to keep it that way.'

She looked into his eyes, not speaking, but obviously understanding what he was saying.

He said, 'Okay, Sadie, we're going to make a run for it. We'll head for the exit behind us. That's the quickest route out of here. And for God's sake keep your head down.' He waited for a second, letting his words sink in. And then he asked, 'Are you ready?' She nodded, her eyes rimmed red with fear. 'Okay, here goes!'

Mason took her hand and said, 'Right! On the count of three. One. Two, Go!'

They rose quickly and headed for the park gate. Around them as they ran, multiple bullets spat puffs of smoke around their feet. Miraculously, they reached the gate without being hit. Mason pushed Sadie down behind the stone wall on the roadside. The shooter had no chance of hitting them there.

'Nick! What's happening?' Sadie cried out.

'Just take a minute. Breathe.'

Mason guessed that once they were on the road, the gunman would leave them alone. Too many witnesses to relate their stories and far too many cell phone cameras to record the event.

'Look, we need to get out of here and put a bit of distance between us and the shooter.'

Sadie pressed hard into the wall behind her and said, 'That's an understatement!'

Mason looked over the wall. There were no more shots. Apart from the traffic from the road, there was no noise. He wondered if the shooter had left his bolthole over the grassy knoll. It was still a little too soon to leave the safety of the park wall.

He sat back down next to Sadie, their backs against the wall, both breathing heavily. He took her hand, to comfort her.

'I think we should probably get back to the Home and warn Ms Reynolds. They'll probably pay a visit their too. It's only a short distance.

'Why would they want to go to the Home?' she asked looking into his cold eyes.

'I don't know for sure. But I think it's a safe bet that they'll want to tie up all the loose ends before they leave town. Me, you and possibly Ms Reynolds are those loose ends.'

She turned towards him. 'I don't understand. Your father's just been murdered, and you don't appear to bat an eye lid, and what has all this got to do with me and Ms Reynolds? It's crazy! We need to call the police.'

Mason turned to face her head on and held her shoulders gently.

'There's lots of things you don't know, Sadie, and probably wouldn't understand. At this point the police are not going to help. In fact, they might even make it worse.' She looked confused, but he continued, 'We'll go around the other way to the Home. With some luck the Shooter has gone, and we can sort all this out. What do you say?'

Sadie looked unsure but agreed to Mason's suggestion.

'Okay, give me a minute.'

'What?' she asked.

'There's something I need to do. You stay here. It'll only take me a minute.' Before Sadie had chance to say anything else, he was up and moving back into the park, keeping as low as possible. He reached his father and knelt beside him.

'I don't think you'll be needing this dad.' He released his father's pipe from his mouth and tapped it on the floor to jettison the warm embers of tobacco. Once empty, he put it in his jacket pocket. He said sadly, 'It shouldn't have ended this way, dad. I'm sorry I couldn't protect you.' A tear fell on his cheek as he closed his father's eyes. 'But I promise I'll get the man responsible.'

CHAPTER 10

The car park of the Lynne Residential Home for the Elderly was almost empty, save for a couple of cars in the staff quarter.

They'd taken the long way around. Now Mason quickened his step and jogged effortlessly up to the door, with Sadie struggling to keep up while digging into her shoulder bag for the key fob. As she lifted the fob up to the key-less entry point, Mason said, 'No need, the doors already open.'

The lock had been shattered, with a screaming mouth of splinters instead of the key aperture.

'O God! What's happened?' Sadie cried into her hand.

Mason knew it was a bullet hole but didn't say. 'I don't know, but it doesn't look good.'

He pushed the door open slowly and peaked inside, looking both ways. As he started to push the door further open Sadie grabbed his arm. 'Nick, I'm scared.'

He put his hand on her arm. 'Me too. But we need to warn Ms Reynolds that she may be in danger.'

'It may be too late for that, Nick. We should call the police. Let them deal with it.'

'No. Trust me. I must do this myself. Lester has killed my father. Next time it will be me.'

'Lester who?' Sadie asked.

'Tom Lester. Look, I haven't got time to explain. Maybe later. Let's do this and talk later.'

'Okay. But you go first.'

Mason slowly walked into the hallway, the reception desk immediately in front of him, looking up and down the corridor. He heard a distant television. There was an eerie feel about the place. His stomach began to quiver at the possibilities on offer. As soon as he rounded the high reception desk, he witnessed the worst of those possibilities at close quarters, death in all its glory. The young red-headed receptionist who he had met earlier was crumpled up in the corner against the wall. There was a mass of blood across her chest, with more on the wall behind her where she had crashed and then slipped down, dead. Her mouth was an open scream, her eyes wide and fearful. She knew death was coming and it had arrived, violently.

'O no! It's Melanie!' cried Sadie who had come around the desk.

Mason turned and pulled Sadie to one side.

'Sadie, it might be better if you stayed outside. I have a feeling there is going to be more of this.' He began to turn her away from the grizzly sight.

'No,' she stopped, her breathing heavy. 'I have to know what's happened here. These are my colleagues, my friends.'

Mason loosened his grip and reluctantly agreed, 'Okay. But I need you to be calm. The killers might still be here.'

'Do you think so?' she asked, visibly shaking.

'I don't know. But we must be careful. Are you ready?'

She hesitated for a moment before answering. 'Yes, I think so.'

'Okay, but don't touch anything.' Sadie nodded, tears falling down her cheeks. 'Let's go,' he said.

Mason led her through to the main lounge. It was carnage. The dead lay where they had been sat. It was a blood bath. This wasn't the bloody battlefield it resembled, it was the wanton killing of defenceless pensioners and carers. There was blood everywhere, on the walls, on the floor and windows, dripping from bodies.

A female worker lay with her arms outstretched in an effort to protect the people she cared for. She lay across two old ladies, her head destroyed by the bullet that had recently passed through it.

Sadie scrunched her hand into Mason's.

In the kitchen, the staff lay on the floor below where they had been working, with pans sat on heated rings, now bubbling over; steam filling the room. One boiling pan of liquid had fallen on top of a cook and had scalded her face; the paler, pinky red a stark contrast with the deep red of the blood that covered the chef-whites she wore.

Sadie couldn't stop crying. She knew all these people. She had worked at Lynne's for five years and counted all these people, staff, and resident alike, as friends, family even. She gripped Mason's hand tighter. He turned towards her in response.

'Who could do such a thing, Nick? Why would they do this?'

He brought her closer to him, laying her head on his chest. He didn't know what else to do. How do you explain the killing of these defenceless old people to someone who hasn't lived in the criminal world?

He said simply, 'They're evil people, Sadie.'

He let her cry into his chest for a few moments before lifting her head and looking into her eyes. 'Come on, we need to find Ms Reynolds.'

She pulled away and, with hands shaking uncontrollably, wiped the tears from her face, only for more to fall down her cheeks.

There was a corridor that led from the kitchen to Reynolds' office. Mason led Sadie as he headed through the corridor. Blessedly, there were no dead bodies there. However, Mason did note a couple of empty cartridges on the floor. He knew this did not bode well for what was coming. He said nothing of his fears to Sadie.

A rectangular area opened at the end of the corridor. To the right lay the corridor leading back to the main reception area. Ahead, there were stairs to the upper levels of the Home. And to the left, Charlie Reynolds office. The door was closed.

They both stopped in front of the door, fearful of what they would find within.

Mason had to take the initiative. He was the most experienced person here, at least in these circumstances. They may be in the Lynne Residential Home for the Elderly, Sadie's workplace, but this was Mason's world, a galaxy apart from what Sadie had ever experienced.

He looked around at Sadie and asked, 'I don't think this is going to be pleasant. Are you ready?'

Sadie was as pale as it was possible for a live person to be. Her hair had become dishevelled at the front and strands hung loosely over her face. The tears had continued to fall from eyes that were now rimmed red.

'I think so,' she said, convincing neither of them.

Mason pulled the cuff of his jacket sleeve over his hand and turned the doorknob to Charlie Reynolds office, anxious to leave no trace of his fingerprints. Once the door was released, he pushed it so that it opened slowly.

The window faced the open door, sun streaming in through the blinds. The desk had been cleared. Mason stepped into the room, fearing what he might see next. The carnage they had witnessed already was tearing at his equilibrium. He didn't know if he could stomach any more bloodshed.

When he looked to the right his fears were realised. Charlie Reynolds was dead, crucified-like, upright between two grey filing cabinets, arms stretched over the cabinets, and tied in place, her head held up, somehow, with blonde hair matted with dark red blood. Her eyes were shut but her mouth was open, blood had dripped from the corner. She was stripped to her underwear. From several knife wounds, peppered over the body, blood had pumped out, leaving hideous trails downward, dripping off her feet that had been lifted from the floor and tied together.

Sadie stood at Mason's side; her hands flopped to the side of her body. She thought she'd seen it all in the other rooms, but this was something else. 'O my God! Who are these people?'

'The scum of the earth, Sadie.' And just to make sure she had heard him correctly, he repeated himself, 'The scum of the earth!'

Sadie picked her way through the debris on the office floor looking for something.

'Sadie, stay here.'

'I'm looking for a blanket, or something, to cover her up. The way they have left her is awful.'

'No, Sadie. We can't move or touch anything. We must leave it as it is. The police will work things out for themselves. The last thing we need is for the police to find our fingerprints and to put two and two together and come up with us, me.'

'So, what do we do?'

'Get out of here. I'm not sure where, but we need to go, now!'

'Why not my place? It's only down the road, on the edge of the moor. It's quiet there.'

'That's a start. Let's get going.'

CHAPTER 11

Sadie was leaning on the wall next to the front door of her apartment block. She lifted her bag and rested it on her raised knee. 'They're in here somewhere,' she said, rummaging around in what seemed like a bottomless pit.

Mason looked around anxiously, checking the busy Bolton to Preston Road. They were completely visible to passing traffic from the apartment entrance.

'Sadie, we need to get inside, quickly!'

'I know. The keys are here somewhere. I know they are.'

'I'd be happier if you proved that.'

'Yes, here they are!' She lifted the bunch of keys from her bag and opened the outer door. The hallway, with its stone floor and lime green walls, was cold and soulless. Bypassing the elevator, they moved quickly up to her top-floor apartment, three storeys up above the street.

Sadie led him into the small lounge. A window stretched the whole length of the wall to their right, under which a small flat-screened TV sat on a long coffee table. Along the wall behind the opened door was a two-seater settee. A matching chair faced it on the opposite wall. Immediately in front of them, and behind the chair, was a small circular dining table with three chairs. To their left, a door led to the kitchen.

'Do you want a drink?' Sadie asked. 'Alcohol-wise, I've only got wine, I'm afraid. I'm not a beer drinker. Tea or coffee, on the other hand, I can do.'

Mason went over to the window and looked out at the main road below, wondering if Lester's men were out there looking for them.

'A drink?' she asked again.

'Oh yes. Wine will be good. Thanks.'

As Sadie turned towards the kitchen, she said, 'Alexa. Play the Music of Darley.' Immediately, the speaker came to life with the music of a local group playing softly in the background.

Nick wasn't sure what he should do. His father was dead and the whole of the Lynne Residential Home, including Charlie Reynolds, had been murdered by Lester and his men. Fortuitously, he had been around to save Sadie. The poor girl had no idea what she was mixed up in.

She returned with two glasses of red wine. Mason took one and thanked her.

Sadie sat on the couch, the furthest seat away from Nick and the window, and tucked her legs under her body.

'Penny for them?' she asked Nick.

He had no idea what he was going to tell her. If he told her everything, she might panic. If he didn't, she might be in more danger. Either way she could go and tell the police. And if she did that, Nick could be in serious trouble. Ashley too.

Mason perched himself on the bare window shelf, took a sip of his wine, and turned towards his host.

As if reading his mind, Sadie said, 'It appears I've got myself into a something serious here, Nick. And I think you should tell me what it's all about. Am I the next in line for a bullet? That bullet that killed your dad could easily have hit me. And then back at the Home, if I hadn't been out, I'd be a corpse by now, for sure.'

Nick was amazed at how calm she had become since the carnage at the Home. 'So, tell me. Am I next?' she asked more firmly, taking a drink.

Despite feeling the beginnings of a headache, Nick took a glug of wine. He had to go for honesty. Regardless, of what the consequences were, he had to tell Sadie what was happening, if only to offload. He had no idea if she would tell the police, but he knew the odds were in Lester's favour if she did. Lester had *Grasses* everywhere. He'd find out where Mason was anyway. It was better to keep Sadie in the loop, for now.

He lifted his head and looked at Sadie. 'Sadie, I need you to keep what I'm about to say confidential. No one, not even the police need to know any of this.'

'So, I'm deep in something that smells, am I?'

'You are, I'm afraid. And it's not your fault.'

'Is it yours?' she asked.

'Partly. Yes.' He took another swig of the wine, his glass already almost empty.

Sadie recoiled a little. 'Should I be worried?'

'No,' he lied. He needed to keep Sadie calm, if only to stay in her apartment for the night where he would be safe. Lester and his men wouldn't know anything about her or where she lives. 'If I tell you what's going on, you must promise me you won't tell a soul. If not for my life, but for yours too.'

She brushed her hair back from her forehead and got up from the settee. 'I have a feeling I'm going to need another drink. How about you?'

He drained the last of the wine and accepted the offer of more.

Sadie returned from the kitchen with a bottle of red wine. She filled both their glasses and put the bottle on the windowsill. She sat back down on the settee, but this time with both feet on the floor, 'Go on. Let's have it.'

Nick took a gulp and began, 'In a previous life I was a driver of getaway vehicles. I got mixed up from an early age in the criminal world. About six months ago, Tom Lester hired me, through an Intermediary called Kosinski, to kill a girl. That girl...'

'Hang on! I thought you said you were a driver. But they hired you to kill someone?'

'Yes, I'm a driver. I accepted the job for the money. They were offering a ridiculous amount of cash for the job. My dream was to get out of the crime industry completely once the job was done.'

'Unusual retirement plan. Bit quicker than a solid pension fund, I suppose.'

'Sadie, this is hard enough. Please.'

'OK. Sorry. Carry on.'

Mason looked down into his glass, looking for inspiration. 'It turned out that the girl was a long-lost sister of mine that I never knew about. My mother was pregnant when she left me with my father.'

'William Mason?'

'Yes, William Mason.'

'So, what happened?'

He took another drink. 'Once I found out, I couldn't kill her. Instead, we escaped to Dubrovnik in Croatia. Lester, I heard, had been charged with various crimes including murder, drug running, a whole list of stuff. Ashley, that's my sister, and I were fine for a while, then she left. I thought I'd left everything in the past until an acquaintance from that time turned up to warn me that Lester had escaped from prison. That friend died because he came to warn me Lester was free. Obviously, the first person I thought about was my father. I got on the first plane back to England.' He looked at the remaining wine and drank the last of it down. 'You know the rest.'

'Shit! So, where does that leave us? I mean, you don't want to go to the police, although I'm sure they'd put you in a witness protection scheme, or something. I don't know where that leaves you, or me? You're going to be on the run for a while at this rate.'

'I'm afraid so.'

'I don't know if you've got a plan, but I suggest you come up with one quickly, or this man Lester will have your guts for garters, by the sounds of it.' She stood up. 'Right! While you're thinking about that, why don't I see what's in the freezer? At least we can have something to eat. How does that sound?'

'Good.' Nick smiled for the first time in a while.

'Why don't you empty the remainder of that bottle into your glass and then get a fresh one from the rack in the kitchen. While you're doing that, I'll rustle up some frozen lasagne.'

'Sounds like a plan.'

She led the way into the small functional kitchen. The small wine rack was to the left of the kitchen sink. He picked a red wine at random and took it back into the lounge with a corkscrew. With a little trouble, he removed the cork intact, and then placed the bottle in the middle of the table.

The speaker was still quietly playing the same local band. Mason thought the sound was calming. Just what he needed at this moment. It was definitely slowing his heartrate.

He returned to the kitchen and asked Sadie if she needed help.

'Get the knives and forks from the drawer,' she pointed to the drawer in question, 'and set the table, will you?'

He did as he was told and waited for her to come back into the lounge. He checked the bookshelf out. He noticed a romance, billed as a bestseller, 'Going Home'. He'd never heard of it. There was also a children's book, 'Inky Stevens, the Case of the Caretaker's Keys.' There was no other sign of children in the apartment.

'OK! The meal's ready,' she finally announced, carrying a tray with two plates of lasagne and a bowl of salad. She placed the meals on the placemats on the table and put the salad between them. Nick poured two glasses of wine from the newly opened bottle.

Nick praised Sadie's lasagne, even though he knew it was the shop-bought microwavable type and not homemade. She accepted the praise.

Just as they were finishing their meal, Sadie said, 'I don't get many visitors.'

'No? I can't believe that.'

Sadie's beauty had not been lost on Nick. Her brown hair, originally tied back in a bun, had been let loose and was now shoulder length. Her brown eyes glistened in the lighted candle she had placed in the middle of the table. Her lightly tanned face didn't need make-up. She had a winning, youthful smile. 'Don't you have a partner?'

Sadie put her knife and fork down, took a drink of wine, and admitted, 'I haven't had a boyfriend in some time.

Unfortunately, the job gets in the way. The unsociable hours are crippling, and as far as pay is concerned, it's a pittance. Once I've forked out for this place, I don't have much left for a social life.'

'Still, it's a nice place you've got.'

'*Spartan*, I'd say. But there's no one else here, so it doesn't matter much.'

'Hobbies? I noticed you're a reader.' He glanced at the small bookshelf in the corner.

She looked at the bookshelf herself and admitted, 'I am. I read as much as I can. They're all library books. I think it's only me and the old dears at the local luncheon club who keep the library in business.'

'You're lucky it's still open from what I hear.'

'We are. Quite a few have been closed with the cutbacks. We staged a few small demos outside council meetings and, fortunately, the library was given a stay of execution.'

'Sounds like fun. I never had the urge to hold a placard shouting at politicians.'

'You should try it. It can be fun. Sometimes you are just a tiny part of the reason things change for the better; hospital A&E's stay open, road safety signs are erected, or maybe libraries are kept open.'

'You sound like a real rebel.'

'Not really. I haven't got the time or energy for most of it. But threaten my library and I'm going to be in your ear until you back off!'

They both laughed.

'Right! It's my turn to do something. I hope you have a pair of gloves because I'm not ruining these hands doing the washing up?'

'You don't look the precious type to me,' she said smiling, 'but yes, the gloves are on the drainer. I'll leave you to it. I'll put my feet up and carry on with this delicious Malbec.' She got up and started for the settee. Just as they were passing, they accidentally bumped into each other. Mason, six foot tall, towered over Sadie at five-six, and for a moment they stood looking at each other.

Finally, Nick broke the awkward silence, 'I should get that washing up done,' but he didn't move. Neither did Sadie. They just looked into each other's eyes.

Sadie was the first to take the initiative. Buoyed by the wine, she lifted on to her toes and kissed Nick on the cheek and said, 'Thank you for saving my life.' Mason's cheeks reddened as she turned and headed for the settee.

Nick had been momentarily taken aback by Sadie's kiss. When he returned from the kitchen, he didn't know for sure what to do. Should he sit next to her, or use the armchair? If he was honest, a relationship wasn't what he needed right now. He needed to sort the situation with Lester out, not get romantically entangled with someone. He picked his glass of wine up from the dining table and sat on the armchair across from Sadie.

Mason took his cigarettes and lighter from his jacket pocket and asked if he could smoke.

'Yes. I'll get an ashtray and open the window for you.' When she sat back down, she asked, 'So, what are you going to do now?'

Mason took a swig of wine before speaking. He couldn't let Lester get away with what he had done. He'd killed numerous people, including Mason's own father and he had to pay for such actions. He needed to get himself armed and find out where Lester was. Without a weapon, Mason would always be at a disadvantage. He told Sadie of his plans.

'Why, Nick? Why don't you just go away and lose yourself? Somewhere Lester can't find you?'

He sat forward and took a drag from his cigarette. 'I'm afraid that's impossible, Sadie. Lester has contacts everywhere. Wherever I land, he'll find me sooner or later.' Mason was still toying with how much he should let Sadie into his confidence. After what had happened today, he decided he might just as well go for broke.

'Sadie, I was living in Dubrovnik. Well just outside, really. A place called *Babin Kuk*. I rented an old house by the sea.'

'It sounds perfect.'

'It is. Sorry, was,' he corrected himself. 'As I said, one of Lester's men came and warned me that his boss had escaped from jail.'

'But who was he? Why did he warn you?'

'He had helped me previously. Bevan, that was his name. He'd had an affair with Charlie Reynolds, your boss, and through her come into some information that persuaded me to abort the mission. He advised me to leave town, just as you're doing now. But Lester, I think, may have found me in Dubrovnik.'

'So, why didn't this Lester chap kill you there?'

'Luckily, Bevan got to me first. It was the last thing he did. As I said, Lester had him killed.'

'But who is this Lester? I've never heard of him?'

'He lives mainly in the shadows. Basically, he runs the criminal underworld north of Birmingham all the way up to the Scottish border. He probably has half the police force on his payroll.'

'Forgive me for saying, but he sounds like a very unsavoury character.'

'That's one way of describing him. Anyway, if I don't get to him first, he's going to get me. And I'd rather not have the latter happen.'

'I know it's quite early, but why don't you sleep on it? Decide what you're going to do tomorrow. I'll make you some breakfast. Take it from there.'

'Sounds good.' He stubbed his cigarette out in the ashtray. It suddenly crossed his mind that he didn't know where he was sleeping. Sadie enlightened him…

'I'll get you a blanket and a pillow. I'm afraid the settee is all I've got to offer.'

'That'll be fine. Thanks.' He drank the last of his wine and took the empty bottle and glasses into the kitchen.

Sadie returned with the blanket and pillow. 'Okay. I'll leave you to it. If you get up before me, just make yourself a drink and settle in.'

'Will do. Thanks.'

Sadie shut the lounge door as she left.

CHAPTER 12

Tom Lester sat behind his desk smoking a fat Cuban cigar, while listening to someone on the telephone. The smoke rings he had just blown from his puckered lips rose, clouded densely, then dissipated above his head. His face was flushed, and his tie had been loosened from his unbuttoned shirt. The lighting had been dimmed except for the desk lamp which illuminated the whole workspace.

The solid oak-panelled door opened and Irwin, the butler, black-tied and suited to perfection, stepped into the room. He waited for his boss to give him the go-ahead to speak, then announced, 'The gentlemen you were expecting have arrived, Mr. Lester. Would you like me to show them in?'

Lester sucked from the cigar slowly, looking towards the ceiling. He retained the smoke in his lungs, removed the cigar from his mouth carefully, then allowed a cloud to escape. 'Please do that, Irwin,' he said away from the mouthpiece. As the butler left the room, Lester turned his chair away from the door and towards the draped windows. The handgun in the back of his waistband dug into the small of his back. He needed some sun he told himself, half-listening to the caller. Once all loose ends were tied up, he was going away for good, to somewhere where the sun shone all year round.

Lester's train of thought was cut when Irwin cleared his throat. 'Mr Lester, your guests. Mr Lloyd and Mr Nesby.'

Lester didn't respond to this new interruption. Instead, he said into the telephone, 'Just keep me informed if Željko meets anyone.' He heard the click as the line went dead.

Lloyd and Nesby looked uneasily at each other as they entered

Lester's office. Irwin retreated and closed the door behind him once they were inside.

Lester still hadn't turned around.

Lloyd and Nesby stood with the bookcase behind them. They knew that Lester would begin to speak when he was ready. It wasn't their place to begin the conversation.

After a full two minutes of sheer agony for the visitors, Lester slowly turned his chair around to face them. His face told them immediately that he wasn't happy. The crimson hue, which even the shadows couldn't hide, spoke volumes. The rims of his eyes circled red with anger.

Lester kept his fury in check and asked in a measured tone, 'What happened?'

Lloyd started to speak, but Lester cut him off, 'No! You!' He pointed the soggy end of his cigar at Nesby.

Nesby stiffened, suddenly afraid, 'I know you said to scare the old guy, but I couldn't get a clear shot to frighten him. I'm sorry, but I took a split-second decision to kill him. A clean shot.'

Lester didn't take his eyes off Nesby, the younger of the two, as he spoke. Once there was silence, he said, 'Spilt milk.' Then he moved his attention towards Lloyd. 'Now your turn.' It wasn't a question.

Lloyd shifted on his feet. 'While my partner, here, was dealing with the old man, we tried to get the information you wanted from the manager, Reynolds.'

'Unsuccessfully, I take it?' Lester asked, already knowing the answer.

'Ye... Yes, Tom.' A bead of sweat dropped from Lloyd's forehead on to the floor.

'So, you decided to run amok with your guns and butcher everyone in the building?' Lester continued, still measured, 'Did you think that would help? Do you think that was,' he seemed to savour the word, *'proportionate?'* His eyes bored into Lloyd's skull. 'Well?'

'We thought if we showed Reynolds that we were serious, she'd tell us where Nick Mason was.'

'And did she?'

Lloyd looked at Nesby, then quickly back to Lester. 'No,' he answered, hesitantly.

'Sorry. I didn't hear that. Speak up, will you?'

'No, Tom,' Lloyd said, louder.

'No. I bet she didn't. You fucking idiot!' he spat. 'Because of what you've done the police will conduct a massive hunt for the killers. It's all over the news for fuck's sake! That's not exactly what we wanted to happen, is it?' Getting no reply, Lester balanced his cigar on the ashtray and walked around the desk, stopping in front of Lloyd. 'They'll be looking for you. I need you to get out of town.'

'Sure, Tom,' Lloyd began. 'I can get away as quick as you nee...' But before he had finished the sentence Lester had drawn the handgun and shot Lloyd in the head, point-blank. Lloyd lay flat on the floor where he fell; a gaping bloody hole was all that was left of his face.

'That's just about quick enough,' Lester said, looking straight ahead at the bookshelf. He pushed the handgun back into his waistband.

Nesby staggered back a step; a splattering of Lloyd's blood having landed on his clothes. Lester's act, Nesby witnessed, didn't register on his boss's face at all. He was focussed on the bookcase behind where Lloyd had stood. Lester stepped over the dead man's body, carefully missing the spreading blood, and perused the books as if in a local library. He picked one and brought it out. The book's spine was damaged, and it was spattered with blood.

Lester walked back and placed the book on the desk, before wiping the blood off his hands. He lifted the phone and spoke into it as he sat down, 'Irwin, there's a mess in my office that needs cleaning up. Sort it now!'

Irwin appeared immediately. He surveyed the scene and, without missing a beat, commented, 'I'll get the *cleaners* in, Mr Lester.'

'Do that, Irwin. And, please, check the books on the shelves.'

He touched the one he'd taken from the shelf. 'This first edition, Casino Royale, is damaged. I want all the damaged books replaced.' He discarded the once valuable book into the waste bin at the side of the desk.

'Yes, Mr. Lester.' Irwin left the room and closed the door behind him.

Nesby had been shuffling from foot to foot since Lloyd had been slain. His heartrate was soring. He couldn't help but wonder what his boss had in store for him. Whatever it was, Lester wasn't rushing.

Lester relit the half-smoked cigar he'd left on the ashtray. He savoured the slight sweetness as he inhaled, rolling the cigar between his fingers as if using it as an aid to his deliberations.

Nesby almost wished he'd taken the bullet, the silence from Lester was killing him. If he was to be Lester's next victim, surely it would be better to get it over with. Nesby had one advantage over Lloyd though, he knew that his boss was packing and where the gun was. Lester wouldn't be able to go for the gun without him knowing about it. And secondly, Nesby had his own weapon, one which he could easily draw before his psychopathic boss produced his own. If it was a gunfight at the Lester Coral, Nesby was certain he'd beat the older man. Escaping afterwards, now that would then be the issue.

Lester looked up, cigar smoke rising above his head and asked, 'Did anyone see you at the Home?'

'No, Tom. I never went there.'

'So, there's no connection between you and what happened?'

'Except for the death in the park, but I'm sure no one saw me.'

'Good.'

He beckoned the young hitman to the chair across from him. 'Sit, please.' Nesby did as he was instructed. His boss rose and went to the drinks table in the corner of the room. 'Look, I'm sorry about all that,' Lester apologised without a single hint of remorse, 'but sometimes, I must act. You see, failure can't be tolerated. If we fail, the business fails. And if the business fails, we all go under.' He poured two generous shots of whisky and offered one to Nesby, who took it, unable to disguise the tremor in his hand. 'Let's not beat around the bush,' Lester continued, sitting back behind the desk. 'I need this man Mason dead. Not only has he disrupted my business, but I now believe he has allowed his sister, a journalist, to live also. Her work has led to another writer, who we can't locate but works for the same Rag, to delve further into our business interests. First, I'd like Mason *dispatched*. Then the reporter.' He took a gulp of the whisky and reflected for a moment.

Nesby had been listening carefully to Lester for any sign that he was the next for the chopping board. He waited for his boss to take a drink before sampling the expensive whisky himself. He let the golden liquid rest in his mouth for a second or two, mulling over why it cost so much. He was damned if he knew, to him it was just alcohol.

Lester began to speak again, 'All leads at the home are now dead, soon to be buried, so to speak. I want you to keep your ear to the ground. Find out where Mason is.'

It was time for Nesby to tell Lester about the actual shooting. He didn't know if his boss would like what he heard. He suspected not.

'Tom, look...' he stuttered, 'at the shooting...'

'Yes?'

'My instructions were to scare the old man. I went further, as I've just told you.' He paused wondering, wanting to choose his next words carefully.

'And?' Lester sat up in his chair and leaned on the desk.

'There was a younger man and a woman with the target when I found him.' Nesby stopped, waiting for Lester to respond. If he didn't like what had happened, the whisky may be the last drink he ever tasted.

Lester didn't reply straight away. He simply looked at Nesby, his eyes unblinking. Eventually, he emptied his glass.

'Do you think it was Nick Mason,' he asked.

'I've never seen him. And my instructions related to the old man only.'

Lester sat back. 'What about the woman?'

Nesby thought for a second. 'I don't know. But they didn't sit close. He arrived separately and seemed to be in a rush.'

'I'd say you've had Nick Mason in your crosshairs. But no matter. You weren't to know.' He took a drag from the cigar. 'About the girl. Any ideas?'

'No, Tom.'

'If they arrived at different times, perhaps the girl worked at the Home with the elder Mason.'

'That would make sense.'

'Yes. Look, I've got some business in London and then I'm off to Dubrovnik. We know Mason was in the city recently. A complete fluke he should be where my next business venture is. I can't imagine he'll show up there again, that would be madness. If you do find Mason, kill him. I don't care how you do it. Just get rid. And the girl, too, if she's with him. I'll make sure you get a good bonus when you complete the task.'

'Thank you, Tom.'

Lester put the cigar between his lips and opened the desk draw. He picked out a brown envelope contained within and placed it in front of him. Opening it, he took a picture of Nick Mason from among the pile of papers inside and threw it in front of Nesby. 'Take this. It's Mason. The next time I see you, I expect good news.'

Nesby sunk the remainder of his drink, got up, and left the office, but not before chancing a final glance at Lloyd's lifeless, bloody body. When he closed the door behind him, his stomach began to heave.

CHAPTER 13

Mason hadn't slept well. Sadie's settee, while looking nice enough, was far too short for his 6-foot frame. He'd scrunched up, tossed, and turned most of the night.

Tom Lester was not a man to cross. And Mason had done more than cross him. He had been party to bringing Lester and virtually his whole organisation crashing down. His old boss was never going to let him vanish into the distance, no matter how far he ran. Mason had picked Dubrovnik because it was a beautiful city, not that far by plane to England. Less than three hours, in fact. It was just damn unlucky for him that Lester had established contacts there.

At about three in the morning Mason had decided to stop trying to get comfortable. He checked in the kitchen and found an unopened bottle of Malbec. He uncorked it and helped himself to a large glass. Opening the window, he lit another cigarette and contemplated his predicament. Mason had to find Lester first, because if it happened the other way around it could prove fatal. He had to get one step ahead. But how was he going to do that? Lester probably had Bolton wired for any sound or sightings of Mason. There was one person he could take a chance on though, Jonas Pemberton, a local mechanic and all-round know-it-all. He kept his ears to the ground and his cards close to his chest. If anyone knew where Lester was, it would be JP.

Sadie was up and in the bathroom at 7am. After she had finished, he showered, then had a breakfast of eggs and bacon. He apologised for drinking her last bottle of Malbec. They left for JP's garage soon after 9.

On the corner of some dilapidated industrial units on the site of the old Railway Works, it was clear the Garage was a one-man outfit. As Mason and Sadie approached, they could see JP's flashy new pick-up truck emblazoned with his initials, address and contact details, along with the promise, 'Whatever the time, Wherever the place, We're on the Case!' Mason wondered which local advertising guru had come up with that little gem. On either side of the oversized garage door were several cars, one with no wheels on, balanced precariously on a stack of bricks. Obviously ready for the knacker's yard, Mason thought. The smell of engine oil permeated the air, reaching high enough into Mason's nostrils to irritate.

As they walked around the parked cars, a pair of overalled legs could be seen sticking out from underneath an aging Ford Mondeo. One of the black-booted feet was tapping to the beat, unsuccessfully, to the tune of *This Ole House* by Shakin' Stevens, which came from the sound system somewhere in the garage.

Mason cleared his throat as loudly as he could. The foot stopped tapping and JP dragged himself from below the vehicle laying face up on an under-car wheeled creeper. He looked up at Mason and then at Sadie.

'Do my eyes deceive me, or has the confirmed bachelor I know and understand to be Nick Mason bagged himself a girl at last?' He seemed to jump up in one clean movement. The creeper flirted back partially hiding under the car. Grabbing a comb from his pocket he back-combed his black, heavily gelled hair into a rockin' DA. Returning the comb to his pocket, he rubbed his dirty hands with a rag from the other hip pocket and offered to shake Sadie's hand. 'Hello, there. JP's the name. Car repair is the game. And you may be?'

She took his hand and replied, 'Sadie Kellerman.'

'It's a pleasure to meet you, Sadie. And what might you be doing with this loser?' He looked across at Mason and smiled. 'No offense, Nick, but I'm sure this girl could do better. Far better!'

'None taken JP. And I'm sure she could. How's it going?'

'Come into my office.'

JP led his visitors past the prone vehicle he'd been working on and into a glass-encased office in the corner of the garage. The smell of a working garage was everywhere. The desk was covered with papers, mostly smudged with oil or dirt. The computer terminal was so outdated it looked like it could have been one of Bill Gates's prototypes. A couple of grey filing cabinets stood behind his desk chair. 'Sit. How about a coffee?'

'Black for me,' accepted Mason, taking his place across from JP. 'And me,' Sadie joined.

Along the side wall, adjacent to where they sat, was a table. Atop was a coffee machine with its glass pot full of hot black coffee. Cups, sugar, and milk sat to one side of the machine. JP poured the hot coffee and offered Mason and Sadie their cups. He moved some papers aside and put the sugar bowl on his desk in front of them.

The smell of the coffee was a welcome distraction from the oil, Nick thought, as he raised the cup to his mouth. The hot liquid burned his lips before he could take a proper drink. He decided to let the coffee cool a little before trying again.

'So, what can I do for you?' JP enquired. 'I didn't see a car in need of first aid.'

'I've got a serious problem, JP, and I need not only your help, but your discretion, too.'

JP sat forward and looked Mason in the eyes. 'Come on, Nick! Discretion is my middle name.'

'But this one is big Jonas. Bigger than you can imagine.'

The mechanic took a slurp of coffee, put the cup down and then opened a desk drawer. Nick wondered if his friend had a weapon in there but breathed a little easier when JP lifted a tin box containing Jaffa Cakes out from the drawer. 'Want one?' their host offered.

'No, thanks,' Mason declined.

'I'm fine, too, thanks,' Sadie agreed.

JP grinned. 'All the better for me. A full box of Jaffa Cakes. Can't go wrong there.' He took one from the box, bit into it, and said, 'Okay, Nick. What's on your mind? And don't skip the details.'

'It's not what, it's who, and it's Tom Lester that's on my mind.'

JP sat up, swallowing hard. He felt a Jaffa Cake scrape down his throat as he said, 'This is serious, Nick. Go on,' he urged, popping another whole cake into his mouth.

'I need to find him.'

'Are you sure? He's one nasty character, Nick.'

Mason looked over at Sadie. 'We know. We've had recent experience of his work.' Nick paused momentarily. 'Have you seen the morning papers?'

'I have. Bad news about all those dead old folks. There are some sick bastards about.'

'Lester.'

'What?!' JP spat a burst of crumbs all over the table. 'I know he's escaped but I thought he'd be out of the country lying low somewhere?'

'Not anymore.'

'How do you know it was him?'

'Let's just say I, sorry, we're sure.'

JP wiped his mouth with the back of his hand, dislodging crumbs that fell down his overalls. Once he was content, he pushed another Jaffa Cake into his mouth. 'So, what do you want from me?'

'I need to know where Lester is, before he finds out where I am. Can you get that information?'

'You'd better leave it with me. I'll ask around. But listen,' he added, pointing a warning finger, 'if you come a cropper with this, don't come blaming me when your legs in plaster, or you've lost both of them completely.'

'I won't.' Mason paused for a moment. 'There's just one other thing.'

'I'm all ears, not that I should be,' confirmed JP leaning back in his chair.

'I need a gun. Can you sort me one out?'

'Nick!' Sadie interrupted. 'Why do you need a gun?'

'You've seen what Lester and his friends are capable of. It's for the best, Sadie. I need to protect both of us, and I can't do it without a weapon.' Sadie looked away from him. 'Look, Sadie, as soon as this is over, I'll dump the gun. I promise.'

She turned back towards him. 'Having a gun makes you just as bad as them Nick.'

'No, it doesn't, Sadie. It just gives us some protection.'

She thought for a moment and then agreed, 'Okay. But promise me you'll be careful.'

Mason looked Sadie in the eyes and promised, 'I will.'

'Are you both quite finished? I have work to do. I should've finished that car off yesterday, but I went to a 'Shaky' Tribute show in Bridlington of all places.'

'Yes,' Mason confirmed. 'Now, how about the gun?'

JP wrote an address on a piece of paper and passed it over. 'This is Gunner Tudge's address. He's got all the tools you could possibly want. Tell him I sent you.'

'Cheers, JP.'

'Now skedaddle! I've got a car to finish repairing. Nice to meet you, Sadie.' Rising from his chair, he added, 'If you ever get lonely, don't hesitate to drop in.'

Sadie stood up, blushing. 'I might just do that,' she said looking at Nick.

Mason took her hand and said, 'Come on! There's no time for that.'

CHAPTER 14

Nesby knew that Lester had eyes and ears all over town, but to have someone at the very heart of the Cop-Shop was a bit of a coup. For the first time Nesby was getting to meet with his boss's go-to man at the Station, Detective Inspector Ferguson. Lester had told him to wait for a call from Ferguson, who would arrange a meeting. That call had duly come as promised and now they were to meet at a pub about five miles north of town, the Hare and Hound's.

A red light stopped his cars progress as he was about to leave town. Just as well, he didn't want to arrive early. Getting to the party early was the biggest faux pas according to an ex-girlfriend of Nesby's. He felt nervously for the gun under his left armpit. Did he need to pack a weapon where he was going? Probably not. Before the light turned to green, he unclipped the gun from its holster, leant over, and dropped it in the glove compartment where it would be safe.

The rural road north was free of traffic, save for the odd vehicle. The open undulating road allowed for speeds which weren't safe, and evidence of patched-up brickwork walls which skirted the route proved some drivers had overestimated their driving ability.

Nesby drove at a safe speed. He had no idea if police cars patrolled these quiet roads and the last thing he needed was to be stopped for speeding. He could imagine the ensuing conversation…

'Where do you need to be in such a hurry, sir?'

'It's nothing important, officer, I'm just on my way to have a drink with a bent copper!'

That was an exchange he could well do without.

Eventually he came to the pub on the right and pulled into the large car park. It was late afternoon, and the sky was a suffocating grey. There were a few other cars dotted around the parking area. Most of the customers would have had their lunches already and left. The dinner patrons wouldn't start arriving for another hour or so.

Flicking open the glove compartment, Nesby took another look at his handgun. He touched the empty holster under his arm. He felt vulnerable without the weapon. If there was trouble, the last thing he needed was an empty holster.

No, he had to take it.

If there was one group of people you just couldn't trust, it was the cops! He slipped the gun back into its holster and headed for the restaurant entrance, clicking the car locked as he went.

Inside, he was greeted by a young red-headed girl with freckles covering her young face. She was slight and dressed in regulation black, as lots of waiters and waitresses were these days.

'Yes, sir,' she smiled. 'Do you have a booking?'

'I'm meeting someone. Mr Ferguson.'

She moved around the reception table, glanced down at her booking's ledger, and nodded.

'Yes. He's already arrived. If you'll come this way, I'll show you to your table.'

He followed as she zig-zagged through the empty tables. Ferguson was sat with his cell pointed towards his clean shaven face, engrossed in whatever was on the screen. He'd taken his suit jacket off and had hung it over the back of the chair next to him. His shirt was white and crisply ironed, his old school tie falling over his lean torso.

'Mr Ferguson, your guest,' introduced the waitress.

Ferguson said 'thanks' and gestured to the seat facing him, killing his cell, and stowing it in his jacket pocket.

'Can I get you a drink, sir?' the waitress asked Nesby. Ferguson already had a sparkling water.

'Honey bourbon.'

'Thank you. The bar staff will bring your drink shortly,' she said, and retreated.

Ferguson glanced out of the side-window overlooking the car park. Beyond his reflection he could see his own navy Beamer parked alone at the far end. He'd worked hard for years to afford such luxuries. Unfortunately, his paltry police salary didn't match the living standards he, his wife, or indeed, his mistress, expected. This meeting, with one of Tom Lester's lackeys, was a necessity if he was to continue living the life he enjoyed.

Lester paid him a monthly retainer through a legit company, and, in return, Ferguson offered security advice, as and when required. Of course, what Lester wanted was inside information about investigations or possible heads-up on issues that may relate to him or his associates, information which Ferguson was more than happy to oblige for the money he was paid.

As Nesby placed his cell on the table, Ferguson shook a finger towards it.

'I think it would be better for all concerned if you discarded the listening device.'

'What's your problem?' Nesby asked. 'It's a phone.'

'I agree. But in the wrong hands, it's a bug. The last thing either of us need is for this meeting to be recorded. Trust me.' The irony of his last statement wasn't lost on Ferguson. Whatever was happening here, there was little trust on either side of the table.

Nesby returned the cell to his inside jacket pocket.

A different waitress, this time a petit blonde girl with sharply defined black highbrows, brought Nesby his drink.

'Bourbon?'

Nesby lifted a hand off the table. 'Please.'

She placed the drink in front of him.

'Will you be ordering food, gentleman?'

Ferguson said, 'No. We'll just be having drinks, thank you.'

She said, 'Thank you,' and left.

As Nesby took a small sip of the bourbon, Ferguson said, 'It'll rot your guts, that.'

'I'll take my chances,' Nesby replied, savouring the smooth honey drink slipping down his throat.

Ferguson took another look out the window. His car still alone; it was as if the other patrons didn't want to be seen parked next to a copper's car. A bent copper, at that. He felt the loneliness constantly. The truth he held was his alone. He couldn't tell his employers what he was doing, he'd be arrested on the spot. Neither could Tom Lester know of the secrets he held back. If he did, he'd be a dead man for sure. His mistress didn't know anything at all. She was just a random highlight for a stressed-out copper. And his wife, if she found out about any of it, life was over as he knew it. Divorce, jail, death, and probably in that particular order too. All stress-related afflictions that ate away at his stomach daily.

Ferguson turned back towards Nesby, Lester's lackey. He could spot a goon a mile away… wears a suit and jacket, probably provided by some two-bit tailor in town who advertises a 'bespoke' service, closely cropped hair that aspired to be 'hardman-military' in appearance, a starling tattoo on his right hand, and that tell-tale bulge under the left armpit. If Ferguson so desired, he could nick Nesby now for possession of an illegal firearm. But, what the hell! He didn't care. He just needed to get this little tête-à-tête over and done with.

'So, what's Tom after this time?' Ferguson asked.

'Just a small favour.'

'And that is?'

Nesby emptied his glass, 'I think I'll have another one of these.' He raised his arm and clicked his fingers in the direction of the waitress. 'Do you want one?' he asked Ferguson.

'I'm fine.'

The waitress came over, took Nesby's order, and retreated towards the bar.

Ferguson then revealed, 'You know I could nick you once you get behind the wheel of that car of yours?'

'Yeah, but you wouldn't, would you? My boss wouldn't be pleased about that. Not at all.' Nesby gave Ferguson a toothy grin.

'Now. Mr. Lester would like to know what information you've got on the massacre at the old people's home.'

Ferguson exhaled deeply. 'Shit situation that. There are some sick bastards about, I can tell you. Got a call over the radio. I went to the location myself. A sickening bloodbath is the only way I can describe it.'

The waitress interrupted Ferguson's flow with Nesby's drink. Once she'd retreated, Nesby asked, 'Anything stand out?'

'How'd you mean?'

'Well, could it have been terrorism? Random slaughter? Disgruntled relative who didn't like the way their parent was being cared for? Or was there some other motive?'

'A motive?' Ferguson laughed. 'What sort of crazy motive could some sick fucks have for murdering thirty-odd pensioners and their carers?'

'I don't know,' Nesby said, taking a slug of the bourbon.

'And you can forget terrorism. Even those deranged bastards wouldn't do that.'

'So, who then?' Nesby asked.

Ferguson sat back in his chair. 'If I was a betting man, I'd say it's just some mental case who had got hold of a gun and went on a bit of a rampage. You read about it all the time about America.'

'Sounds plausible.' Nesby liked this line of thought; it took the police away from Lester. He then noticed something in Ferguson's eyes. An almost visible question mark sat in the middle of each pupil. Ferguson was thinking that there was more, and he had questions to which there were no answers. That much was clear.

'What's on your mind?' he asked Ferguson who'd fallen silent.

After a beat, Ferguson said, 'Wait. There was a snippet of a conversation I caught. When I got back to the Station, I heard that an old guy had died from a gunshot wound in the local park.'

'Coincidence?' Nesby asked, knowing it was no such thing.

'Could be. But I doubt it. There was no one with him, so how did he come to be there? Poor bastard was still strapped into his wheelchair. Couldn't have got there all by himself.'

'Do the Coppers have an ID?' Nesby asked taking a deep gulp of bourbon.

Ferguson shrugged.

'Mr Lester will need to know when you find out who he is?'

'And why's that? He's just some random old guy. If you ask me, the gunman did him a favour. Instead of him suffering a slow painful death, he's put him out of his misery with a single bullet.'

'Just keep us in the loop, will you?'

'Tell Tom, I'll be in touch the minute I have something of use.'

'Just one more thing.'

'I'm all ears.'

'Do you have a person of interest, anyone in mind for the murders?' Nesby asked.

'Not that I'm aware of. Like I said, it's probably just some mental fuck lost his way. He's gonna end up in somewhere like Broadmoor when all this is over.'

Nesby laughed to himself. Little did Ferguson know that the gunman who saved Mason Senior from all those years of old age agony was sat across the table. He wondered if Ferguson did know, would he arrest him for the killing?

Now that really would be interesting...

CHAPTER 15

Just on the outskirts of Bolton, northwest, was a stone cottage, its upper windows and roof peeking over the higher road. The dilapidated structure was covered by crawlers, as if trying to suffocate the life out of the structure. It was evident the windows hadn't seen a chamois in months, if not years.

Mason nosed the SUV through the tight stone-walled gateway. He parked next to a battered Land Rover and killed the engine. There were tyres and other car parts haphazardly discarded around the area.

'This place looks a mess,' said Sadie looking at the debris-strewn driveway.

Mason opened the door, 'I don't think ascetics are a gunsmiths' top priority. Do you?'

'I suppose not. But I hope the inside is a bit cleaner.'

'Don't bank on it,' he said shutting the car door.

Mason pushed the doorbell. There was no immediate answer, so he pushed the button again, impatiently.

After a short interval, there was a click from a speaker somewhere above the door and a metallic voice instructed, 'Hold your Driver's Licence up to the doorbell. It's a fish-eye camera too.' Mason took the card from his wallet and did as instructed. After a beat, a buzzer sounded, the door-lock released. Mason pushed the door open as the voice commanded, 'Come in and follow the hallway down to the end.'

Mason and Sadie entered the house, closing the creaky door behind them.

The hallway they found themselves in was musty, a smell which cut deep into Sadie's nostrils. Cobwebs arced between the walls and ceiling, 'Does he ever clean this place,' she whispered.

'It would appear not.' Mason took hold of Sadie's hand. 'Come on. There's no time to stand and admire the fixtures and fittings.'

There were two exits on either side of the hall with a fifth lying straight ahead, slightly ajar. A light shone between the door and the frame. When they reached the door, Mason pushed it fully open. Stairs led down into a cellar and at the bottom a bald-bespectacled man stood waiting for them. With the limited light available, Mason guessed he was in his fifties. He had a gun slung under his left armpit.

As they descended the stairs, Mason got the feeling he'd seen Gunner Tudge before. In his circles it wasn't unusual, but he just couldn't place him. Tudge's sideburns, cut off at the top of his ears, met the stubble that wrapped around his chubby chin, which seamlessly joined the chest hair which escaped from an open-buttoned shirt at the top. His exposed skin was clammy in the claustrophobic cellar. His half-moon glasses had slipped down his nose and both his armpits were dark with perspiration.

The only light came from a single bulb hanging from the ceiling.

Tudge wiped his hands on a napkin and made to shake Mason's hand. 'Hello. Jonas said you'd be coming.' He swept his arms out in an effort to widen the cluttered cellar, 'Welcome to my humble abode.'

Shelving covered all four walls, and on them boxes were piled high. Facing the stairs was a desk. Tudge made for it and sat down. 'Please, sit. You don't mind if I finish my lunch, do you?' He didn't wait for an answer and took a large bite from the half-eaten Big Mac, washed down with a slurp of cola from the large drinking carton.

Mason and Sadie took seats across the desk from Tudge, Sadie more hovering than sitting.

Once Tudge had finished chewing, he asked, 'So, what can I do for you?'

'I need a gun.'

'Not surprising. You've come to a gun dealer.' He took another slurp of the cola. Sadie tried not to look as Tudge put the carton down and indelicately extracted bits of burger from his brown teeth. 'Anything in mind?'

'Not really. It's just for protection. They're not really my thing.'

'But you've suddenly found yourself in some trouble and you need a little life insurance,' Tudge interjected.

Mason looked at Sadie and she at him. 'Sort of,' he agreed.

'Well, you've come to the right place. Do you have any preferences?'

'As I said, it's not my sort of thing, but something easy to conceal.'

'Have you used a gun before?' Tudge asked.

Mason raised an eyebrow.

'Good! I hate showing people how to use guns. Some people get the idea I'm a teacher, that I can turn them into Dirty Harry in ten minutes. I say to them, "I'm a seller, just like your local newsagent. And just like he can't teach you how to read the news, I can't tell you how to use a gun and,' he paused a beat, 'who to point it at.' Tudge got up and wiped his hands on his already smeared shirt. Picking a box up from a shelf to Mason's right, he opened it and peered in. He picked the gun out of the box and assessed the weapon. 'Magnum. This is too big, I think.' He replaced the box and picked another from a shelf above. As he lifted its lid a smile lit up his face, 'Now we're talking. Feast your eyes on this little doozy. A Glock. The Old Bill like this little doozy.' He offered it to Mason who took it from him and weighed it carefully in his hand. 'Just what you want, in my humble opinion. I have a belt clip for this and plenty of ammunition. What do you think?'

'Just the job. What's the damage?'

Tudge took the gun back from Mason and put it back in the box on the table while he collected the ammunition and belt holster. 'I'll work it out.'

Once everything was on the table, he scribbled a series of calculations on a notepad. Having finished, he turned the pad around so Mason could see the total cost.

'Bit steep, but you've got me over a gun-barrel, so to speak.'

'I'm a reasonable guy, my friend. These things cost money and are very hard to come by. Non-traceable. If you can find another supplier at a cheaper rate, be my guest...' Tudge pointed back up at the stairs behind Mason and Sadie.

'No offence, meant,' Mason said, taking the money from his jacket pocket and counting it onto the table.

'None taken, Mr Mason.'

'Nick, please.'

Tudge got to his feet and, tucking his bulging shirt back into his trousers, he approached a shelf on Sadie's side of the room. He picked out a bottle of Glenfiddich, and three glasses. Cracking open the bottle, he poured a small amount in the glasses and passed one each to Sadie and Mason. He sat down with his glass in front of him. Sadie wasn't keen on whiskey but took it anyway. Anything to get the smell of the cellar out of her nostrils.

'Let me give you some advice, Nick,' Tudge started, after a generous slug. 'I've heard on the street that Tom Lester is looking for someone who fits your description.' He shifted his gaze over to Sadie. 'No word about a lady friend though.' He looked back at Mason. 'But if you are that guy, I would be very careful. Lester is one nasty bastard. Beggin' your pardon,' he said in Sadie's direction. 'Now, my guns will kill anyone, and to be honest, I couldn't give a baboon's red-hot ass who, but if it's Lester you're pointing it at, make sure your aim is good and you get the first shot in.'

'I have every intention,' Mason said taking a swig of the whiskey.

Sadie felt obliged to take a drink, to join the party. She coughed as the fiery liquid went down. Both men looked at her. Her face had turned red. Once she'd cleared her throat, she asked, 'What do you know about Lester?'

'Just that he's one bad dude.'

'Have you sold guns to him?' Sadie asked.

Tudge laughed. 'What are you? A cop?'

'No. I would just like to know about your allegiances.'

Mason cut in. 'Sadie, I think we should let Mr Tudge get on with his work. It's no concern of ours.'

'No concern of ours? What are you talking about?'

Tudge poured himself a second measure. 'This is a first. I've never had a domestic in my office before.'

'Sadie, calm down.'

Sadie jumped up and turned away from both men. 'Calm down! How can I calm down?' She felt her head was about to exploded. Tears began to flow, and they escaped through the fingers that covered her face. She abruptly turned back, wiping away the tears and regaining her composure, to Mason and Tudge. She pointed at Tudge. 'This man could have sold Lester the guns that killed all my friends, and your father.'

'Which friends are we talking about?' Tudge cut in.

Mason rose from his chair and gave Sadie a comforting hug. He could feel the tenseness in her body.

He turned to Tudge and said, 'We need to keep our heads down. Can we trust you?'

Tudge crossed his heart with an index finger.

'The old people's home...'

'That was Lester?' Tudge took a slug of whiskey and quickly refilled his glass.

'Yeah. Not only that, but we think he was looking for me.'

'Holy shit! You *are* in trouble.'

'You could put it that way.'

Sadie sat down and took a drink, 'So you see. My friends have been butchered and the guns responsible could have come from here.'

'No.' Tudge stopped her in her tracks. 'No. The guns didn't come from here. Lester has a private supplier. I've never met the man or any of his associates, as far as I'm aware.'

'That's good,' Sadie said, staring at Tudge.

Mason's burner phone came to life, buzzing in his inside pocket. Mason apologised and moved towards the stairs, answering the phone.

'Yes.'

'JP here. I have news.'

Mason didn't really need JP to identify himself as there was the unmistakable sound of Shakin Stevens in the background. There was only one person he knew who played Shakey none-stop.

'Go on.'

'Lester's back in town. My contact says he's been in Amsterdam tying up a deal. He's back at his house on the moors just north east of town.'

'How many men does he have with him?'

'No idea. But it's safe to say he'll be well protected. Look, Nick. Do you really need to be getting mixed up with Lester? I mean, this man thinks killing people is sport.'

Mason glanced over towards Sadie. He'd not only got himself mixed up with the biggest drug dealer in the north of England, but he'd dragged her into his affairs, too. This girl had no idea what she was mixed up in. So not only did he have to neutralise Lester for himself, but also for Sadie, too, because she'd never be safe again while Lester was alive.

'I haven't much choice, JP. He'll find me eventually. I'd rather it was on my terms.'

'What are you going to do?'

'I don't know yet. I'll have to play that as we go. Look, do me a favour.'

'Anything...'

'Just keep your ears to the ground. Anything, anything you hear about Lester, get it to me asap.'

'Sure will, Nick.'

With that, Mason rang off and returned to his seat. Sadie and Tudge had been talking and drinking. 'Any chance of a top-up?' he asked.

'Sure.' Tudge refilled Mason's glass.

'You two good now?' Mason asked.

'We've had a little chat. Sadie was still a little sceptical to begin with, but I've convinced her that I don't deal with Lester. The death of her friends is a tragedy. We have raised a glass in their honour, and to your father's.' Mason looked across at Sadie. 'You okay?'

There was no evidence of her previous tears or anxiety. 'Of course. I was just letting everything get to me for a minute. I'm calm now. Let's just target the right people, shall we?'

'Good.' He took a drink. 'I've just heard Lester is back in town. We should go.'

'Nick, you need to be careful if Lester's your target,' Tudge warned.

'There's no need to worry. Careful is my middle name.' He emptied his glass.

'And you're sure you can use this gun,' Tudge asked, glancing at the Glock sitting in the box on the table.

'I'm good,' Mason assured.

'Nick, honestly, I don't care who this gun kills. But know this, there will be repercussions!'

Mason stood up and clumsily fitted the holster to his belt. He slipped the gun home, patted his jacket down over it, and put the two boxes of bullets into his jacket pocket.

'There will be no repercussions for you, Mr. Tudge. Come on, Sadie.' Mason didn't wait for him to respond. He led Sadie back up the stairs and out of Tudge's ramshackle house.

When they got in the SUV, Sadie said, 'You'd think he'd have a nicer house with all that money he makes from those gun sales.'

CHAPTER 16

Mason parked the SUV on the poorly lit country road and killed the headlights. The gated entrance to Tom Lester's private estate stood open at the side of the road to their left.

Sadie looked across at Mason who was staring at the entrance, 'So what do we do now, Sherlock?'

'We take a look,' he answered casually.

They got out of the car, shutting the doors in unison. Beyond the gate there was a curtain of darkness with the flicker of starlight above. No light from the road penetrated beyond the gate. They traced the meandering tarmac which cut through the lawns. Mason imagined that a century or two before this road would have been a dirt path with a horse and carriage bringing Jane Austin-type characters hither and thither.

He estimated they'd walked almost a third of a mile into Lester's estate when a stone wall set waist high, lay before them. There was another open-gated entrance. Rising tall, trees traced this inner barrier. Mason motioned for Sadie to crouch down and sit with their backs to the wall.

He whispered, 'You sure you're up for this?'

'About as sure as I can be.'

Mason reached for his gun and checked everything was in working order. Satisfied, he replaced it back in the holster.

'Right, let's go.'

They moved through the gate into the inner compound. The house was an imposing stone structure. Mason guessed the main building was constructed sometime during Victoria's reign. Other parts may have been built earlier. He whistled, 'Wow! What a pad.'

'You're telling me,' Sadie whispered. 'I once stayed in a hotel this size. Cost me an arm and a leg.'

'Yeah?'

'Yeah. I had to throw in the other leg to get a full English Breakfast,' Sadie joked.

The spotlights that hung under the high gutters provided the only light and, whilst not flooding the whole area, they did project an arc of clear vision around the building. Anxious not to be seen, they skirted the brightly lit area around Lester's home, using the trees as cover.

'I think we should go around the back. But stay out of the light,' Mason cautioned.

The pair ran from the trees to the side of the building. There were no windows on this gable end.

Sadie followed Mason around the edge of the building. They walked through an arched stone gateway built on to the side of the structure. Once through, the garden opened in front of them at the back. The closely lit area of the garden was all they could see. The old stone residence was dotted with windows criss-crossed with lead. Mason could imagine children playing noughts and crosses with their fingers on the windows in the winter condensation.

He motioned for Sadie to crouch down again as they walked past the first set of darkened windows. Beyond those, a bay window jutted out over the rear gardens. Mason peered in at the near side window. Inside was what he presumed was Lester's office. Beyond his chair and desk, wood-panelled shelving stretched around most of the walls, only stopping for the window and a door which stood to the far-left corner as Mason looked in.

'We need to get in and have a *butchers*, Sadie. Are you comfortable with this, or would you rather wait here?'

Sadie took hold of his hand and whispered, 'Where you go, I go.'

'Sure?'

'Sure!'

AN INVITATION FOR REVENGE

'Good. Then let's move.'

Mason checked the window. It was locked. No surprise there. The main glass panel was solid with no opening. Amazingly, he found that the far side window was slightly ajar. He pulled the frame slowly open, hoping that it wasn't wired to an alarm. Fully opened, and with no siren activated, he said, 'In for a penny...' then lifted himself onto the window ledge. Once he'd had a look around, he jumped down into the office. He immediately turned around and beckoned Sadie up onto the ledge. She jumped up and joined him inside.

They crouched down between the window and the office desk and chair.

Sadie broke the eerie silence, 'So what now, Raffles?'

Mason pulled his handgun from the holster and took the safety off. 'This could get messy. If anything happens, keep your head down.'

Sadie's eyes widened as she saw the gun, 'Don't worry! If you don't mind, I think I will!'

Mason rose and checked the desk drawers. There was nothing inside apart from the usual assortment of pens, pencils, paper clips etc. He scanned the amassed books and noticed a large gap on one of the shelves opposite. 'Come on, I think I've found a safe.' He led Sadie around the desk over to the shelving. He studied the gap in the books, head high, running his hand along the shelf. 'Well, it's not a safe, but there is something.'

'And what's that?' Sadie asked, seeing nothing but a gap in the books.

Mason's eyes were unblinking as he looked at a dark stain on the shelf. 'If I'm not mistaken, I'd say this is dried blood.'

'Shit!' Sadie whispered.

'"Shit", indeed. This doesn't look good. I know it's stating the obvious, but we need to be careful. Come on, let's have a look around.'

'You first, Rambo!' she whispered.

Sadie followed him, both creeping, out of the office and into what looked like the main reception area of the house. A grand staircase reached up from the middle of the room to their right. At the top it split into two, heading to the East and West Wings. Down the side of the stairs, where they now stood, lay a couple of wooden doors, both closed. To their left, facing the stairs, was the main entrance to the house. On the other side of the hall were another couple of doors. The area was tiled and cold. But for a couple of paintings on the wall and a chandelier that dropped from the ceiling, decoration was limited.

Scanning the area carefully as he moved, Mason crept across the hallway and passed the bottom of the stairs. The first door he came to was shut. There was a crack in the second and a light framed the opening. Mason raised an arm across to stop Sadie passing him. He needn't have bothered. She was a couple of steps behind and not rushing to advance. He pointed towards the light with his gun and then crouched, signalling for Sadie to do the same.

'Look,' he whispered, 'Lester might be in there. I'm going to have a listen at the door and if I think it's clear, I'm going in. You stay here. If you hear anything you don't like, run.'

'What happens if there's more than one person in there?'

A shadow crossed Mason's face, 'I'll have to deal with the hand that's dealt on this, Sadie.'

'Okay. But just for the record, I think you've lost your mind. There's no way he's going to be sat in there on his own. He'll have bodyguards. *Armed* bodyguards.'

'You may be right. But until I get him, I'm always going to be looking over my shoulder. Right! Now stay back.' Sadie did as she was told while he slowly moved towards the open door. He leaned into the door, listening carefully, gun held head high with its barrel pointing up towards the ceiling. Classical music from the room. There was no conversation as far as Mason could discern. Did that mean that the occupant was on his or her own, or was the music a shared experience? Mason needed to find out.

He slowly pushed the door open with the flat of his hand, trying to get a better view of the room as the door opened slowly. Just like the office, this room was filled with bookshelves.

A figure, grey haired, sat with his back to Mason, his head just above the chair's backrest. An arm rested lazily on a chair arm, where a bulbous half-full glass of brandy sat on a side-table. A book lay open next to the glass, face down, its spine tortured. Mason was careful not to make any sound. He quickly looked around the back of the door…

No one there.

The man was alone and oblivious to the intruder's presence.

Mason tip-toed around the side of the room as quietly as possible, holding the gun up, ready to respond if the man made any threatening move. He was now square-on to the coffee table, almost within reach of the glass. He felt his mouth drying, desperate for a sip of the dark liquid.

Mason knew this wasn't Lester, of course. The man was much too old. His tell-tale butler-like black suit being another giveaway. The heavy nasial breathing didn't reach a full snore, but it was noticeable. The round stomach stretched his shirt to the limit, his black tie falling to the side. A black jacket was thrown over an adjacent chair.

Mason saw no sign of a weapon.

The orchestral music filling the room provided excellent cover. Mason knew that if he could keep any noise below the level of the speaker volume, he'd be free to interrogate this old man. Yet before he had chance to wake the sleeping butler, Sadie burst into the room. 'Okay! What's happening? This place is empty!'

The butler woke up with a start and attempted to jump from his seated position. Mason moved quickly, pushing him back and putting a hand over his mouth while pointing the gun squarely at his forehead. 'Shut up, old man!'

The butler's body stiffened under the pressure Mason was exacting on his face.

Mason looked up at Sadie. 'Will you shut up and get over here,' he ordered through gritted teeth. 'Someone's sure to hear.'

Sadie walked over towards Mason and casually took a drink from the butler's glass. 'Nope. No one here. I've checked the master bedroom and most of the other rooms. Not a soul in sight. This guy,' she stuck a thumb out, 'is home alone. Do with him what you will.' She put the glass down. 'Nice brandy!'

Mason looked at her, eyes wide with disbelief. 'I can see I'm not going to be able to leave you for a minute. You could've been hurt, killed even.'

'Well, I wasn't.' She looked at the butler, tapping at the glass. 'You haven't got any more of this have you?'

The butler's trembling hand pointed at a drinks table in the corner of the room. As he began to speak, Mason eased the pressure on him. 'Help yourself,' the butler said.

The man retrained his fear-filled eyes on Mason. 'What do you want?' he stuttered.

Mason looked over his shoulder and asked Sadie to fill him a glass. He returned his gaze to the butler. 'What's your name?'

'Irwin,' answered the butler.

'Well, Irwin, I'm looking for Tom Lester. You wouldn't happen to know where he is, would you?'

Sadie offered Mason a glass of brandy. He took a gulp.

'I haven't the foggiest. He doesn't tell me anything about his movements. I just pack his bags.'

Mason brushed the gun barrel tip gently down Irwin's nose. When he reached the end, he pushed forwards a little, creasing the butler's skin. Irwin's eyes followed the gun barrel. He sank back into the seat attempting to move away from the weapon. But there was no escape.

'Are you sure?' Mason pressed.

'Of course, I'm sure. I'm just the hired help. I know nothing of Mr Lester's dealings or whereabouts. I'm not privy to that information. Please,' he begged, 'I know nothing. I can't help you.'

Mason turned towards Sadie, 'What do you think we should do with him?'

Sadie took a drink and chewed over the question. 'You could kill him,' she said eventually.

Irwin's gaze shot from Sadie to Mason. He was sweating

uncontrollably. 'No! Honest, I know nothing. I can't help you.'

'Bit drastic that, Sadie,' Mason cautioned. 'Remember, we're supposed to be the good guys here.'

'Sorry. I thought we were playing good cop, bad cop. I've always wanted to be the bad one,' she said casually.

'No problem,' said Mason.

Irwin exhaled.

'Irwin. Do you have a first name?'

'It's Ted, sir.'

Mason pulled away sure he was safe to do so.

'No need to call me "sir", Ted.' Mason thought for a moment. 'Okay. I'm going to disregard my friend's suggestion, but instead I'm going to tie you up. I'm sure you have cleaners and other staff arriving in the morning. You'll be safe here for a while, and more importantly, we will be.' He turned his gaze back to Sadie, 'Go find something to tie him up with.'

'Okay. As it happens, I've seen some rope in the house. Can't think where. I'll…'

Irwin interrupted, 'Yes, there's some rope at the side of the kitchen table. I was using it earlier.'

'Very helpful, I'm sure,' Sadie said and set off for the kitchen.

Mason watched her leave, then asked, 'Let's not get the feeling we're too chummy, Ted. I'm the one with the gun.'

Irwin felt a bead of sweat trickle down his back, his face bright red. 'Now, I'm going to ask you once more while the little lady is out of the room. I'm sure you wouldn't want her to witness what a mess this gun would make of your head. Do you agree?' Irwin nodded uncomfortably. 'Now, once more,' Mason began with added steel, 'Where is Lester?'

'Please!' Irwin held his hands up in surrender. 'I don't know.'

'Okay. Let's start with what you do know.'

'Mr. Lester left earlier today. I don't know his destination. Honest. He'd only just got back from a business trip to Amsterdam. This time he wanted clothes for a warmer climate. That's as much as I know.'

'Good. Now we're getting somewhere. So, we're thinking out

of the country. I mean, you wouldn't wear shorts and sandals in this God-forsaken shithole, now, would you?'

'No,' Irwin agreed. 'Only he didn't say where, or for how long he'd be gone.'

'Is that normal?'

'I suppose. I just look after the house.'

'Can you think of anything else that might be of interest?'

Irwin took his time answering.

'Come on,' Mason hurried. 'Out with it!'

'It's just that...' He paused, then continued, 'Yesterday, Mr. Lester had two guests.'

'And? What's so special about that?'

'Only one left!'

'Only one left?' Mason repeated.

'Yes. Well, when I say *only one left*, what I mean to say is, only one left alive. The other left in a body bag.'

'A body bag? Is that his blood in the office?' Mason asked.

'It is, I'm afraid. Mr. Lester has a man who cleans up for him. A sort of trouble-shooter.'

'Why did Lester kill the man?'

'I don't know. I don't listen in. Mr. Lester is very keen for me to keep my nose out of his business affairs. And to be honest, so am I.'

Sadie returned carrying a length of rope. 'How's our little friend?'

'Singing like a bird. It's a shame you missed it.' Mason took a drink of brandy, then offered Irwin his glass, 'You'd better have a drink. You won't be getting another until the morning at best.' Irwin took the glass and had a long pull on the drink. 'Tie him to the chair, Sadie.'

Sadie did as she was told while Mason looked around the library. 'Does Lester read all this shit?'

'He does.' Irwin winced as Sadie pulled tight on the rope. 'Says it's the only thing that relaxes him.'

Mason peered at the titles on the shelves. One caught his eye, and he picked it up from the shelf. He flicked through the pages.

'Hard to believe reading Jane Austin's Northanger Abbey would be relaxing.' He closed the book and dropped it on the floor. 'O well, horses for courses, I suppose. Have you done with that rope yet?'

Sadie looked up. 'Instead of picking your next library book you could give me a hand.'

He joined Sadie and between them they made sure Irwin was tied down securely. Both took a final drink.

'Look, Mr. Irwin; as they say, this isn't personal. It's just necessary.'

'I understand, sir,' replied Irwin. 'Be on your way before anyone comes back. I'll clean up tomorrow.'

CHAPTER 17

Tom Lester clipped his watchstrap together as he sat on the side of the hotel bed. His bronzed body was toned and sculptured. His peppered grey hair, normally gelled to perfection, was slightly ruffled after his recent exertions.

He'd now had meetings in Amsterdam, Marseille, and London. The final leg of his negotiations to land the drug deal of his life was set for Dubrovnik in the coming days. If he could tie up a deal at the supply end with Željko Kovačić in the Croatian city he'd be set for life, with the money and the power to put all his worries behind him.

He hadn't forgotten his time in prison, and he didn't want a repeat of that experience. Cushioned from the extremes of prison life with a bribe or a bung in the right envelope, Lester had had time to reflect on why he was there and who was to blame. Bevan, his trusted confidant, and right-hand man for many years, had stabbed him in the back. He'd regretted not being there when Bevan had paid the ultimate price. Lester had always experienced pleasure when watching people beg for mercy. The first person he'd killed had cried like a baby. Begging, pleading, snivelling to be allowed a second chance. He'd revelled at seeing his victim breathe a sigh of relief when he gave him a slight indication that all would be well, that a stay of execution had been granted. Only to dash all hope for the victim when he'd pistol whipped him back into the jaws of hell, with the realisation that he wasn't going to survive his ordeal after all.

Even though Lester was only 18, he had prepared for that first killing meticulously. He was desperate to get it right. The lock-up he'd prepared was out in the sticks where no one would hear any screams, close to a multitude of suitable dumping sites. The victim's body could be dropped anywhere and with some luck, never be found, he had reasoned. Alas it was and the police had visited, notifying him of his own father's brutal demise.

The lead copper didn't spare the younger Lester any of the details about his father's death, before asking him if he knew why anyone would want to torture his father. 'Why on earth would anybody want to severe your father's hands and feet, and bludgeon "his manhood" into such a state that only a pathologist would know if his body was male or female?' Lester feigned ignorance and shock as best he could, after all he was no actor. He had a feeling the copper didn't believe a word he said, because just before leaving the detective said, 'What I don't get is why after going through all that, the cutting, the dismemberment, the brutality of it, the killer then blasts the body with a few bullets in the back. Makes no sense to me at all.' Lester just shrugged, and said, 'If it makes no sense to you, why should it to me?'

If he'd wanted, before they left, he could have told them that the murderer might have had some vital information about his late father that the police had failed to act on for many years. The information that Lester senior had regularly been beating his mother for years. Lester junior had witnessed it himself. He'd seen his father kick and beat his mother to within an inch of her life on numerous occasions. Lester senior had kicked his wife out of the car at the hospital door many times. And the authorities hadn't lifted a finger to help. When he'd asked his mother why she never ran away, it was obvious to him that she was too scared and too fearful to ask for help. When his father wasn't beating her up, he was raping her. She was constantly in pain. His father had turned his mother's life into one of fear, pain, anguish, and torture.

One day, his mother had obviously had enough. Having dropped her son off at school with his lunchbox and kissed him goodbye, she walked to the nearest station and waited for the next train, the 9.15am from Blackpool North to Manchester

Central. As the train approached the platform, commuters all around bustling for position to jump on, she calmly stepped out onto the track. The train did stop… but not before ending her misery.

Lester could have told them all that, but he didn't. Justice had been served. There was no more to be said or done on the subject.

He was brought back into the present by a blaring car horn coming from outside the hotel window. The noose was tightening around Nick Mason's neck. Nesby would find him; Lester was sure of that. With some luck, he'd be involved in Mason's last moments on this earth.

The bathroom door opened behind him. A woman, naked but for a pair of black panties, came into the bedroom. She was maybe twenty-five, with blonde wavy hair which brushed her shoulders. Her small breasts hardly moved as she glided through the room towards Lester, a man old enough to be her father. She sat next to him and put her head on his shoulders. Lester lifted her chin and looked into her bright blue eyes. He kissed her gently on the lips.

Drew sighed as Lester cupped her left breast. She knew already that Tom wanted her a second time. His tongue was exploring her again and he was gently pushing her back down flat onto the bed. Just as his hand was moving up her inner thigh, Lester's cell rang out. He stopped immediately and sat up. He picked the phone up from the bedside table. 'I need to take this,' he said. Drew sat up beside him, again leaning on his shoulder.

'Lester.'

The voice on the other end said, 'It's Irwin, sir. I have important information.'

'One moment.'

Lester didn't want Drew to overhear any of his conversation. She was a little too close to the phone. He put his arm around her back and gently guided her off the bed. Instinctively, Drew knew what Lester wanted. He'd pushed her head down there many times before when he was taking calls.

Once Lester was sure Drew couldn't hear his conversation, he said to Irwin, 'Go on.'

Irwin cleared his throat of the brandy he'd just swallowed. 'You had visitor's last evening, sir. A man and a woman. They were very anxious to know your whereabouts. Of course,' he stressed, 'I couldn't enlighten them.'

'What did the man look like?' Lester asked.

'Muscular, with dark hair. Carried a gun. Very threatening.'

'It sounds like Mason. Did you catch the woman's name?'

'No, sir. She did take a liking to your Remy Martin though. While they were questioning me and tying me up, she drank quite a lot of it to be honest. If it wasn't for Doris, the cleaner, coming in early this morning, I'd still be tied to the chair now.'

'That's okay, Irwin. There'll be a nice bonus in your pay packet this month.'

'Thank you, sir,' Irwin accepted cheerily. 'Is there anything else you'd like me to do while you're away?'

'No. Just make sure the house is in order for when I get back.'

'Of course, sir.'

Lester rang off without saying anything further. He looked down and watched Drew's head moving slowly up and down. He was reluctant to stop her. For such a young girl, she was doing a very good job. But needs must. He pulled her head away and ordered, 'Go and get dressed. I have business and I need to leave soon.'

Drew looked disappointed.

'Oh Tom! I never get more than a couple of hours with you. Please stay a little longer,' she implored. 'I promise I'll make it worth your while.'

She put her head between his legs again, but he lifted her up again.

'Look, why don't you go and get dressed and then if you're lucky I'll take you on a nice little trip.'

She brightened immediately, clasping her hands together. 'Of course, Tom. Where are we going?'

Lester could see she was bubbling at the news that he'd take her with him.

'Calm yourself. I'll tell you when I've finished my little bit of business and we're both dressed. Look, I'll order room service. We'll have the works, eggs, bacon, croissants, coffee, the lot. And then we'll talk.'

Drew stood up and kissed him. 'Okay, Tom. I'm off to the bathroom.'

He watched her and waited till the door was shut before standing. Naked, he drew the curtain aside a little checking the weather. It was wet and grey, in complete contrast to where he was heading.

He punched Ferguson's number in his cell.

'Tom?'

'Yeah.'

'What are you ringing me here for? I'm at the station. I can't take your calls here, you know that.'

Lester let the curtain fall back into place and walked towards the desk, picking up the breakfast menu. While looking at it, the venom was clear in his tone, 'Listen to me, and listen carefully. I don't give a fuck where you are. I pay you good money and it's time you delivered.'

'But Tom! Just let me get out of the building.'

'Just fucking stay where you are and listen!' he spat.

'Yes, Tom.'

Lester noticed the menu had a platter of breakfast items that covered all the bases. He'd order that once this conversation was over.

'Nick Mason was round at my home last night. Terrorising my butler, of all things. He had a girl with him. Drop whatever you're doing, find out who she is, then contact Nesby immediately.'

'But Tom, I'm in the middle of an investigation. I can't just…'

Lester butted in. 'Drop the fucking lot and find out who this bitch is!'

He rang off before the copper could say anything else. Lester resolved to jettison Ferguson once this business was tied up. He threw his cell onto the bed, picked up the house phone, and ordered the so-named Comprehensive Breakfast Platter for Two.

He'd then have to let Drew down gently. There was no way she could accompany him on this trip. Maybe the next.

CHAPTER 18

Mason entered the front door of the house behind Sadie and passed her at speed. He sped through the hallway and the galley-styled kitchen and approached the rear door, which he opened using the key lodged in the lock. Leaving keys around for burglars to use is a bad idea, he thought. Standing at the open back door, he surveyed the garden. It was well maintained. A rectangular lawn, surrounded by a multi-coloured flower border. Around this central space ran a crazy-paved pathway. At the top right-hand corner stood an expensive-looking metal shed. Bordering all this was a panelled fence that had obviously had a fresh lick of creosote. At the top left of the garden a gate offered the only break in the fencing. He skirted the lawn and opened the gate. Beyond was an open field. Where it led, Mason had no idea, but it wasn't a place he'd like to get stuck. If this was to be their escape route, they'd be sitting ducks in an open field, for sure.

He returned to the kitchen where the kettle was starting to whistle. Sadie was getting two cups from the cupboard.

'Are you sure your sister isn't coming back soon?' he asked.

'Positive. She's away on business. Works for a multinational company. I can't remember the name. Something to do with fashion. She's always jetting off somewhere. Milan one week. Paris the next.'

Sadie poured the boiling water into the cups and stirred in the milk. She opened the cupboard looking for sugar but didn't find any. 'I'm afraid you're out of luck. No sugar. She normally texts to ask me to collect the essentials for her return.'

'No worries,' said Mason, turning away with his cup. 'Come on.

AN INVITATION FOR REVENGE

We'll have a drink and then think about what comes next.'

Sadie followed him into the large open lounge. Before sitting down, she lit the fake coal effect gas fire. Once ignited, it began to heat the room up.

She took a seat on the armchair facing him sipping her coffee.

'So, what's the story with you and your sister? This is quite some place she's got here,' he observed.

'In stark contrast to mine, you mean?'

Mason looked around at the wall paintings and the expensive furniture.

'There's a little bit of a difference. Your place, if nice, is a little stark. Whereas this is, how can I put it, *richly decorated*? I would imagine if they put the two homes side by side on TV and asked who lived there, no one would guess at siblings.'

Sadie pushed up onto her feet and stood with her back to the fire, wishing she had a stronger drink in her hand instead of unsweetened coffee.

She looked down and said, 'Well, hand on heart, I'm the black sheep of the family. To my family's dismay I didn't get the grades at school. Unlike the prodigal daughter who owns this place. Passed all her exams, went to a fancy university, studied like the girly-swot she is, and then got a prestigious job at the first time of asking.' She stopped in her tracks and decided she did need something stronger.

Opening the oak drinks cabinet in the corner, she selected a malt whiskey, not her favourite, and two cut glass tumblers. Generously pouring two, she handed one to Mason, who didn't have time to thank her before she continued with her story. 'I, on the other hand, achieved nothing. Absolutely zilch. Our parents were devastated. It ruined their view of our family being strong and resourceful. And self-reliant. Instead of *poor kid making it rich*, I managed to lose my silverish spoon and became poor.'

Mason sat up straight. 'Don't your family help you out? Money-wise, I mean?'

Sadie's eyes darted a look at him, ready to throw spears. 'No, thank you. I don't do handouts! That is one thing that dad did instil in me that stuck. I've worked for what little I have, and I wouldn't take a penny off anyone, even my rich dad.'

'Nothing wrong with that,' he agreed. 'What about your sister? Could she not have helped get you a job? It looks like she's in a prime position to get you on the ladder without giving you something for nothing.'

Sadie took a large gulp of whiskey which wrenched at the back of her throat and took her breath away for a second. 'No way Pharaoh! Work in business? I wouldn't know where to start. Meeting deadlines? Competing with others for favours from the nobs at the top? Not a chance! I like working with people. Caring for people in need is where I get my kicks. Not looking at some spreadsheet and salivating over rising profits.'

Mason tested the whiskey. He was no connoisseur, but it tasted like Glenmorangie to him. Sadie confirmed as much when he asked.

'Sadie, you know, we all have our place in society. We all do necessary jobs. If there was no need for someone to work in business, there wouldn't be such a job.'

Sadie took another slug of the Glenmorangie, 'I saw my dad pour over sheets of paper at his desk until all hours. Always satisfying someone else higher up the food chain; people sat comfortably watching their investments grow while my father's health and quality of life declined.'

'It's the way of the world, I'm afraid. There's always someone else in charge taking a bigger slice of the cake, whipping the cream off the top. In an ideal world everyone would earn what they deserve. Until then, we're stuck with this imperfect one.'

'I'll drink to that,' she said, draining her glass. 'Want a top up?'

'Please,' he said, offering his glass.

She refilled both and, after passing Mason his, sat back in the chair facing Mason.

'So, what are your plans?'

'For what,' she asked.

'Going forward. I mean do you have any ambitions?'

'Before I got involved with you, there was no plan. Apart from to continuing to work at the Home. I enjoy my job.'

'No dreams? A better life? Getting married? All that stuff.'

'I've been saving. I did toy with the idea of moving to Spain or Greece, somewhere like that. But since you came along, all that seems to have been put on the back burner.'

Mason lifted his glass in a conciliatory salute. 'Sorry about that.'

Sadie took a large gulp of whiskey and asked, 'So, what's our next move, then, Nick?'

He looked down into the glass as if emulating a sea-side fortune teller, considering his next move. Eventually, he said, 'Well, to be honest, I'd like to have had some news from Ashley, my sister, but I've had no reply from her. That's to be expected, I suppose. She said as much when she left. Next,' he paused for a beat, 'I must return to Dubrovnik. I know Lester will be there at some point. And I need to be there to meet him.'

'Then you have to take me,' she snapped.

'No,' he cut her off sharply. 'It's too dangerous.'

But Sadie persisted, 'I'm going and that's the end of it. My future is tied up in all this mess now. You can't leave me here at the mercy of Lester's henchmen.'

'Sadie, this isn't a game.'

'Don't you think I know that?' she accused. 'I saw your father murdered in cold blood.' She paced over to the drink's cabinet. Pouring more whiskey into her glass, the emotion began to well up in her body. Her voice started to break as she recalled, 'My friends have been slaughtered. How dare you suggest I think this is a game.'

Mason rose and went over to Sadie. He put his arms around her shoulder. Her breathing was heavy, erratic. She responded to his affection by embracing him tightly, pulling him in as close as she could.

'I'm sorry, Sadie. It's a lot to take in, I know. You've been through a lot; we've been through a lot,' he corrected.

Mason pictured his father's dead body still in a seated position, anchored to the wheelchair in the park. Eyes wide open, his life extinguished. One minute talking and smoking. The next, *nothing*. The only link he had now was his father's pipe. At least that was something tangible, something to bring his parent closer. Along with the pipe came that horrible memory though. The end of his father's life, which was brutal and unforgiving. He wouldn't forget that. Neither would he forget Tom Lester's part in it.

A tear slid from his eye and rolled down his cheek. Finding nowhere else to go, it fell onto the back of Sadie's sweatshirt and disappeared as if it had never existed.

Sadie lifted her head and looked directly into Mason's eyes. For a moment, Mason wanted to kiss her. Just before he succumbed, he pulled himself away and stood in front of the fire. He nodded slowly to himself.

'If you're insistent on joining me, I'd better book us a couple of tickets on tomorrow morning's flight to Dubrovnik. Have you got your passport?'

Sadie smiled. 'It's in my bag.'

'Good. I'll check the flight times. How about you order a pizza delivery?'

CHAPTER 19

The weather had turned distinctly chilly. The brisk air had replaced the warmer weather of late. Fortunately, the sky was clear of cloud. If he was honest, Nesby liked it like this. Not for him the holiday hotspots with golden-sanded coastlines.

He sat in the car park of the Hare & Hounds. The pub was open. Several vehicles dotted the parking area, but his meeting with Ferguson would have to be conducted out on the tarmac, his time was precious.

Opening the door, he got out of the car, buttoned up his black woollen overcoat, and hugged the collar under his neck. He watched cars pass by as he paced around his vehicle. Eventually, Ferguson's navy-blue BMW came into view. The copper parked it up leaving a bay between his car and Nesby's.

The policeman opened the window and said, 'Do you want to get in? It's bloody freezing out there!'

'No. Get out and we can stretch our legs.'

Nesby could see Ferguson muttering something as he closed the window before getting out.

'Jesus Christ, Nesby! Are you trying to fuck with my health?'

'Don't be a soft bastard! You get paid, work or play. What's your problem?'

Ferguson stamped the ground a couple of times, 'My problem is that I hate the fucking cold. Now get on with it. What is it you want?'

The policeman dug into his jacket pocket and plucked his cigarettes and lighter out. He offered one to Nesby, who refused, before lighting up himself. He blew the smoke out and it swirled around his head for a moment before disappearing into the cold air.

'Have you found out who the girl is, yet?' Nesby asked impatiently.

'I have,' the detective admitted, blowing out more smoke. Nesby waited for Ferguson to tell him, but he didn't. His patience ran out.

'Are you going to tell me, or what?'

'Her name is Sadie Kellerman. Worked at the Home where Mason's father lived. It's assumed down at the Shop that she was with Mason Senior when he took the bullet.' Although Nesby knew the circumstances of Mason Seniors death and Kellerman's flight, he didn't enlighten him. 'She must have taken a hike, and sharpish, because she wasn't there when the real shooting started.'

'What do we know about her?' Nesby asked.

'Mid-twenties. Worked at the Home for two years.'

'Where does she live? Local?'

Ferguson stubbed out the cigarette under his shoe.

'Yes. Within walking distance of the Home. But don't bother going there. She's not returned home yet. We have a stakeout in place if she does.'

'So where is she?' Nesby pressed. 'I swear, you coppers are fucking useless!'

'We may be,' Ferguson agreed as he ignited the tip of another cigarette, 'but we do have one lead that hasn't been followed up yet.'

'And what's that?'

Ferguson watched a car park up behind his. He watched closely as the occupants got out and set off for the pub door, chattering. He waited for them to disappear before he answered.

'She has a sister who lives in a house, over New Road way.'

'How'd you know?'

'Her sister was stopped for a dodgy break light last year by a traffic cop. Sadie, the passenger, wasn't exactly happy at the inconvenience of being stopped by the 'fuzz', as she called the copper concerned. He had to give her a warning to calm down.

Her name ended up in his report and, just like a paedo with a computer, her name is forever digitalised for future reference.' He took a drag from the cigarette. 'If only people would stay calm and keep their head down, they'd never get themselves noticed by anyone, especially the police.'

'What's the address?'

Ferguson handed him a piece of paper from his jacket pocket.

As Nesby reached for the note, his cuff rode up his hand. Ferguson noticed the web tattoo on his hand between his thumb and finger. He disliked tattoos. It was just another reason to dislike Lester's errand boy.

Nesby read the note with interest. He knew the area the house was in.

'So why aren't the cops staking this house out?'

Ferguson took a deep drag from the cigarette.

'Look, are you sure you don't want to go in for a drink? I need to warm up a bit if we're going to keep talking.'

Nesby looked at his watch. He didn't know when he was going to get his next meal. And if he had to stake out Kellerman's sister's house, he'd never get anything proper to eat. 'Come on. Let's go in. I might get a quick sandwich at the bar.'

'Good man.'

'Hey! Don't get any ideas we're bosom buddies because we're having a drink together,' Nesby warned. 'I'm here on Mr Lester's business. That's all.'

The policeman looked over his shoulder as he led the way to the door and said, 'Of course. You're a crook. I don't have crooked friends!' He threw the half-smoked cigarette in a plant pot as he entered the building.

They took a seat at the bar and ordered drinks. Nesby also ordered a sandwich and a side of fries.

Once the barman had retreated to stock some shelves further down the bar, Nesby asked, 'So what's the update on the Home murders?'

'From what I can gather, the police have no motive for the murders. They just think it's a random nut-job.' He took a drink of sparkling water. 'I poked my head into the situation room. Just pictures of dead bodies, location, times etc. Grimes, the Senior Investigating Officer, is a friend. We go way back. I found him in his office, puffing so deep on an e-cig he was nearly choking on the fucking thing. Hadn't a clue, the poor bastard. Didn't know where to start. Mind you, he's never known his head from his arse. They'll have a bunch of cold cases in years to come that he couldn't solve. Useless bastard!'

'If he's that useless, why do they keep employing him?' asked Nesby, taking a drink of his honey bourbon.

'Family connections. The whole family are coppers. Dad was a Chief Constable down south somewhere back in the day. Uncle's an ex-detective. Even his mother worked for an ex-Chief Constable in this force. Rumour has it she kept him sweet in the office, if you know what I mean?' said Ferguson tipping his glass in Nesby's direction.

'I get the picture. So, where are the cops heading, if anywhere?'

'Like I said, as far as I can tell, absolutely fucking nowhere. Grimes couldn't solve a murder if someone plastered the culprits name to his fucking forehead!'

'Looks like some sick bastard got very lucky. Probably the biggest mass murderer this country has ever seen, and he's got away with it. Modern policing, absolutely fucking amazing!'

Of course, Nesby knew who the killer was. If he dropped Lloyd's name down at the station Grimes, by the sound of it, still wouldn't get a result. Lester's man would have put Lloyd's body where no one could find it anyway, and the case would still end up a cold one, with its chief suspect missing, presumed to be in some dodgy Spanish villa.

'Is there any way you can get into the investigation proper? I mean, be on the inside, day to day?' Nesby asked. 'Tom would really appreciate your proximity. You'd find information out much quicker.'

Ferguson took a drink of his water and thought for a moment.

The barman approached and placed Nesby's food on the bar. 'Sorry for the delay, sir.'

'No problem,' said Nesby, picking up the ham sandwich. He took a bite and waited for Ferguson to confirm he'd get in on the investigation.

'I'm not sure I can swing that.'

'Well, you'd better. Tom wants all the information as soon as it's available. Not days later.'

Ferguson decided he needed something stronger to drink, even though it was only 7pm. He ordered a brandy and another bourbon for Nesby.

'I suppose I could hand my work over to my number two. They've been wanting to promote her for some time. My boss has been badgering me about giving her more responsibility. I could come up with some serious bullshit about giving her a leg up and me being more help to Grimes and his squad.' Ferguson paused. The barman left them their drinks and went back to cleaning bottles on the shelves. 'Hang on a minute.' Ferguson said. 'What do *I* get for this? I won't be getting a promotion by shifting over to Grimes's squad, so that means there's no money in it for me.'

Nesby finished the first half of his sandwich and brushed his mouth with a napkin.

'Well, you'd be assisting Mr Lester. And he doesn't forget people who help him. Funnily enough,' he added without a smile, 'he doesn't forget the people that don't help him either.'

Ferguson felt the steel in Nesby's voice. He didn't need it spelt out. He had to get in on the Grimes case, and fast!

'Look, I can't promise anything. All I can do is try.' He took a gulp of brandy.

Nesby had almost finished his sandwich and was now starting on his fries.

'Look, Mr Lester pays you a lot of money, so I suggest you try very hard.' He washed a couple of fries down with the remainder of his first glass of bourbon. 'If you need to grease a few palms, let me know. I can get some cash over to you.'

'That might help,' Ferguson conceded.

'I need to warn you though. I give you money that's meant for greasing palms and it ends up buying nice lingerie for that slut you are shagging behind the wife's back and you're dead meat!'

'What?' Ferguson was taken aback. He didn't know anyone knew about Petra. They'd been careful not to be seen in public. 'I don't know what you're talking about,' he protested.

'Look, I'm not judging you. But who isn't shagging their secretary? Especially when they look like her.' Nesby bit his chip in half and pointed the remaining half at Ferguson and said, 'Must give you a serious hard-on fucking someone half your age.'

Ferguson was frantically looking around to see if anyone was listening. He couldn't afford for this to get out. His wife would screw his balls up so tight he'd be singing like Aled fucking Jones for the rest of his life. He had to act to stop this getting out.

'Look! I'll get in on the investigation. Let's leave my mistress and wife out of this, shall we?'

'Your decision,' said Nesby, pushing his plate away and picking his glass up. 'Right, I'm off,' he said. 'I expect you to be in touch soon.'

'I will be,' Ferguson said emptying his own glass. He watched Nesby leave. Once the door shut, he called the barman over and asked him if there was a table for two available.

'Yes, sir. I can sort that out for you.'

'In about forty-five minutes?'

'Yes, that won't be a problem."

'Good. I'll sit at the corner table until my guest arrives. Could you bring me another brandy over, please?'

Before the barman could say, 'OK sir,' he had left the bar and was tapping on his phone.

Ferguson sat at the table and waited for the line to be opened.

'Petra, it's me. Look, I need to see you. Get down to the Hare & Hounds as fast as you can. I've got a table reserved.'

CHAPTER 20

Nesby pulled up at the entrance of the cul-de-sac where Kellerman's sister lived, off the New Road. It was a new-build of million-pound stone houses, with just five residences on the plot. If Mason and Kellerman were hold up here, he'd find them. He killed the engine and paused for a moment. The car was warm and would remain so for a while, keeping the evening outside chill at bay.

He'd spoken to his boss, Tom Lester, after leaving Ferguson and asked for some final instructions before he went ahead. 'I want the two fuckers out of the picture, permanently,' Lester had barked down the phone. His intent was unequivocal; he wanted them dead. A message had to be sent out; *mess with Tom Lester and you're dead*!

Nesby had stopped off at his own apartment first to get a travel bag and passport. Lester wanted him in Croatia as soon as he had finished his work here. If Nesby was honest, he wasn't looking forward to that trip. The work didn't disturb him. At best he'd be a bodyguard holding Lester's hand, at the worst there would be a killing or two. Either way he wasn't concerned. A job was a job. It was the baking sun he wasn't enamoured with. He'd packed sparingly, bagging the lightest loosest clothes from his small wardrobe. Once the job was completed, he'd head to a hotel near Manchester Airport and wait for the next available flight out to Dubrovnik.

Nesby got out of the car and popped the boot open, shivering. He'd stashed his handgun in a hiding place he'd created especially inside the spare wheel well. To anyone else, a toolbox was a toolbox, but he'd built a secret compartment into this one, and with the flick of a switch the bottom would open to reveal a handgun. It was a bit 'nineteen-sixties spy movie', but it worked for him, and it was safer than the glove box. The gun had never been found despite him being stopped by the police on a couple of occasions.

Getting back into the relative warmth of the car, Nesby checked the gun was loaded. It was. He'd packed a few spare rounds from the apartment, too, so he was well prepared for any eventuality that might present itself.

He holstered the gun and got out of the car. Either he was getting older, or global warming hadn't reached this part of the world; he needed a coat. He took his padded coat from the back seat and put that over his suit jacket and set off to kill Mason and the girl.

*

Nick Mason was feeling tired. He had that many plates balancing in the air, he felt that if he dropped one his whole life would come crashing down. He wished he was back in Dubrovnik with Ashley, his sister. It seemed much safer there then. Yes, they'd made a run for it, and to all intents and purposes they'd never been safe, but at least he'd settled into a tranquil lifestyle where he could sleep at night and be himself without fear.

But now?

Now he was all butterflies and anxiety. It didn't help that he was saddled with Sadie. Yes, she was beautiful. Yes, she was very good company. But meeting her now, amid this cluster-fuck of a situation wasn't ideal. At any other time he'd be asking her out for a drink, no problem. But she had no idea about the world he lived in. A world he had been unwittingly dragged back into. She was innocent of all the things that were happening around her – to her. He had to find a way to convince her that going to Dubrovnik wasn't in her best interests. And yet, it could be the safest place for her. He'd bought the last two tickets online for the first morning flight out to Dubrovnik. With her close he could keep her safe, safer than if she stayed behind at the mercy of Lester's men. He was sure by now that they would know who Sadie was. And with that knowledge, it wouldn't be long before they found her.

What to do for the best?

No, he had to take her. If he had any chance of saving Sadie from Lester, it was in Dubrovnik.

Mason looked across at her. She was curled up on the settee. He'd told her to get some rest before their flight. She'd fallen asleep in seconds. If only his mind would allow him to relax that easily.

Mason rose and climbed the stairs to the bathroom. He was leggy, lethargic. He'd done nothing physically and yet his body was dying on him.

The bathroom was spacious with a large retro-styled tub and a separate shower; the type with jets that attack you from all sides. He used the toilet and flushed. He had to admit that this bathroom was special. It had small towels to dry your hands with that you dumped in a small silver bucket by the side of the sink. He'd only ever seen that before in five-star hotels.

A chill wind struck him from the open window above the sink, which overlooked the back of the house. He reached over for the handle, but just as he was about to close the window, he glimpsed a shadow moving behind the fence to the rear of the garden. With the minimum of movement, he reached over to get a better view. He caught sight of a man crouched down, partially hidden, but still just about in sight for Mason to see.

Time to move, and fast!

Despite the fatigue, Mason took the stairs two at a time. Once down in the lounge, he shook Sadie out of her slumber.

'Sadie, come on! We've got to go!'

She sat up slowly. 'What?' she asked drowsily.

'Get up! There's someone here. Lester's men have found us!'

Sadie came around all too suddenly. 'Shit! I'll get my bag.'

They collected their things, crouching down as they moved

around the house. At the front door, Mason stopped suddenly. 'I've seen someone at the rear. There may be someone out front as well. Keep low and make sure you stay close to me.'

'This is getting a bit "Butch and Sundance" if you ask me.'

'Sadie, just trust me,' Mason pleaded.

'Sure thing,' she agreed.

He turned the key in the lock and took hold of the handle.

'On three I'm going to open the door. Then we're going to run to the back of the car. Once we get to the vehicle, I need you to split towards your side and jump in. Once there, duck down. You got that?'

'Gotcha!'

'Right, let's go! One, two, go!'

Mason flung the door open, and they both ran for their lives. Each had a bag in their hand and as they ran, the bags dragged against their legs, slowing them down. As they reached the SUV, with no sign of any other gunman, they split, Mason to the driver's side, Sadie to the passenger's. They jumped in and Mason kicked the engine up while Sadie ducked down as instructed.

The tyres dug deep into the stones as Mason sent the car into overdrive from a standing start. In the mirror, he saw a figure running around the front of the building, arm held out straight ahead of him, aiming a weapon towards them. Mason didn't hear a sound, but the passenger wing mirror abruptly exploded into a thousand tiny fragments.

'Keep down,' he yelled at Sadie.

He had to get as far away as possible, and fast!

'Have we lost them?' Sadie shouted as they reached the main road. Mason turned right without looking to see if it was safe. Luckily it was.

'I doubt it. I don't know how many of them there are. I only saw one, but there could be more.'

He checked the central mirror. A vehicle was already closing in on them, its headlights bright in the rear-view mirror. He pushed the accelerator as far as he dared. He quickly turned right off the main road and sped down a sharp decline that ran parallel to the cul-de-sac.

The chasing car rear-ended them, momentarily lifting the vehicle's rear wheels off the road. Mason quickly regained control. His getaway skills were coming into their own. Little did the jerk behind know who he was dealing with. Now they were on Mason's territory.

As the road bent down left, Mason deliberately left room on the inside track.

The pursuer approached on Mason's inside. Good, he thought, the idiot had fallen for it. He could see the other driver had both hands on the wheel and didn't have a gun prepared. Mason waited until the car came alongside and then abruptly turned the wheel inward and smacked the SUV into the chasing car, causing it to veer into the kerb violently.

Mason looked in his mirror and sped off, leaving the other car floundering at the side of the road.

The driver, after being shaken by the collision, eventually got the car moving again and was once again in the hunt.

Mason turned right at the lights onto The Queen's Road, narrowly missing an oncoming vehicle. Thankfully, there were few cars around. He had to get this jackass off his tail, and quick. He went across the lights and on to Montford Road, a dual carriageway. He saw a couple of vehicles coming towards him on the other side of the central reservation. They were safe there.

The chasing car was only a matter of ten feet away now. In his mirror, Mason could see the determination in the pursuing driver's face. He was accomplished, for sure. Other drivers would have given up after being shaken further up the road. This guy was persistent.

Where could he go where it was safe? Mason had to get this lunatic away from any built-up area and where he could take the initiative.

At the lights at the top of the hill, Mason's speed, a cool ninety already, caused the car to lift off the tarmac for a split-second.

Beside him in the passenger seat, Sadie was being shaken around uncontrollably. 'What the hell is happening up there?'

she screamed over the roar of the engine.

The car jolted back onto the road.

Mason glanced down, 'Stay where you are! He's just behind us. I'm heading to the motorway. Hopefully I'll shake him off there.'

The SUV was fast approaching a set of traffic lights. The top light glowed red. Mason would have to turn right there. On the right-hand corner was a Shell garage. Mason knew that he could cut a corner there if there were no cars filling up. He checked as best he could, saw the lot was free, and turned sharply right. The car dipped and then hit the rising tarmac onto the forecourt. He drove through the floodlit lines of pumps, little more than a blur on the forecourt CCTV.

He checked the rear-view mirror again, seeing the pursuing car whacking the rising tarmac he'd hit just moments earlier. Sparks flew up around the low-slung bumper as it scraped the tarmac of the forecourt.

Mason's SUV was now on the road rising towards the 61 slip-road. There, he was hoping to lose the chasing car. Although that was proving increasingly difficult. His pursuer had guts and determination. To stay on the tail of someone of Mason's calibre like this was impressive.

Hitting the slip-road up to the motorway, the cars were now almost touching. They'd hit more traffic than before. This was what Mason had wanted; to make it harder for this guy to follow them. The speedometer passed a hundred, as the car swayed a little in the wind. Mason didn't like the feel he was getting on the road; this car could lose manoeuvrability any time if he wasn't careful. A lesser driver would have been off the side of the road by now as he swirled between the cars.

'The fucker's good,' he shouted at Sadie. 'He's still behind us!'

'Then lose him!' Sadie ordered. 'You're supposed to be the driver around here.'

Mason dipped the car between two Jags and raced away from them.

The hunter's car slowed suddenly. Mason could see smoke grinding out from the tyres as the pursuing driver slammed his breaks on.

He'd now gained a little space on the car behind. He had to find a winning move that would leave the chasing car behind for good. The clump of cars ahead didn't enthuse Mason. If anything, they were going to slow him down and allow the other car to catch up.

Sadie sat upright and declared, 'Right, I've had enough of this. I'm breaking my back down there!'

'Keep your head down, for God's sake!' he shouted across at her.

She turned to look through the rear window.

'He's gaining on you.'

'I can see that.'

'Well, what are you gonna do about it?'

Mason zipped between two cars and held his position. 'Let's see, shall we?'

Their pursuing vehicle had gained on them again and was now only two cars behind. Mason could tell his pursuer was determined and wasn't going to give up easily. He was desperately trying to get past the Sunday driver in front of him but was unable to. If Mason could time it right, he could force the driver into a big mistake, one he may not be able to escape from.

Mason had to get his timing right. He waited, looking into his rear-view mirror, the one remaining side mirror, and then, once the cars were lined up as he wanted, he shifted the car out into a space and thumped the accelerator down hard, leaving the cars behind him in his wake.

The pursuing driver attempted the same manoeuvre. His fatal mistake was not watching his own rear-view mirror. Just as he'd made his move, the oncoming car in the outer lane had almost passed him. He clipped the car's bumper and at that speed there was only one outcome; the car flipped high into the air, summersaulting as it did. The car turned several revolutions before landing half on a trailer carrying prestigious sports cars, and half on the tarmac.

Seeing this, other drivers slammed their breaks on in an

unsuccessful effort to avoid the crash. It didn't work. They just compounded the problem. Cars smacked against each other. Within moments the southern carriageway was completely blocked with smashed and dented cars.

Horns blared. Tempers flared!

The mayhem behind the SUV left the road ahead clear for Mason and Sadie to speed away and leave the driver of the chasing car to his fate...

CHAPTER 21

The following morning, the wall-mounted clock above the exit door showed nine-thirty. The Situation Room at the police station was a hive of activity. Several plain-clothed officers were getting on with their personal tasks in relation to the investigation.

Phil Grimes, the Senior Investigating Officer – or SIO – for the murders at the Lynne Residential Home. was sitting at his desk. Sat opposite was Gregg Spaulding, Assistant Chief Constable, six-feet-four and looking every inch of it even though he was seated.

The door to the office was closed.

Grimes pleaded, 'But why, sir? I don't need the assistance of another DCI. My team will get a result soon, I'm sure of it.'

If he had been sat in Grimes's seat, Spaulding knew he'd be arguing the same case. But needs must...

'Look, Phil,' he interrupted his subordinate, scratching his clean-shaven chin, 'we need this case wrapped up with a bow tie put on it, rapid like. With an extra pair of eyes, some more experience around the place, I'm sure you'll get a result. It's simply a matter of optics, and you need more resources.'

Grimes stood, hiding his e-cig in his pocket, and turned towards the map of the town on the wall. He heard Spaulding's cup scrape against the saucer. Cup and saucer for the Assistant Chief Constable... everyone else got a mug.

'That's strange.'

'What is?' Spaulding asked putting his cup down.

Grimes answered still looking at the map, 'It's normally the other way around.' He turned towards his superior officer.

'You're usually taking resources away, not adding to them.'

Spaulding rose from his seat, towering over Grimes. He picked his cap with the force insignia above the peak off the desk, and then placed it carefully on his head.

'There's no turning back on this, Phil. Expect Ferguson to call in.'

Grimes could feel his rage starting to rise. He'd never had another DCI foisted onto him. It was as if the bigwigs didn't trust him to get a result.

'For God's sake, sir, when was all this decided? It's all a bit sudden, isn't it?'

Spaulding leaned over the desk, facing the SIO. 'All I know is that I got a call so early I hadn't even had time to scratch my arse. The Chief said I was to put Ferguson on the case to work alongside you. No pleasantries. Just do it.'

Grimes threw a pen on the desk in frustration. 'Great!'

'What's the problem, Phil? You and Ferguson get along okay. You go back years.'

The DCI sat at his desk, resigned to his new orders, but clearly not happy. 'This is the biggest case I've ever been involved in. I was the duty officer when it came in. Everyone else was off doing some mediocre shit.' He sat back and let out a sigh. 'I just thought it could be a great way to finish my career, sir. Do something big. Achieve the impossible almost.' Grimes' eyes had become glassy with the emotion.

'And you still can,' Spaulding said. 'You're still in charge. Ferguson's only here for support, a sounding board, if you will. You're still calling the shots.'

'Come on, sir, you know the score as well as I do. It'll be like having Woody Woodpecker on my shoulder constantly hammering away at my temple. "Have you thought of this?" and "What about him? Where was he when the shooting started?" You're putting me in a difficult position here, sir.'

'Look, Phil, I know it's not ideal, but they're the cards you've being dealt. Neither you nor I have an option here.'

Grimes raised his head and looked Spaulding in the eye.

'Would you be doing this if it was your call, sir?'

The Assistant Chief Constable shifted uneasily. 'Thankfully, it's not a decision I have had to make.'

'But would you have done?' Grimes persisted.

Spaulding stiffened, 'Just get someone's fucking head for this. I don't care who works on it or who feels the collar first. I just want a result!' He paused to let his words sink in and then asked, 'We all good?'

Grimes rose from his chair, rounded his desk, and shook the senior officer's hand. 'Yep. Don't worry. We'll sort it.'

Spaulding turned away. 'Good man,' he said as he opened the door and left the office.

CHAPTER 22

Two hours after Spaulding had informed Grimes of the Chief Constable's decision, Marc Ferguson came through the Situation Room door. He was dressed immaculately in a navy suit with his old school tie pinned at the middle. He carried two Starbucks take-out cups on a cardboard tray.

He went straight into the glassed-cornered office without knocking. DCI Grimes was standing in deep thought, looking at a plan of the town on the wall behind his desk. Coloured pins marked out areas of interest on the board in front of him.

Ferguson cleared his throat and said, 'Here you go. A double shot of black coffee with three sugars piled in there. That should help the wheels turn in that prehistoric skull of yours.' He placed the cup on the desk and sat down.

Grimes turned around in deep thought and then sat at the desk opposite Ferguson. He wanted to ask his colleague something, but he couldn't bring it to mind. Then he remembered, this was time to be civil, not petty, 'Welcome aboard, Marc.'

'Cheers, Phil.' Ferguson raised the cardboard cup in salute. 'Good to be here. How's it going?'

'If I'm honest, I can't get my head around all this shit.' He quickly drew on his e-cig and spewed the smoke out. 'Why would some fucker want to kill dozens of old timers and their carers? Plus, some old dude out in the park on an afternoon jolly?'

Ferguson crossed his legs and declared, 'Some sick bastard if you ask me.'

Taking a slurp from his drink, Grimes admitted, 'I've got to admit, this is all doing my head in. I'm getting all sorts of shit from above. They want all this wrapped up, and quickly.'

'With your expertise I'm sure it will be, Phil. From what I've heard, you've got all the bases covered.' Ferguson lent forward, 'You're the best they've got. If you can't crack it, no one can.' Ferguson's own two-facedness was not lost on himself. He'd be hard pushed to admit Grimes knew where his own arsehole was. 'Look, crack open that bottle of whisky you've usually got hidden. I'll have a tiny drop in this coffee with you, for medicinal purposes, you understand?'

'Yeah, why not?' Grimes stood and went over to the grey cabinet in the corner, opened the top drawer, and lifted an unopened bottle of Johnny Walker out. He cracked the seal and poured some in his coffee, then some into Ferguson's cup. Sitting back down he screwed the top closed and placed it on the desk between them. He took a sip of the drink.

'I'm getting too old for this, Marc. Computers? All this modern policing shit is passing me by. I can't even get into my cell phone half the time. I had my fourteen-year-old grandson opening my cell for me yesterday. Know what the first thing he saw was?'

'Your porn stash,' Ferguson teased.

'A picture of a fucking corpse.'

Ferguson smiled.

'Well, if nothing else, it should put him off this shit job.'

'No such luck.' Grimes took another sip. 'First thing he said was, "I can't wait to be a copper and get to see this every day!" Fucking weirdo!'

A knock on the office door broke off their conversation. A plain-clothed female officer stood in the doorway. 'Sir, I've got some information I think you should know.'

She was dressed in a navy business suit with slim-cut trouser legs, shiny black shoes, and a crisply ironed white shirt open at the neck. An ID badge hung close to her belt. Ferguson couldn't make out the name.

'Yes?' There was irritation in Grimes's voice. 'What is it? You can see I'm in conference!'

The young officer approached her superior and put a sheaf of paper down in front of her boss.

'It's Sadie Kellerman's sister. I've just spoken to her. She's in Paris, at some fancy Champs Elysée hotel. Must be costing her a fortune.'

'Get on with it, Strickland!' ordered Grimes irritably, inhaling from his e-cig.

'Yes, sir.' She brushed her hair behind her left ear before continuing. 'Anyway, she's not heard from Sadie for at least two weeks. That's not unusual. She's not expecting to be back in England herself until late next week. She asked if she should come back. I told her she didn't need to and that there was nothing to worry about.'

'Good. Good.' Grimes repeated. 'Get yourself over to the sister's house. See if the Kellerman is there.'

Strickland looked at her watch. She had a lunch date with a colleague that she was hoping might turn into something a little more serious.

'Don't worry about your lunch. You can pick up a meal deal from Tesco on your way.'

'Yes, sir.' Strickland left her boss's office, picked up her jacket, shoulder bag, and cell phone. She left the Situation Room without talking to anyone.

Ferguson watched her through the glass-walled partition before speaking.

'In the old days you'd be chasing that girl's skirt, Phil, not running her out of the office. She looks well pissed off.'

Grimes put another capful of whisky into his coffee. He offered Ferguson more, but the DCI declined.

'Not anymore, Marc. It's not in the modern copper's manual. I've given up chasing young skirt. They all know their rights. Besides that, the wife was getting a bit fed up with my, how can I put it?' He paused for a beat. 'My little *indiscretions*. I'm strictly a pipe and slippers man when I clock off now.'

It looked like Grimes had given up to Ferguson. Pipe and slippers? That'll be the day, he thought. He had a hot date with

Petra later and he wasn't giving her up for anyone. It's what kept him going, he'd convinced himself.

'Shame, that, Phil. You were a bit of a ladies' man back in the day.'

'Yeah,' Grimes mulled Ferguson's words over for a moment, and then remembered what he wanted to ask. 'Hey Marc, what's the score, you coming on board with this one? I didn't ask for any help. And no offence, but I've got all the hands I need.'

Ferguson had prepared for this. He knew another DCI wouldn't be happy about a copper at his own level poking around in his case, especially a sensitive one like this. He wouldn't want it himself.

He got up and closed the door, as if hiding his answer from the outside world.

'Look, to be honest,' which was the exact opposite of what he was intending to be, 'I'm feeling the pressure a bit myself. I'm on the verge of quitting.'

'No!' The surprise in Grimes's voice was clear. He took a gulp of coffee.

'Yeah. I've got an in-tray full of the usual crap and I can't make a dent in any of it. For every file I close, there's another ten awaiting a conclusion. It's relentless. Tick this fucking box! Tick fucking that!'

'Tell me about it. The missus keeps going on at me to jack it in, but I keep putting it off,' Grimes admitted, tapping the e-cig on his lip. 'What would I do? With a stomach this size I can't take Pickleball up. And with my inability to spot a rose from a daffodil, that puts gardening on the back burner.'

'Anyway,' and here was the killer to build Grimes up, the *useless fucker* in Ferguson's mind, 'I just thought coming here, working with you, someone I admire, well,' he hesitated for effect, 'I thought it might take some of the pressure off. So, I asked for a move down here.' He took a drink of his whisky-laced coffee and pulled a mock-sad expression.

'Aww fuck, Marc. You shouldn't be feeling that bad. It's not worth it. What about your work? Is it going to get done?'

'No problem there. Got a right fucking know-it-all in the office. Desperate for promotion. They were more than happy to let me come down here. It'll be another feather in their cap if they can promote another female officer. There aren't many here and I heard they need to get their quota up.'

'Shit! It's all a numbers' game now, isn't it? Spreadsheets and money rule. Not like the old days when you got the rank you deserved through merit.'

Merit? Ferguson smiled to himself. Grimes hadn't earned a Sergeant's badge, never mind a DCI position. Nepotism had always lived in the police force, and always would.

Ferguson's personal cell bleep-bleeped into life. He looked down and checked who the text was from. Shit! The text banner read 'Lofty', the code for Tom Lester. What the hell did he want?

'Phil, I just need to take this. Personal.' He winked at Grimes and stood to leave the office. 'I'll just nip out for a minute.'

'No worries.' Grimes waved his colleague away.

Ferguson tapped the green button and said 'Yes,' as he was walking out of the Situation Room into the main corridor. The long corridor had doors leading off either side, all painted a dull beige. A strip light was blinking, giving the hallway an eerie feel.

'It's Lester.'

'I know. I'm in the office. Can't this wait until later?'

'No, it fucking can't,' Lester barked down the phone. 'And just remember who pays your wages,' he reminded.

Ferguson opened the first Interview Room door that didn't have a red light shining above it. The room was empty, save for a table with four chairs placed around it. Light streamed in from windows lined high above the side wall.

He closed the door behind him and attempted to calm Lester, 'Okay, okay, Tom. You're my top priority, you know that. It's just that it's difficult to answer the phone here.'

'When I call, you answer the phone wherever you are. Have you got that?' Lester demanded down the line.

'Of course, Tom. Always.' Now, conscious that he needed to get back to Grimes, he asked, 'What can I do for you?'

'This girl. Kellerman. The one that did a runner.'

'Yes,' Ferguson asked, wondering about Lester's interest in her.

'Get her name out.'

'What?' he asked.

'Release it.'

'I can't do that, Tom. I'm not in charge of the investigation. It's not my call.'

'You're right it's not. It's my call. Now leak the fucking information. Whatever. Just get it out there.'

Ferguson heard footsteps out in the corridor. When he was satisfied the person had walked past the room, he said, 'It's not that easy, Tom. If I give that information to my usual contacts, there'll be questions. They'll burrow down, ask even more questions, try to find out why the name's being leaked. It's bound to get back to the Station and come down on my head.'

'I don't give a shit who it gets back to. Just do it!'

Lester cut the call dead.

The policeman looked at the 'call ended' sign on the screen and wished with all his heart he hadn't stopped smoking.

CHAPTER 23

Marc Ferguson put his glass of red wine down on the kitchen island and walked up behind his mistress, Petra Antonucci. She was rinsing dishes and placing them in the dishwasher beside the sink. He reached around her and squeezed gently.

'That meal was beautiful, Miss Antonucci.' He moved her hair over her ear and gently kissed the side of her neck. 'May I be so bold, and ask what's for afters? Or have I already found it?'

'Come on Ferguson! Let me finish this and then whatever your heart desires…' She let the words hang in the air.

'Mmm, that sounds good to me.' He put his hands on her hips and swivelled her round to face him. She lifted her arms in submission. 'So, what happens if I can't wait?' He began to undo the buttons of her blouse to reveal her cleavage.

Petra made an unconvincing effort to pull away, not wanting to admit she was enjoying the moment.

'Now you're taking liberties, DCI Ferguson.'

Ferguson leaned in and whispered into her ear, 'So write an article, Miss Antonucci. It's what you're good at, surely.' He nibbled gently on her earlobe.

Unable to resist, Petra began to kiss his cheek and neck in return.

He brought her closer to him and whispered into her ear, 'I can see the headline now. *After taking advantage of her excellent culinary skills, Detective Chief Inspector Ferguson ravages innocent reporter in her own home. DCI reported to disciplinary panel for enjoying himself farrr too much.*'

She reached down into the front of his trousers and gently cradled him. 'And yes, it can be confirmed, he was enjoying himself far too much!'

'I'm sure your evidence against me will be invaluable, Miss Antonucci. Although I'm not sure,' he paused and gently kissed her on the lips, 'if I'd get de-truncheoned or given a commendation.'

Petra smiled and said, 'Look, if you want a commendation, you're going to have to work a little harder; if you get my drift?'

*

Later, they lay naked under a white sheet on the bed. An air freshener shaped like a Chinese lantern gave off a zest of lemon odour that permeated the room.

Soft music from a small Bluetooth speaker was playing in the background.

Petra's head was on her lover's chest. She wasn't a fan of the mass of black hair that carpeted his torso, but she had to admit she enjoyed the power and tautness of his muscular body. He was fifteen years her senior, but in a lot better shape than most of the men she'd slept with.

She knew Ferguson's marital status but remained unconcerned. That was a side of his life that she wasn't interested in. The complications of a full-blown relationship were something she didn't need or require. She lived and worked at her own pace and would not have it dictated to her by any partner. Petra had always been straight with people... she wasn't interested in children, box sets or animals, and she never would be.

Petra had had a gruelling day at the work, getting nowhere on the murders of the old people at the Lynne Residential Home. Wherever she went, she'd faced stone cold responses. If the police knew anything, they were keeping it very close to their chest – for a change. When she'd contacted relatives of the deceased, they'd just shut the door in her face. Her boss had been giving her aggravation for days. He wanted progress, and if he didn't see it soon, he'd threatened to move her to the *small crappy local stories* she hated with a vengeance.

Petra was always stumped as to what to say after sex. She always had been. What was there to say? If she was honest, she'd have been happy for Ferguson to go the minute he'd seen to her needs, but even she knew that wasn't the correct etiquette. You should be considerate to one's lover so as not to hurt their feelings, or so the magazines always advised. If Petra was honest, she wasn't sure Ferguson had any real feelings for anyone.

The policeman broke the elongated silence, 'So, what have you been working on?'

As Petra sat up the sheet fell slightly revealing her petite breasts. Her blonde tussled hair fell to her shoulders. She picked up the glass of red wine that sat on her bedside cabinet and took a sip.

It was the first time Marc had asked about her work since they had first started their affair. A topic they'd agreed should be off limits. The journalist took a moment before answering. She put the glass back on the cabinet, and answered honestly, 'Well, I've been knee deep on that nursing home story. The only problem is that I'm drawing a big flat blank wherever I go. It's been so frustrating.'

'I'm sure you'll find a way through it soon,' he encouraged, running his hand up and down her inner thigh. He sat up and took a drink from his own glass of wine. It was a tasty Merlot he'd bought from the wine shop on his way over to Petra's apartment. For a moment, he pondered whether to tell her he was now on the investigation team himself but decided against it.

'I'd better do, otherwise my boss is going to take me off the story completely.'

He began gently stroking her arm.

'Look Petra,' Ferguson started, hoping to convey reluctance, 'if you promise to keep my name out of this, I might be able to help.'

She sat upright and perched on her heels excitedly. The beauty of her young naked body wasn't lost on Ferguson, even as he concentrated on the job in hand.

'But you must promise to keep your source secret.'

'I will.' She made the sign of a cross over her naked left breast.

Ferguson half turned and put the wine glass back onto the bedside table.

'I don't know if I should get involved,' he said in as weak a voice as he could muster. 'I mean I've never done anything like this before.'

'Look, I promise not to reveal any sources. I never would. I never have. They could water-board me, and I still wouldn't talk,' she added.

He took another drink, trying to appear nervous, avoiding her gaze.

'Can I trust you, Petra?' he asked, lifting his eyes back to her. 'This isn't just my livelihood. It's my whole life. I could be jailed for leaking information about an ongoing investigation.'

'Of course you can. Just tell me,' she pleaded. 'It looks like it's something you need to get off your chest.'

He returned his glass to the bedside cabinet and turned back towards her. Her bare chest was heaving with anticipation.

'Look, this may be nothing.'

In her excitement, she interrupted a little too quickly. 'Let me be the judge of that.' She needed a breakthrough, and it looked like this might be a golden opportunity.

'Okay.' He stopped for a beat before continuing. 'I called in to see an ex-colleague of mine today. Phil Grimes. He's the SIO, that's the Senior Investigating Officer...'

'Yes, I know what an SIO is, Marc. Get on with it,' Petra pushed.

'Anyway, we go back a long way. While I was having a coffee with him, a young detective came in and said they'd identified a woman of interest. She worked at the Home but miraculously survived.'

'Shit-a-brick! How the fuck?' Petra regained her composure. 'What was her name?' Petra asked impatiently.

'Just let me think.' He paused again, watching Petra get more excited by the second.

'Well?'

Then he said, 'Yes, it's Kellerman. Sadie Kellerman.'

'Fuck!' She exclaimed at the same time as reaching into her bedside cabinet draw to grab a pad and pencil. Petra flipped a few pages over to find a blank sheet and then scribbled 'Sadie Kellerman'.

'What are you going to do with the information?' he asked as she threw the pad on the floor beside the bed.

'Let me worry about that.' She straddled his naked body and said, 'Now what can I do to help you in return, Mr Ferguson?'

CHAPTER 24

Mason and Sadie had got through 'check in' and customs without a hiccup. In fact, it was easier and quicker than Mason had expected. If anyone had been looking for them, their names hadn't come up on any of the country's exit point databases, otherwise they'd have been hauled into a side room and strip-searched on the spot.

He'd encouraged Sadie to surf the terminal shopping area while he found an uninhabited corner in one of the bars overlooking a stationary plane. He needed to catch up with Gunner Tudge.

'Mason?' There was no surprise in Tudge's voice when he answered the cell, he'd been expecting the call. 'What can I do for you?'

'Gunner. Good to speak to you. Listen, I've left that piece of equipment we talked about on the inside of your garden wall.'

'You have?'

Tudge already knew that Mason had been around earlier that morning and secreted the box containing his handgun and ammunition behind the wall at the entrance to his yard. Mason obviously underestimated Tudge's security precautions. The gun-seller had cameras installed all over his property. Everything was recorded 24/7. On reviewing this morning's footage over a bowl of Cheerios, Tudge had been surprised to see Mason crouching down and hiding the box underneath a tyre leaning up against the garden wall.

'Yep. Earlier this morning.'

'Now that is a surprise. You're not looking for a refund, are you?' There was a note of caution in Tudge's voice. 'There's no buy-back scheme around here, Nick.'

'Nothing like that, no.' Mason confirmed. He just needed to get rid of the gun and couldn't think where else to put it. 'I've finished with it, and I thought who better to leave it with than Gunner Tudge himself.'

'I'm not a storage facility, Nick. Once I've sold an item, that's it. There's no further discussion.' He paused for a second, and then continued, 'Unless, of course, you'd like to purchase a new product? I have a fine selection of equipment; for all occasions, in fact.'

'No nothing like that.' Mason checked himself and looked around to see if anyone was listening into his conversation. As far as he could ascertain no one was within earshot. All good. 'I'd like some information.'

'I'd love to help. Is it of a confidential nature?'

'It is.'

'Then I could be your man. What is it you want?'

'Can I trust you, Tudge?'

'You rang me, Nick. I'd be quite happy to put the phone down now. I'm expecting a nice little package from Deliveroo any minute.'

'It's just that this one's a bit delicate.' Mason tapped the table in front of him. 'Especially over the phone.'

'I think you'd better get on with it, Nick. As they say, there's no time like the present.'

Mason couldn't be sure if this was the best thing to do, telling someone else where he and Sadie were heading. He needed information though. And he needed to get it independently of Željko Kovačić.

'I'm taking a trip abroad.'

'Go on,' Tudge encouraged, intrigued.

'To Dubrovnik, in Croatia. I'll need something while I'm out there. Is there anyone out there I can contact that you know?'

'You mean who could get you something for personal protection?' Tudge asked.

'Exactly,' Mason confirmed.

'I do know someone, as a matter of fact.'

'Contact number?'

'Do you know that you're the second person to ask me this question in only the last week or so?'

'Who else?' Mason asked with some urgency.

'Well, I don't suppose it matters now. Confidentiality is redundant in this situation.'

'Why's that?' Mason fired back, wondering if their conversation would lose its confidential status as soon as the phone went dead.

'An old acquaintance of mine, known him for years, went out there recently and asked me the same question. This acquaintance never made it home. In fact, he was found a day after going missing.'

The sudden upheaval in Mason's stomach was making him wretch. He knew all too well what was coming next.

'His body was washed up on the shoreline at a place called Copacabana Beach. Brings to mind Lola, the showgirl,' Tudge mused. 'I wonder if she's out there doing a turn for the locals. Apparently, whoever killed him tried to sink his body in the ocean. They obviously didn't think about the cruise liners churning the shit up every day as they pass through.'

'Not sure I know who you're talking about. Or where even,' Mason lied.

'Fella called Bevan. Worked for Tom Lester. Always came to me for advice on items of need, if you get my drift?'

Mason did.

'Called in and said he was off to Dubrovnik and wanted the name of a specialist out there; didn't fancy going through customs with a package that would draw attention.'

Mason ignored Bevan's name and asked, 'And whose name did you give him?'

'Chap called Zlatko Vlasić. Nice fella, if a little paranoid. He's got a small army of boys and girls out there, armed to the back teeth.'

Mason pointed out the obvious, 'He's playing the same

dangerous game as you, then, if you don't mind me saying.'

'It's the Wild West out there, Nick. It's all a little bit more sedate around here.'

Mason glanced around and caught sight of Sadie approaching with a plastic bag full of purchases. He needed to cut the conversation.

'Okay, Gunner, where do I find this Zlatko guy?

He beckoned Sadie over.

'You'll find him at his café, "Zlatko's" in Gruž. It's a nice little place, by all accounts. Near the market. I'm sure you'll find it. I'll let him know you're coming.'

'Cheers for that. I'll be sure to pass on your regards. Bye.'

Without waiting for a reply, Mason pushed the red button on the cell screen just as Sadie reached him. She plonked herself down on the armchair next to him, dropping her bag on the floor.

'It's pandemonium out there. I've never seen anything like it.'

'There've been a lot of delays recently. French air traffic controllers' strike, I think.'

Mason looked up at the flight information screen hung on a column behind Sadie, something he'd completely forgot about while talking to Tudge.

'It would seem our plane's bang on time. I think we'd better make our way to the gate. It's almost ready for boarding.'

He shouldered his carry-on bag, then picked up Sadie's plastic bag.

'Come on,' he said. 'We don't want to miss our plane.'

They walked side by side towards the gate. In a quiet part of the corridor, Mason stopped and turned towards Sadie. She stopped too, surprised at his sudden halt.

'Sadie, have you got a cell phone?' he asked.

'Yes. Why?'

'Open it and give it to me.' She fumbled inside her bag then duly produced it. 'Are there any numbers in this cell that you can't do without?'

'Apart from my sister's, no.'

'Her name?'

'Beckie.'

Mason scrolled through the unlocked cell and found the number. He scanned it, memorised it, then killed the cell. Next, he took the sim out, bent it in half and deposited it in the bin next to them.

'What're you doing? I need that.'

'Not anymore, Sadie. It's a tracking device. You carry that around and anyone can find you.'

Mason then dumped the dead cell phone into the next bin along.

'Great!' she said. 'How am I supposed to contact my sister now?'

'All up here, Sadie,' he tapped his temple reassuringly. 'Come on. We'll miss our flight.'

Mason turned on his heels and headed off in the direction of the boarding gate.

On board the plane, they took their seats without much hassle. Sadie was flicking through her new book, a Richard Osman 'Thursday Murder Club' story, when Mason tapped her on the arm.

'Here. Look at this.'

He held his cell between them so that they could both see the screen. After pressing the start button on a report from the BBC news website the short video playback began...

A heavy-set man stood behind a bank of microphones. According to the banner at the bottom of the screen, it was DCI Phillip Grimes. A tall, suited woman was standing next to him. She checked her wristwatch intermittently. The policeman held some notes just below the line of the microphones. Someone with headphones wrapped around his neck ducked from screen-right to screen-left, low, but not low enough not to be seen. Without turning his head, DCI Grimes, followed the individual with his eyes. The woman glanced at her watch again, then tapped Grimes on the shoulder.

The DCI lifted his notes and glanced at his prepared statement.

'Good morning,' he began, 'My name is DCI Grimes, Senior Investigating Officer looking into the murders at the Lynne Residential Home.' He paused for a beat, scanning the assembled press pack before him. After a moment, the policeman continued, 'I want to reassure the community that my officers and I will not settle until the perpetrators of this barbaric crime meet the full force of the law. We will move heaven and earth to locate these callous killers and put them where they belong, behind bars.' He lowered his notes, 'Now, if anyone has any questions, I'll be happy to answer where I can.'

From the pack of reporters, hands were raised, and a multitude of voices rang out, all vying for Grimes' attention.

The woman stood next to him pointed to a reporter at the front of the pack.

'State your name and publication, please, and then DCI Grimes will answer your question.'

'Yes, Simon Brick, the Guardian. You said "perpetrators". How can you be so sure that there was more than one person involved?'

Grimes leaned into the microphones and answered, 'The sheer scale of the killings and the spread of the victims' bodies in the Home indicate more than one person. Other than that, for operational purposes I can't go into detail.'

Again, the woman next to Grimes pointed, 'The lady in the white blouse.'

'Petra Antonucci, Eyewitness North. Can I ask DCI Grimes where Sadie Kellerman fits into this investigation?'

DCI Grimes hesitated, momentarily taken aback. He quickly regained his composure, 'I don't know where you've acquired that name, Ms Antonucci, but I think we should leave the questions for now.' Grimes began to turn away.

The reporter persisted, 'But Miss Kellerman? Surely you can tell us who she is?'

Grimes half turned back towards the microphones.

'Miss Kellerman is a person of interest. We have been trying to locate her.'

'Do you think she has something to do with the killings?'

'I didn't say that,' the policeman snapped. 'Now if you'll allow me. I must get back to work.'

Mason shut the video down.

'Oh shit!' Sadie said out loud.

Mason put his hand over hers and attempted to reassure her that everything would be okay.

Sadie half turned to him and said in a voice louder than intended, 'What the fuck!' She realised how much her voice had carried when an old lady turned towards her from across the aisle. She immediately lowered her voice to more of a whisper. 'Look! I'm not sure if you've grasped the nettle here, but I've suddenly turned into public enemy number one and I'm on a plane leaving the country. How's that gonna look when I'm up before the Beak?'

'You're not gonna be up in any court. At worst you'll be a witness, and best you'll quickly be discounted by the cops and never hear another word about it again.'

'But what about when we land? Won't the Croatian's want a word?'

Mason said, 'Just because some pot-bellied, balding copper from Manchester says you're a 'person of interest', doesn't mean every gendarme in the world's gonna be on your tail.'

She mulled his words over for a beat, then said, 'As soon as they get this plane up in the air, I want the largest drink they supply, and double it. And it's on you!'

CHAPTER 25

Against his better judgement, Nesby sat on the leather couch in the corner of the bar area at the local Premier Inn. He always felt settees were for courting couples, not for single blokes getting pissed.

The left side of his body felt like someone had hit him with a baseball bat. After the crash he'd been taken to hospital where the quacks had given him the once-over. They'd wanted him to stay in, but he'd checked out anyway, telling them he'd speak to his own doctor if there were further complications. The staff had put up a token struggle, but the A&E doctor had found it hard to hide his delight. Nesby wondered if another admission would go down on the Quack's record. Would that push his monthly figures up? At any rate, he was gone and away from that stench of suffering that permeated hospitals.

Nesby checked into the Premier Inn because he didn't want to deal with the cops if they came snooping, as they surely would. He could easily guess their line of questioning… 'Why were you driving so fast, Mr Nesby?' 'Who were you chasing?' 'Do you have any information as to their whereabouts?' He knew how their shit-filled brains worked, and they wouldn't stop probing until they'd found out the exact size of his knob, both hard and soft. Perverted bastards!

The barman brought over a second large brandy and, with a nod, placed it on the coffee table in front of Nesby. What the hell, he wasn't driving. He reached over to down the dregs of his first drink and winced. His left shoulder and side were black and blue all the way down to his waist. When the car had turned and landed, Nesby's side had been smashed against the door.

Luckily the airbag had activated on impact. This had caused some bruising to his face, but he'd mend. It was his side that was causing him the most discomfort. The pills the hospital had given him weren't touching the point of pain at all. If only the brandy would kick-in quicker and ease the healing process.

Two men in grey suits came into the bar, their chatter instantly irritating Nesby. He wished they'd just get their drinks and leave as soon as possible. They sat on stools at the bar while the barman uncorked a bottle of red. He picked two glasses from the shelf behind him, checked they were clean, and placed them in front of the two men. He started to pour but was stopped by the louder of the pair.

'We're going for a smoke outside, mate. I'll take that.'

'Yes, sir.' The young barman put the bottle down and retreated, leaving the men to take the bottle and glasses out with them. They passed Nesby and exited through the open patio doors near where he was sat.

It was only 2pm and the light streamed through the patio door with a slight breeze wafting against the heavy purple curtains. Nesby took another gulp of the brandy. If he carried on like this, he'd be drunk by six.

He caressed his shoulder to soothe the pain, but the discomfort was too much to bear so he refrained and sunk back into the settee.

Apart from the chatter Nesby could hear emanating from the two men outside, no one encroached on his solitude. The barman was busy cleaning behind the bar. He downed the last of the brandy and waited a moment. Did he want another? Would he stay alert if he continued drinking?

As tired and intoxicated as he was, Nesby knew that he had to find Mason and kill him. It wasn't a question of *if*, it was only a question of *when*. He'd killed Mason Senior. Now it was the son's turn to die.

'Nesby.' A voice interrupted his thoughts. It was Ferguson striding in from the door to his left.

Nesby began to rise from the settee but then thought better of it.

Ferguson winced standing over Nesby, 'Jesus! You are a mess. You look like you've gone through ten rounds with Tyson Fury.'

'Don't fret, I've looked in the mirror. I know how bad I look.'

'But does your mother?'

'Fuck off and get me a double brandy. And make it an expensive one!'

'Keep your hair on, mate. All in good time.'

Nesby snapped, 'I'm not your mate!' then immediately wished he hadn't, as a spasm of pain erupted in his side. 'Just get the drink.' He watched Ferguson get their drinks and return, placing them on the table between them.

'So, what's the story with the face?' Ferguson asked, taking a drink of his water.

'Shut up!' Nesby grimaced as soon as the words had left his mouth. 'Just tell me what's going on with the cops.'

Ferguson moved uncomfortably in his seat. 'Look, the investigation is at a standstill. It's what happens when they put a useless prick in charge. Grimes would be hard pressed to find his own cock!'

'Look! Mr Lester isn't going to be pleased if I've got no news for him.'

Ferguson picked his glass up, 'Just tell Tom there's nothing new to report. He'll understand. He knows how the police work.'

'The police don't work, you moron,' Nesby spat. 'That's why he employs people like me.'

'You can fuck off!' Ferguson hurled. 'I'm not taking that from you. I've not come here to be insulted by a minion.'

Nesby sat forward on the settee with considerable discomfort and said with as much menace as he could muster, 'You've come here to listen to whatever I have to say and do whatever I tell you to do.' He flinched and took a moment to compose himself before continuing. 'I'm here to represent Mr Lester. And whatever he wants, you do. Have you got that?'

Nesby stared at the policeman, daring him to contradict what he had just said.

Ferguson didn't. He just sank back into his seat instead, 'Take a chill pill, would you? Just relax. Look, we're all friends here. We're all working toward the same end point.'

Nesby took his glass and sat back himself. Taking a sip he asked, 'So what have you got for me?'

'Like I said, absolutely nothing. Grimes is fucking clueless. They're pinning all their hopes on this Kellerman woman and they're desperate to locate her. From my point of view, there are two possibilities. One, she was in on the murders. Or two, she's been killed herself and we just haven't found her body yet. Either way, I'm not helping Grimes in any significant way.'

Nesby knew that none of this was true. Kellerman was alive and was currently with Mason. He wasn't going to provide Ferguson with that information though. The more the cops were stuck in a revolving door, the better.

Nesby took another drink, 'Right, it's time you were back at the station. I want you to let me know of any new developments and quickly. I'll be here for the foreseeable.'

Ferguson shuffled in his seat again, 'Look, Nesby, it's getting far too difficult for me to continue passing on information. Eventually, they're going to twig who's been feeding the information to the journalists. If I get caught, I'll be completely useless to Tom. So, I need to back off a bit. Take a low profile.'

Nesby swished a little of the brandy around his mouth, pondering, before starting to speak.

'So, you want out. Is that what you're saying?'

'No. No.' Ferguson reassured but knew what he was saying was a gamble. If Lester had no need for him there was no telling what he would do. But Ferguson had to take a chance. He'd decided to leave the police, his marriage, and ask Petra to live with him permanently. This would be hard, but he had to do it. 'I just want to take a back seat for a while. I'm a little too close to this investigation. It's going nowhere. Tom isn't in any danger at all from Grimes or the police on this. I just think it would be wise for me to lie low for a while.'

Nesby knew what his boss's reaction would be but didn't

enlighten the copper. This would be Ferguson's problem down the line, not his.

'Okay. If that's what you want, I'll pass your message on to Mr. Lester. You know your retainer will cease immediately?' he warned.

'Look, the money isn't an issue here. I want to be more helpful to Tom later, when I'm sure I can be more useful.' He was lying. He wanted out forever. But that's something he couldn't say out loud. He just hoped Tom Lester would find another informant in the police and forget all about him. 'When all this has blown over. I'll be back.'

'Right then. When I speak to Mr. Lester, I'll tell him of our conversation. I'm sure he'll be fine with it. Now I have one last request before you fuck off out of my sight.'

'What's that? Anything? I can see you're in a lot of pain.'

'Get me another drink!'

'Sure.' Ferguson returned with the drink and placed it on the table in front of Nesby. 'Okay. I'm off. Take care of those injuries.'

'Piss off!' Nesby spat back and took a drink as Ferguson left.

CHAPTER 26

As they produced their passports for the border guard at Dubrovnik International Airport, Sadie squeezed Mason's hand hard. It was a relief to him when the guard ushered them through with little formality; he didn't think he could take the pressure Sadie was putting his hand under much longer. Sadie exhaled, 'Phew!' under her breath as they moved further away from the border kiosk. With only carry-on bags there was no delay waiting for luggage at the carousel.

The comfortable air-cooled atmosphere of the airport was extinguished quickly as a woosh of hot air swept passed Mason and Sadie when the exit doors automatically opened.

'Crap a frappe!' Sadie exclaimed. 'Back to the stall over there. I need a hat and sunglasses.'

She turned on her heels leaving Mason in her wake.

He followed obediently.

The tourist stall not far from the exit contained all sorts of *tat*; stuff that Mason would never buy in a million years. A girl, no more than twenty years old in Mason's estimation, sat behind the counter looking down at her cell phone. She welcomed them without much enthusiasm, 'Dobar dan.' – Good day.

Sadie didn't respond. Mason gave a weak smile.

For no reason, he turned the book carousel around. Glancing at the titles, he noticed one that he'd seen on a shelf at Sadie's apartment. He remembered it because the character had such a distinctive name, Inky Stevens. He couldn't read the title because it had been translated into Croatian.

Sadie nudged him in the ribs and asked, 'What do you think of this?'

She was wearing a cowboy-style straw hat. The rim had been tied up, forcing the hat's brim into a point at the front.

He wanted to say, '*You look gorgeous*', but settled for 'It's good.'

'Well, your enthusiasm does indeed over-floweth, Mister Mason.' She turned away and said, 'Get your cash out, I'm taking it and these sunglasses.'

Mason did as instructed, throwing Croatian Kuna notes onto the counter. The shop assistant put the money into the sales register and, as she gave him the receipt, said with little enthusiasm, 'Hvala.' – Thank you.

Sadie had already left the small shop when Mason turned around and headed for the exit door. He picked his pace up and reached her as the door whooshed open in front of them. Hot air immediately won the battle with the air-conditioned atmosphere inside. They stepped outside and Mason immediately felt at home. In the few short months that he'd stayed in Dubrovnik, Mason had settled into life and acclimatised very well to the Croatian weather.

Straining to look up at the hot sun clearly hanging in the vibrant blue sky, Sadie announced, 'I need lotion. And plenty of it!'

'We can get everything we need from the Konzum store at the port.'

'Great! How do we get there?' she asked.

'We'll pick the SUV up at the long stay car park and head over to my place at Babin Kuk. Then we'll sort out whatever we need from the Konzum.'

'You've got a house here?'

'Yes. Well, a rented one, actually,' he corrected. 'But it's mine.'

'Is that where we're staying?'

Mason had been giving this some thought on the flight over. Lester must know, or have friends who would know, where he was living. How else would he have known where to dump Bevan's body? A still image of Bevan dead in the water in front of the Old Yacht Club flashed in front of Mason's eyes. Eyes wide, arm stretched out pleading for help. Help that Mason could not give, it was too late for that.

Mason had decided the Old Yacht Club wasn't the smartest place to lay low. They'd have to find other accommodation, and somewhere cheaper than the hotel prices.

'No. I have a good friend, Luka. He might be able to help. Come on. Let's get the car.'

As they drove along the shoreline high above the Adriatic Ocean, Sadie declared, 'This is beautiful. I've never seen anywhere like this.'

'Stunning, isn't it?' Mason agreed.

Passing the viewing point over Stari Grad, - the Old Town, Sadie exclaimed, 'Wow! That's awesome!'

Once at the Old Yacht Club Sadie jumped out of the car like an excited teenager. She stood looking out to sea across the inlet towards the Franjo Tuđman suspension bridge. 'What a view! Oh my God! Is this where you live?'

Mason joined her. 'I did for a few months.'

'I can't believe you left. I'd do anything to live in a place like this.'

He went into the house and checked everything was in order. No one had been in since he'd left for England.

When he came out and locked up, Sadie was sat at the edge of the ocean and was dangling her feet into the cool water, basking in the summer heat. He toyed with the idea of telling her that that was the exact spot where Bevan's body had been dumped. In fact, his lifeless hand would probably be touching Sadie's feet if he were still there.

He decided not to spook her, he leaned on the car and said, 'Come on. Get in. We should go.'

Sadie clambered out of the water, put her sandals back on and then got into the vehicle.

'So, where to now?' she asked.

'To the Konzum in Gruž,' he said, putting the vehicle into Drive and setting the SUV on its way.

'Where's that?'

'It's the port area across the inlet. We can get all we need from there.'

'Well, I need suntan lotion quick, or I'm going to burn to a crisp!'

'I need a new cell and some alcohol.'

'I hate to point this out, but when you dumped my phone, you kept hold of your own.'

'True,' he said, looking towards her for a moment, 'But I need one that can't be located easily. If Lester or the police have connected us, it won't take them long to locate me via my cell. I never use one for more than a few weeks anyway, so mine will be going in the *drink*.'

'God! That must be exhausting! How do you keep up with your numbers?'

'You just do,' he said dully as they drove around the harbour.

'Look at all these boats,' Sadie said, excitedly. 'Do you have one?'

'No. But I have a friend who does.'

Mason had decided that after they'd been to the Konzum, he would contact Luka. If anyone had any worthwhile news it would be him. He might also know of a place they can get their heads down for a few nights.

After they had got some basic items: deodorant, lotion, drinks, cell phones and sim cards, etc. they headed back to the SUV. Mason ripped open a box containing a cell phone. He assembled the device and inserted a new sim card into the side slot. Luckily it had enough charge to start using it straight away. From memory, he punched in Luka's cell number. After a few short rings, the Croat answered.

'Molim?' – Please.

'Luka, it's Mason.'

'Nick! Where are you?' Luka asked in accented English. 'One day you were here, the next day you were gone!'

'I'm in Gruž. Can meet up for a drink? I need some advice.'

'I'm at your service, my friend. Meet me at the bar just down from the Gas Station in the harbour.'

'The one near the old winery?' Mason asked.

AN INVITATION FOR REVENGE

'Yes, that's the one. I'll be there shortly.'

'That's great! I'll have a large glass of Plavac waiting for you.'

'You're an English gentleman, for sure.' With that, Luka killed the line.

Mason looked over towards Sadie, who was flipping through an English copy of the local tourist guide. He'd told her it was a waste of money as they wouldn't have time to be tourists. 'It's your money!' she said, unconcerned.

'Come on, it's time for you to meet my friend Luka.'

'Is he trustworthy?' she asked.

'Solid as they come,' he confirmed.

'Good! Because I get the impression lots of the people you know are a little on the suspicious side.'

'Not this one.'

'Okay. Let's meet him.'

*

The square jetty was tethered snug to the quayside. The fake green grass covering the deck was worn and ripped. Ten tables, with four chairs and an umbrella at each, stood on the gently rocking structure. All were free when Mason and Sadie took their seats. Almost immediately, a waiter came across from the main bar area which was across the road.

'A bottle of Plavac, please. And for you?' he asked Sadie.

She looked up at the waiter who was dressed in pristine white shirt and black trousers, 'A large gin and tonic, please.'

'Thank you,' the waiter said with a slight accent and retreated to the main bar across the small road.

'So, why are we meeting this Luka?' Sadie asked.

'First, we need to find a place to stay. After that, we can talk about Lester and what he's up to.'

'Sounds like this is going to be a riveting conversation,' she said sarcastically. Looking around, she asked, 'Is there a beach near here?'

'Yes, just further up the shore.'

'Good,' she said. 'I'd like to give that a try while we're here.'
'If we've time.'

Mason lit up a cigarette and threw the pack and lighter onto the table between them.

The waiter came out with the tray of drinks. He placed the bottle of Plavac down with a wineglass, then placed Sadie's gin and tonic in front of her.

As the waiter began to remove the cork, Mason asked, 'Could we have another glass for the wine, please? We're meeting someone.'

'Of course,' the waiter answered. Opening the bottle, he poured Mason a taster and remained for his approval. Mason nodded after he'd sampled the wine and put the glass on the table. The waiter filled his glass and then retreated to get the extra glass.

When they were alone, Mason sat back and exhaled. He needed to breathe. He felt like he hadn't stopped in days. He doubted he'd ever forget the things that had happened since he'd found Bevan's dead body, only a short distance from where they were sat. He had seen enough carnage and death to last him a lifetime. His father, slain for nothing but being his parent. Charlie Reynolds and the old folk slaughtered, and for what? Tom Lester's insatiable appetite for paying a debt he felt he was owed. Not forgetting Kosinski, Lester's henchman, who had been the first man sent to kill him. He had died at the hands of Bevan, but the death had been sickening; shot through the head at point blank with little remorse.

And the sad thing about all this was that he knew the killing wasn't finished. It would not stop until Tom Lester or Mason were dead. Only then would the spiral of death reach an end.

Mason felt sick as he took a deep drag from his cigarette.

'Penny for them?' Sadie asked as the waiter returned and left the glass on the table.

He looked at the girl across the table sipping her drink, hair flickering in the breeze. She was an innocent in all of this. She'd been dragged into Lester's murderous vendetta. Sadie's life had been turned upside down. Her job blown out of existence. Her colleagues, and the people she cared for, massacred. And all for the gratification of Tom Lester.

Sadie didn't have a clue about the world she had walked into when she'd escorted his father to the park just days ago. Mason had to find a way to get her to safety. If only she'd let him.

Mason put his drink down, 'I'm just thinking it would have been nice to be here under different circumstances.'

'Dead right! It feels like I've been chased here at gunpoint.'

Before Mason could respond, he heard a boat engine getting louder. He turned and saw Luka's vessel approaching the quayside.

His friend waved from the boat and pointed towards a jetty next to the where they were sat. Mason rose and went over to the jetty. Cutting the engine Luka allowed the boat to drift in. He threw a line for Mason to catch.

Mason tied the boat up and watched Luka disembark and secure the stern.

The two men met with a handshake.

'Good to see you, my friend,' Luka greeted. 'Where have you been? I was beginning to get a little worried.'

'Unfortunately, I had to return home in a hurry.' He gestured towards Sadie and said, 'Come, I have someone for you to meet and a glass of Plavac to whet your appetite.'

'I'm always ready for a drink.' He clapped his hand on Mason's shoulder as they walked away from the boat.

As they got to the table, Sadie started to rise. Luka said, 'Don't get up on my account. He shook her hand, 'I'm Luka, a good friend of Nick here.'

'Sadie Kellerman,' she said.

He sat next to her, while Mason sat opposite Sadie, as before. Mason poured his friend some wine and then topped his own glass up.

Looking over towards Sadie, Mason asked, 'Do you want another gin and tonic?'

'Yes, please.'

Mason waved towards the waiter, who was now standing at the bar entrance looking out over the harbour. When the waiter came over, he ordered a gin and tonic for Sadie.

As the waiter had left them, Luka asked, 'What can I do for you, my friend?'

Mason put his glass down, 'All in good time. Did I tell you this is Sadie's first trip to Croatia?'

'No,' Luka said lighting a cigarette up. 'In fact, you never mentioned you had a lady friend.'

'That's because I never had one to tell you about,' the Englishman replied.

'I see. So how do you find our little country, Sadie?' Luka asked.

'Beautiful,' Sadie said, sipping the last of her drink. She swirled the remains of the ice around her glass and admitted, 'I don't think I've ever seen a sky so blue in my life.'

Mason had deliberately kept the conversation low-key for a while. He was reluctant to get into a serious discussion with Luka while Sadie was with them. She had experienced a lot in the last few days. He didn't think replaying it all would help her at this stage.

Just as Mason poured the last of the wine into the two glasses, Luka took a pull on his cigarette, 'So what can I do for you, Nick?'

'We need somewhere to stay.'

'What about the Old Yacht Club? Has your lease ended so soon?'

'No. We need to lie low for a while. Bringing attention to ourselves is something we could do without.'

'I see.'

The waiter placed the gin and tonic in front of Sadie.

'Još jedan Plavac, molim vas!' – Another bottle of Plavac, please, Luka ordered.

'Naravno' – Of course, the waiter said retreating towards the bar.

'Could you find us somewhere?'

'Nick, I have the safest place you could imagine.'

'Where?' Mason asked.

'My apartment,' he said, smiling. 'It's perfect. There's just my wife and me. We have an extra room since my mother-in-law passed away five years ago. You must stay with us.'

The waiter brought the bottle of wine and placed it in the middle of the table. He then took the empty bottle away.

'Shouldn't you ask your wife first?' Mason suggested.

Luka took a drink and shrugged his shoulders, 'She will be very happy to have guests. We haven't had anyone stay with us since her sister was here, and before Covid hit. I'm not sure which was worse, having her sister around us all day, or the pandemic.'

'That's very kind. I do think you should at least call and make sure she's okay with it.'

'No need to worry,' Luka assured, taking a drink. 'We'll finish our drinks and then go speak with her.'

Mason paid the bill after they'd finished their drinks and they all got into the SUV for the short ride to Luka's apartment.

The apartment's entrance, at the top of some grey steps, was squashed in between two shops; a delicatessen on one side and a fashion boutique on the other.

As Luka led them through the door, he called out, 'Manuela! Manuela! We have guests!'

He ushered them through the hall and into the sitting room. Manuela came out from the small galley kitchen that was open off the main room. A petite woman, her long dark hair was combed back from her face into a ponytail that fell halfway down her back. Her olive skin gave her a healthy glow, yet a couple of lines stretching from each eye indicated she might not have been as young as her youthful smile suggested.

She wiped her palms on her apron and extended a hand. Sadie smiled and shook their hosts hand, 'Hello, I'm Sadie.'

'Manuela.' She then looked over at Mason and shook his hand, too.

'Nick,' he said.

Luka asked, 'Manuela, would you get the Badel for my friend.' He then looked across to Sadie. 'And for you?'

'A wine will do, thanks.'

'That's settled then. Let's sit and have a drink.' Luka offered them both a seat on the settee facing the galley kitchen.

Mason and Sadie sat without talking, waiting for Manuela to return with their drinks. Once she had returned, Luka offered them his cigarettes. Sadie refused, so he lit his own and passed the lighter to Mason who lit his own, as did Manuela who had sat next to her husband facing the English couple.

'By the way, Nick, I heard about your friend. It was a tragic business. To drown like that? Terrible.'

'Yes, it was,' Mason agreed.

Manuela rose to her feet and asked, 'Are we talking about the man who was killed near Nick's house?' Her husband nodded. 'Then I'm glad this conversation is happening now, before we eat. Sadie, do you want to come with me? We can leave them to their morbid discussions.'

'Yes, of course.' She picked her glass of wine up and joined Manuela in the kitchen.

When the women were out of earshot, Mason took a drag of his cigarette and asked, 'Has Tom Lester arrived in Dubrovnik?'

Luka removed the cigarette from his mouth and answered, 'Not that I know. Although I don't know this man by sight. Is he the man Željko is meeting?'

'He is. And he's a very nasty person.'

'I knew something was happening. My old bones can always feel bad things in the wind, my friend.'

'I'll need you to keep your ear to the ground. If Lester arrives, I need to know. Immediately,' he stressed.

'I will know when anyone new arrives,' Luka confirmed. 'But tell me why this man is important to you, Nick.'

Mason recounted his dealings with Tom Lester, including the events of the last few days, missing nothing out.

'And so you see, if I don't kill him, he will kill me, and most probably Sadie too.' He took a drink of the badel and pointed at Luka. 'And if he finds out you and Manuela have helped us, he'll most likely take his revenge out on you too.'

'This man does sound nasty. Let's make sure he's unsuccessful in his pursuit of you both.'

'I'll drink to that.' Mason raised his glass as did Luka.

CHAPTER 27

The small armchair was the only place in his hotel room that Nesby could get comfortable in. Lying flat on the hard mattress had been a nightmare with his bruised side and by one-thirty in the morning he had given up all hope of a full night's sleep. He'd resorted to catnapping in the chair with CNN on the TV in the background. The odd slurp of the brandy on the side table helped.

He'd showered and felt refreshed by the time room service arrived. Even though there was still a lot of bruising, much of the pain had subsided and he felt he could take on the day in a much better frame of mind and, crucially, in a better way physically. A tray of bacon and eggs, toast, and a pot of fresh coffee had been delivered by a young waitress. He'd seen her in the bar area the previous day after Ferguson had left. There seemed to be a sheen to her short auburn hair which contrasted with the milky-white youthful skin of her face. He admitted to himself that the tattoo peeking out from beneath her cuff interested him. Inked-up bodies definitely attracted him.

His cell phone sprang into life just as he was finishing his breakfast, and he wiped his mouth. It was Lester calling for an update.

Nesby brushed his hands together, jettisoning crumbs of toast from his fingertips, before picking the cell phone up. He swiped the screen right to answer.

'Nesby,' he introduced, even though he knew who was on the other end of the line.

Without preamble, Lester asked, 'What have you got for me?'

'Morning, Tom. Where are you.' Nesby hadn't yet decided how

he was going to tell Lester that he'd lost all trace of Mason and the girl.

'I'm about to leave for Bosnia, to catch up with a colleague. You need to meet me in Dubrovnik as soon as you can.'

Nesby hesitated slightly. He knew that his boss wouldn't be happy that he'd lost contact. 'Tom, about Mason and the girl.' He paused for a beat, then ploughed on. 'I had them cornered at a house owned by the girl's sister, but then I lost them. He's a damn good driver and, unfortunately, he gave me the slip. Ended up trashing my car.' He then added, 'and nearly me too.'

'No matter,' Lester replied, seemingly disinterested.

'Look, Tom, you've no need to worry. I'll locate them and finish the job. It shouldn't be too hard.'

'I don't worry, Nesby. Worrying is a useless emotion. I leave that to other people.'

'Yes, Tom. Like I say, I'll find them.'

'I already know where they are,' Lester revealed.

'But how?' Nesby asked, confused.

'My contact in Dubrovnik informed me that Mason and the girl are there. The house Mason is renting is empty, so he's not staying at his own place. After what happened to Bevan, he'll know we're watching it. I suspect he's trying to avoid the same fate as his deceased friend.'

'So what do we do, Tom?'

'You are going to get on the first available plane out to Dubrovnik. Contact me when you land. I know a nice lady called Marta who has a small B&B where you can stay. In fact, it's not far from Mason's rental, so it will be an ideal place in case he does return there.'

'Will do, Tom.'

'Is there anything else I need to know?' Lester asked. 'I need to catch that plane.'

'Just one more thing.' Nesby hesitated.

'Spit it out!' Lester was beginning to sound impatient.

Nesby took a further beat, 'It's about the copper. Ferguson.'

'What about him?'

'He wants out. Says he needs to lie low for a while. He thinks the cops will suss out he's been leaking information and he's scared he'll get caught.'

'Is he now? Well, you can tell him from me that I don't give a fuck if he gets caught.' There was venom in Lester's voice. 'He keeps his mouth shut and does as he's told.'

'I've, er, told him Tom. He still insists he's out.'

'People don't resign from my employ, Nesby. I decide when they leave.'

Nesby was beginning to get nervous. The last time he'd heard Lester talk like this was at Cranborne Hall when his boss murdered Lloyd in cold blood.

'So, what do you want me to do, Tom?'

'I could have done without this now. It's come at an awkward time.' Lester was thinking out loud. 'Luckily, I've been in conversation with another copper down at the station. Ferguson isn't my only inroad down there now. I think it's time Ferguson's contract is terminated.'

'How do we do that,' Nesby asked, already knowing the answer.

'Pay him a visit. Explain the situation to him, and then eliminate him. And Nesby...'

'Yes?'

'I don't want to hear any more about Marc Ferguson, except when I see his death announced in the obituaries.'

'Of course, Tom. Consider the job done, and I'll be in Dubrovnik as soon as I can get a flight out.'

Nesby heard the line cut. His boss had given him his orders and there was no more to be said.

It was time to check out. He packed his rucksack. Remarkably, his side felt a lot better now. It's amazing what a box of pills and a few glasses of brandy can do.

Nesby did a final sweep of the room before chucking a tenner on the desk for the cleaner, then exited towards the lift.

A few doors down on the left-hand side of the corridor, the young girl who had delivered breakfast was standing in the doorway of a room.

'I told you I wanted The Times, not the bloody Guardian,' a man shouted from inside. 'Do I look like some hippy, climate change, freak to you?'

The young girl moved uneasily from foot to foot.

'I can get you a fresh newspaper, sir. It will only take a few minutes.'

A hand thrust the unwanted newspaper into the girl's chest. She grabbed it and shifted her weight onto her back foot to avoid falling.

'And get me another bottle of this shitty red plonk you lot are passing off as wine.'

The young girl was clearly upset. Nesby noticed the reddened colour of her face and tears were beginning to fall.

He had to make a split-second decision. Should he get involved or not? He hated people who bullied young girls, so it was a no brainer for him.

'Can I help you, miss?' he asked as he reached the door.

The girl looked at him for the first time. He could now see she was really upset.

She said, 'No, it's okay. I'm just helping this gentleman.'

The loud-mouthed customer from the bar the previous day suddenly came into view. He hadn't even dressed properly, sporting a pair of boxers and an unbuttoned shirt that hung down over his waist. His hair was ruffled, and he hadn't shaved.

The irate businessman turned to Nesby, pointed at him, and snarled, 'This has nothing to do with you, so shut the fuck up and piss off!'

Nesby looked at the man impassively, then back at the girl. He put his rucksack down, 'I'm sorry about this man's rudeness. I hope all guests aren't like this.'

'It's okay,' she said.

'No, it's not,' Nesby affirmed. 'You need to go and get his newspaper while I deal with this neanderthal.'

'And how're you gonna do that, you...' the man spat out as he stepped towards Nesby.

Before he finished his sentence, Nesby had punched him in the midriff.

The businessman doubled up, a lungful of air forcing its way out as he crumpled to the floor. He struggled to get his breath as he knelt face down in the tan carpet.

The young girl was glad she hadn't moved away too quickly. She would have been upset to have missed the felling of the obnoxious guest in Room 242. He'd given her a lot of grief the previous evening and again this morning. Unfortunately, hotel guidance doesn't allow you to tell customers to *go take a hike* if they're rude. Thankfully, this other guest didn't have to follow such rules.

'Thank you,' she mouthed in Nesby's direction.

He nodded, then watched her turn away and leave.

Nesby heard the heavy breathing of the man on the floor who still hadn't recovered from the punch he'd received.

'Okay, dipstick! Time to get up. You're making the corridor look a mess.'

Nesby dragged the man up to his feet and pushed him back into the room, closing the door behind them.

The businessman bleated, 'You've no right to treat me like that. It's assault. I can sue your fucking arse off,'

'Is that right?' Nesby asked, sarcastically.

'Yeah, it fucking is! Now get out before I call the police.'

The businessman turned towards the telephone at the side of his bed. But before he could pick up the receiver Nesby had withdrawn the pistol from his waistband and smacked him on the back of his head with the butt.

'Ouch! What the fuck did you do that for?' the man shouted, half turning while clutching the back of his head.

'Because I can,' Nesby informed him.

Sitting on the bed, the businessman looked up at Nesby, saw the handgun and visibly moved back away from his assailant.

'What the hell? You've got a gun.'

'You're so perceptive, I can hardly believe it.'

'But what... do you need that for,' he stuttered.

'What do I need it for? For pricks like you who need teaching a lesson from time to time.'

'Look, just go. I don't want any trouble with you.'

'That's nice. But what about the young girl you've just been abusing out there? I think she needs to be treated with a little bit more respect. Wouldn't you agree?'

'That was just a little bit of playful banter. There was nothing to it.'

'That's not how it sounded to me.'

Shifting on the bed, the businessman said, 'Course it was. I wasn't being serious. She knew that.'

Nesby tapped the muzzle of the gun on his chin and said, 'I'm not sure she did. In fact, I'm positive you've upset her.'

'No, honestly. She's fine.' Realising he was in big trouble, the businessman continued, 'Look, I'll leave a big tip. I can't say fairer than that, can I?'

Nesby said nothing.

Rising from his bed, the businessman pleaded with Nesby, 'Come on, mate. I've had a really heavy schedule. My boss has been the absolute pits recently and if I don't land this deal I'm working on, I'll be out on my ears. And where will that leave the little lady at home and the kids at boarding school? You can see where I'm coming from here, can't you?' Nesby remained quiet. 'I've got pressures, mate. Up to my fucking eyeballs in it. So, I blow a bit of steam off. Don't we all,' he spread his arms wide? 'I didn't mean any of it,' he tried to explain.

'I'll tell you what, *mate*,' Nesby said, emphasising the word. 'When I blow off steam it means someone's in trouble. So, you need to be very aware that at the moment I'm not blowing off steam, I'm simply explaining things to you.'

'Yes right,' the businessman said, looking very carefully at Nesby's gun which was now most definitely pointing in his direction.

With a swift movement, Nesby grabbed the man by his collar and pushed him into the wall.

The man's eyes widened in terror as he saw the gun moving

slowly towards his forehead. He thought all this was movie stuff, not real life.

He tried to put his hands up in front of his face, but Nesby smacked them down with the gun.

'I've got kids! Please,' he pleaded, visibly crying.

'I pity them having a father like you, you snivelling little shit!'

Nesby pushed him hard into the wall and forced the muzzle of the gun into the man's forehead.

'O shit! No!'

Nesby heard something and looked down at their feet. A trickle of liquid ran down the man's leg.

'Fuck me!' Nesby laughed. 'When it rains it sodding pours. Or it does in your case, you soft fucker!' He loosened his grip slightly and continued, 'You'd better leave this girl alone. In fact, when I come back here, if I hear from anybody about you mistreating any of the staff, I'll find you and rip your fucking balls off. Do you understand me?'

There were tears running down the reddened face of the man against the wall.

'Yes, I understand.'

'Good. Now don't let me down.'

'I won't,' the businessman agreed.

A sudden noise in the doorway took his attention away from Nesby. It was the young girl with the Times newspaper.

She stopped in her tracks when she saw what was happening.

'O God!'

Nesby looked around and saw the girl. He pushed the man back onto the bed.

'It's okay. I've dealt with your guest. He won't be giving you any more trouble.'

The girl couldn't take her eyes off the gun.

Nesby realised and instantly re-holstered the gun.

'Look, it's okay. Honest. No harm done.'

CHAPTER 28

Tom Lester's flight to Sarajevo, the capital of Bosnia and Herzegovina, was uneventful. The Cessna Citation private jet was as comfortable as luxury travel comes, apart from the landing, which was a little rocky for Lester's liking.

He'd chartered the private flight from an old business associate who had assured him that he could be in and out of Bosnia without attracting any attention from the authorities. Following his escape from prison, Lester had learned that he had been added to Interpol's most wanted list, and the last thing he needed now was to be picked up by some ambitious Bosnian copper yearning for an extra stripe.

Lester looked up at the grey clouds and immediately wished he'd landed somewhere brighter. Thankfully, it wasn't a cold day. He was met at the foot of the aircraft steps by Željko Kovačić, who whisked him through a private area of passport control at Butmir Airport with a simple nod to the security guard. For Lester, this would be a routine trip that he should have taken earlier. Instead, he had left Bevan to make contact, do the groundwork and arrange the preliminary deal with the Croatian.

If Lester was honest with himself, several good things had come from Bevan's visit to the former Yugoslavian republic of Croatia. The first being confirmation that Željko was the man to supply the drugs he needed to expand his own empire back in Britain. Secondly, Bevan had managed to employ a spy within the Croat's retinue who had been supplying him with information throughout their discussions. And thirdly, the new recruit in Croatia had informed Lester that Bevan had a very cosy relationship with an Englishman out there – by the name of Nick Mason.

Lester believed Mason to be dead. Bevan had assured him of that. Tom Lester didn't like liars in his organisation. Bevan had to die, and he'd asked Željko to *do the honours*. He hadn't told the Croatian the real reason he wanted Bevan dead, simply saying his underling had become 'surplus to requirements'. The Croat understood, he was in the same business, and he duly dispatched Bevan.

Željko had booked Lester in the Hotel Europa in the heart of Sarajevo and, after arriving, they sat at a coffee table facing each other.

After a few moments' contemplation, the Croat asked, 'So why did you want to come to Sarajevo, my friend?'

The Englishman didn't answer, Instead, he took a drink of the *Rémy Martin Tercet* that Željko had ordered. Lester savoured the fresh fruity cognac with the large ice cube floating in the middle.

Receiving no answer, the Croat asked, 'Good? I always have this drink here. They serve it perfectly.'

'Yes, very good, thank you.' Lester removed a pack of cigars from his inside jacket pocket and said to his host, 'I believe we're allowed here?'

'Of course,' Željko confirmed. 'We wouldn't have it any other way. You English are far too precious about these things.'

Lester lit a cigar and offered one to Željko, who took it gratefully.

Once they were both comfortably smoking, Lester revealed, 'I've always wanted to visit this place. It seems to have a wonderful, exotic history, if a little dark, with the assassination of Archduke Ferdinand.'

'Ah, yes. The touch paper for the first great war of the 20th Century. But the city has more to it than that, my friend. It has a history of cultures mixed, free to mingle and experience life together, and has done for many years.'

'And the recent civil war?' Lester asked.

'An aberration that my fellow people should never have

embarked upon. It's the people, not the lying politicians, who are important. If it had been up to the ordinary people, nothing like that would ever have happened. And it's best we leave such things in the past, my friend. For the good of everyone.'

Lester glanced up as one of Željko's men came over. The young man concerned had been sitting in the front of the car which they had travelled from the airport in. They had not been introduced. The man bent down, cupped a hand near his boss's ear and spoke briefly.

Lester couldn't hear what passed between them.

Željko nodded and the young man stood straight and glanced at Lester without leaving his boss's side.

While taking a drink of the cognac, Lester eyed the butt of a pistol housed in a holster under the man's bomber jacket. It didn't worry Lester unduly.

'Petar, please refresh our drinks,' Željko ordered his subordinate. Once Petar had left, Željko asked, 'So why do you come now, Mr Lester? I thought our deal was complete. Especially after I, how can I say, removed the problem of Mr Bevan for you.'

Lester finished the last of his cognac and took a deep drag from his cigar. A speech-cloud of smoke formed above his head, 'Yes, that was very helpful. Thank you for that. He had become something of a liability. I'm sure you know about these things?'

Željko looked up as Petar brought them fresh drinks, putting them down on the table.

'I do indeed, Mr. Lester,' he said scratching his stubbled chin. 'Thank you, Petar.'

'Call me Tom,' Lester encouraged.

'Of course. Tom it is.' He paused for a beat, then asked again, 'So have you come for a holiday, Tom, or is there something you want to talk about more specifically?'

'A bit of both really. I've heard how beautiful it is here from lots of people. Also, I just wanted to touch base with you, make sure all is well with our shipments and merchandise.' Lester took another deep drag from the cigar, then stubbed the remainder of the brown stick out in the ashtray on the table between them. He surveyed the area. Once he was sure only the three of them could hear their conversation, he continued, 'Look, you're transporting a lot of merchandise, and I'm putting a lot of faith in the men I have enlisted to receive your deliveries. I need to be sure this operation is watertight.'

Lester lit another cigar up and offered his companion another one. Željko declined. He was still smoking the cigar he'd been given earlier.

'Tom, there is no need to concern yourself. Everything is in hand. My suppliers are ready to go. Once I give the word, they will deliver the merchandise to my depot here in Sarajevo. My men will then travel overland using a secure route to my compound on the coast of Croatia, and then the cargo will continue by boat to your designated dock at Marseille. Of course, there will be several stops along the way.'

The Englishman took a deep drag from the cigar and, before the smoke cleared his face, asked, 'And where are those stops, Željko?'

The Croat picked up his glass. 'They're in ports that need not concern you, Tom.'

Lester lent forward. There was an urgency in his voice, but he tried to keep it low. 'Millions of pounds' worth of drugs waiting to be seized in various foreign ports wasn't in the prospectus. I don't like the risk.' When he didn't get an immediate response, he looked up at Petar, but if the young man knew anything, his expression gave nothing away. 'If we're going to be in business together, Željko, we must trust each other. And I have to say, it appears you don't trust me.' A bead of sweat fell down the side of the Englishman's right temple. He looked up at Petar again, but still, there was no reaction.

The Croat inched to the front of his seat, 'Tom, everyone who has done business with me has been thoroughly satisfied with my work. It's late, but if you want to pull out now, I can always find another partner to supply His Majesty's England with this much needed cargo.'

AN INVITATION FOR REVENGE

The Englishman bristled. 'I didn't say that I wanted out, Željko.'

Lester had sunk too much money and put too much effort into making this deal a reality, to pull out of it now. He had paid off various transit groups. He'd made promises that couldn't be broken. If he backed out of these deals, Interpol would be the least of his worries.

'Look, Tom, all you need to worry about is that when the cargo arrives in Marseille the boat will be safe to dock. Can you be sure this will happen?'

Lester held the cigar between his teeth. This part of the deal had been entrusted to his French contacts. He'd had dealings with these people before and was certain they were trustworthy. The same organisation had helped him traffic North Africans through Marseille and into Britain. Removing the cigar from his mouth, he told Željko, 'The dock at Marseille is secure. I have a facility for storage before ongoing transit. You don't have to worry about that.'

'Good. Then we are both on the same page, as you English say.' The Croat took a drink of the Cognac in front of him before continuing. 'The only question now is payment.'

'And how do you suggest we complete the transaction?'

'I will give you an offshore account number. It is safe for all purposes. My men will arrive in Marseille with the merchandise. They will protect the cargo until I receive notification payment has been made. They will then, and only then, hand over possession to your representatives. They'll leave the port and return for the next consignment.' He waited a beat. 'Does this meet with your approval?'

Lester took a drag from the cigar and then sunk the last of his Cognac, mulling over the Croats words.

'I think this calls for Champagne!' Lester said, smiling. He looked at Petar, 'Could you get us the best Champagne from the bar, please and put it on my tab?'

Petar smiled and said, 'Of course. Would you like me to get you some cigars? Your packet seems to be empty.'

'Yes, that would be good. Thank you.'

CHAPTER 29

The evening had a chill in the air. Luckily for Nesby he was sat kerbside in a hired BMW SUV with the heater on to take the coolness out of the air. Spots of rain fell intermittently onto the windscreen. The vehicle's previous user had left the radio set on some benign golden oldies station. He'd had to retune it, otherwise he'd have fallen asleep on the job. The talk show host on LBC was now keeping him from *dropping off*, droning on about the state of relations between the UK and the USA since the ill-fated, in his words, 'Brexit vote of 2016'. Nesby couldn't give a damn about such trivial matters, but the inane chatter stopped him from losing consciousness.

The street had been darkening gradually over the two hours he'd been parked up. From his vantage point, he could see Petra Antonucci's third floor apartment in the corner block. It was an old red-brick building, obviously re-purposed to house apartments in the small town centre.

On this side of the building, he could see Antonucci's lounge and kitchen windows. The kitchen light had been dimmed in the last half hour, but there was still light coming from the lounge window. He'd wait until that light had been extinguished too before making his move.

He popped a piece of chewing gum in his mouth and pondered his next move. Once he'd fulfilled his boss's instruction – taken Ferguson out – he'd ring his contact at the airline and get a ticket for the next flight out to Dubrovnik. Flights were normally full to holiday destinations, but he was certain the airline operative would get him a seat, even if it meant bumping someone else onto a later flight.

It wasn't in the prospectus to kill Antonucci, but he had a job to do, and she may end up being collateral damage. He recalled Lloyd making a judgement call at the old folks' home and it didn't work out for him. Lester had brutally murdered his partner in front of Nesby because he'd made the wrong decision. He wasn't going to make the same mistake.

There was a difference between the call Lloyd had made at the old folk's home and the one that Nesby found himself having to make now. Killing all those people had made life very difficult for his boss. This murder, on the other hand, could never be attributed to Lester. No one knew of his boss's attachment to Ferguson, and there was no link with Antonucci.

Nesby couldn't see a way to avoid killing them both. If he killed Ferguson on his way home the police may focus on his connection to the ongoing investigation into the murders at the Home. If he murdered both Ferguson and the reporter, the cops may conclude it was a jealous ex-lover of the reporter. Or more amusingly, the coppers wife who had caught them *in flagrante*.

He checked his watch. It was just before 9pm. Ferguson would have to be getting back home soon. If he didn't get his mistress bedded fast, he'd never get back in time to tuck the children in.

The lounge light was extinguished. Good, he could start to make his move.

Nesby leaned over and opened the glove compartment. He picked a handgun out and a small box of ammunition. Reaching further into the recess, he found the tubular accessory he might need. Checking the gun was fully armed, he put it in the waistband of his trousers. He then emptied a few extra rounds into his jacket pocket – for insurance.

Checking the mirrors for passing people or vehicles, he decided it was safe to get out and cross the road without being seen. He threw the chewing gum on the path and trotted across the road to the side of the Antonucci's building.

Luckily, the big car park iron gate had been left open. Walking with his back to the wall in the shadow he made it to the doorway without coming across anyone. Nesby hoped there wasn't any surveillance equipment to speak of. If there were cameras, then the police would have a very sharp picture of him.

He slipped on some thin latex gloves to prevent stray fingerprints. Nesby then tried the large wooden outer door. It was locked.

One of the advantages of working for a man like Tom Lester was his contacts. His boss knew people that could help in any situation, legally or illegally. At Lester's suggestion, Nesby had telephoned Rob Ginty who was the best locksmith around. He ran a small shop, Locksmiths, on the high street that served as cover for his more lucrative work – helping the underworld achieve its goals. Ginty was able to bypass any entry point, be it a conventional lock or a more complex computerised system. Nesby had given the locksmith Antonucci's address and asked him to furnish him with keys for the entrance and apartment. Ginty had obtained copies of the keys with ease, and at a reasonable cost.

Reaching into his inside jacket pocket, he found what he needed, a ring with three keys. He selected one and tried it in the lock. It opened the heavy door. He slid inside quickly, holding the door all the time, easing it closed so it didn't bang shut.

Ginty had told him there was an inner door that had been locked when he himself had reconnoitred the building earlier. He'd supplied a key for that too. Luckily this, the fire door, was held open by a magnetic arm fixed to the wall, which would presumably release if the fire alarm sounded.

Nesby waited for any reaction from inside before moving further into the building. The hallway was quiet, eerie.

Once past the inner door, there were two elevators facing him. To their right lay the emergency staircase. To the left a utility room.

When he was sure no one else was around, he moved to the stair's entrance, pushed it open and entered the spartan staircase. The stairwell was quiet and cold, with scuffed whitewashed walls.

He took the stairs one at a time, leaning back against the wall, always making sure he had a clear sight of the exits leading on to the staircase.

A bold number 3 was written above the door on the third floor. A small square window gave him a view of the hallway. Three apartment doors led off this corridor. 3C was the apartment Antonucci rented.

He hesitated before going through the door and onto the third-floor landing. A man stood in front of the elevator doors, waiting. Dressed in a suit and clutching an umbrella, he appeared to be dressed to impress.

Nesby didn't have long to wait. After a few seconds the elevator door swished open, and the man got in. The door closed almost immediately. Nesby entered the hallway and checked the elevator information panel. It delivered its occupant to the ground floor quickly.

It was now safe for him to go into the journalist's apartment.

He stood at the apartment marked 3C, put his ear to it, and listened. It was quiet, but for some muffled music. Slipping the apartment key out of his pocket, he turned it in the lock and darted inside as quietly as he could, while closing the door gently behind him.

Standing with his back to the exit, so that he could see the hall in front of him, he grabbed his handgun from his holster and screwed the barrelled silencer to the end.

Antonucci had cooked fish, Nesby could almost taste it from the smell that filled the apartment.

Nesby knew from Ginty's visit that the bathroom was the first exit on the left, next to that was the bedroom. The bathroom was ensuite. On the right-hand side of the hall were the doors for the lounge and kitchen.

Creeping along the corridor, Nesby could now hear some movement coming from the bedroom. The music was still suppressed by the bedroom door which was slightly ajar.

Suddenly, he heard footsteps coming towards the hallway. He darted back and stood inside the bathroom where he had a clear view of the hallway.

The journalist came out of the room and headed towards the kitchen, wearing nothing but her black underwear.

'I'll get a fresh bottle of wine and then we can talk about the weekend,' she called out over her shoulder.

Nesby tip-toed out of the bathroom, across the hallway and into the kitchen behind Antonucci. Before she was aware he was hovering over her, he had grabbed her from behind and covered her mouth so she couldn't scream. The latex of his gloves was in her mouth.

The journalist scrambled frantically to look over her shoulder but couldn't get a clear view of her assailant. She did, however, catch sight of a tattooed web which poked out of the glove on her assailant's hand. Kicking out behind her, she inflicted a painful blow on Nesby's shin. He doubled down on his grip and brought her under control. Her breathing was heavy against his hand, her chest rising and falling deeply.

Placing the handgun in front of the girl's face, he leaned into her ear and said, 'You need to calm down, missy.'

Antonucci's eyes widened in terror, and she stood deathly still as instructed. 'I'm not here for you. It's your boyfriend I want to speak to.' He forced her to turn back, towards the direction she had come, then said, 'Now, we're going to walk calmly into your bedroom and I'm going to have a brief chat with Mr Ferguson. While I'm doing that, I want you to stay in the bathroom and I must stress, you're not to come out.' He paused for a second, then asked, 'Do you understand?'

Petra nodded as best she could while in the vice-like grip of her assailant.

'Good. Now you lead the way.'

She led him out of the kitchen and through to the bedroom door. He stopped her before she went any further.

'Don't get any heroic ideas about this, please. I wouldn't want either of you to get hurt needlessly.' Lying came easily to Nesby. 'Now just walk in slowly. I'll do the talking. Do we understand each other?'

Petra nodded through the grip he held her in.

'Now go.'

She led him into the bedroom. Over her shoulder, Nesby saw Ferguson lying with white briefs on, reading from his cell phone.

The policeman casually glanced up, saw Petra and Nesby, and suddenly leaped up from his position.

Nesby revealed the gun from behind the girl's back and pointed it at the policeman.

'Nesby what are you doing here?' Ferguson demanded. 'Petra come to me.' He beckoned the girl over to him.

Nesby let her go. She immediately stepped over and put her arms around Ferguson. She began to cry.

The gunman grinned, weapon pointing towards the lovers. 'Nice little party you've got going on here, Ferguson. Is it just for two, or is your wife expected to join in the fun?'

'Don't be a pillock, Nesby! What're you doing here?'

'Put some clothes on, will you? You're making me sick.' He turned his gaze to the girl and pointed the gun towards the bathroom door. 'I'd like you to go into the bathroom, please. This little chat is of a private nature.'

Petra looked up at Ferguson, tears falling. He said, 'Go on. I'll just speak with Nesby here for a few minutes and then we'll get sorted.'

She reluctantly stepped through the bathroom door, not taking her eyes off the gunman.

'That's it,' Nesby said. 'Now shut the door behind you.'

Petra did as she was told.

Ferguson picked his trousers up from the chair in the corner and put them on. He grabbed his shirt and fastened the buttons quickly.

'So what's so urgent you have to come barging in here, Nesby?' he asked angrily.

'We'll get to that,' Nesby said. 'Let's go into the lounge.'

Nesby beckoned Ferguson through towards the lounge. He followed at a safe distance, keeping the gun pointed at the policeman's back. Once they were in the room, Nesby told Ferguson to sit down. The policeman did as he was instructed.

Looking up, Ferguson asked, 'So what's all this about? I told you I was finished for a while. I thought I'd made myself clear?' There was no fear in Ferguson's voice, just an air of superiority that he'd practised over many years in the police force. 'And what's with all this wild west shit, anyway? Carrying guns can scare young woman.'

Nesby leaned on the wall next to the door and looked over at Ferguson. The policeman had no idea why he was here. He still thought he could resign from Tom Lester's organisation as if it was the local golf club.

'I've come to talk about your future employment.'

'What?' Ferguson asked.

Nesby scratched his chin. He needed a shave. The stubble was beginning to annoy him.

'I've had a little chat with Tom about what you said the last time we met.'

Ferguson sat forward. 'And…?'

'Well as you can imagine, the boss wasn't too pleased.'

'I can't help that,' Ferguson said, beginning to get up. 'It's getting too dangerous for me down at the station.'

'I didn't tell you to get up! Sit down.' Ferguson did as he was told. 'To be honest, all that's irrelevant. You work for Mr Lester and shouldn't forget that.'

'But Nesby! I can't. They're going to find out who's behind the leaks and when they do, I'm finished anyway. I won't be of any use to Tom in jail, will I?

'That's very true. But you're no use to us if you're not helping. It's a bit of a Catch22 isn't it? What would you suggest we do?'

'Leave it awhile. When the heat's off, I'll get back in touch. And where I can help, I will. How does that sound?'

Nesby gave it some thought, then replied, 'Sounds a bit wishy-washy to me. You'll have to give me more. Something I can take back to Mr Lester. Something that will make him happy. It's his birthday soon. I'm sure he could do with some good news.'

Ferguson shuffled in his seat. He didn't know what more he could say. He needed to get out of this dangerous situation, and fast. Planting his feet down, he tried to get into a position where he could rise quickly and make a run for Nesby. He had to make some sort of move.

'Look, just tell Tom everything's going to be fine,' he said, attempting to buy some time. 'I'll be back in the fold before he notices I've not been around.'

Shuffling his feet, Nesby asked, 'Do you think Tom will be happy with that?'

'I'm sure he will,' Ferguson confirmed looking carefully at Nesby. Checking to see if there was a chink of light in a situation that could see him live or die.

Nesby started to walk towards Ferguson and had lowered the gun slightly. The policeman noticed. As soon as the gunman was within striking distance, Ferguson jumped up quickly and rushed the oncoming Nesby. He grabbed Nesby's gun hand with his left and pushed his face back with his right. Nesby began to fall back, pulling the policeman with him.

They fell through the wooden coffee table with a thud, Ferguson above the gunman. A shot of pain pierced through Nesby's side. The painkillers he had been taking were wearing off and this crash to the floor inflamed the injury.

The policeman spat in Nesby's face. The spittle stung his eyes but didn't deter him. Nesby struggled to get back in control of the situation. He pushed at Ferguson for all his worth. The aching was beginning to burn.

Fury contorted Ferguson's face. He was determined to be alive at the end of this tussle. Every muscle in his neck was stiffened with the energy powering through his body.

Their grappling was ferocious, neither was willing to give an inch. To the death!

Nesby managed to move his right hand a little and the gun's silencer wedged between their two bodies. He was getting the better of the policeman even though his body was in agony from the fall backwards.

Ferguson watched the gun arching slowly towards him. He couldn't let the gun complete its rotation. If it did, he would be a dead man. Suddenly releasing his right hand, he punched Nesby in the face. Nesby's head banged against the floor. The gun moved away from Ferguson slightly. He had some breathing space.

A scream from Petra suddenly rang out from the doorway.

Ferguson looked up. She was now wearing the silk dressing gown that he had bought her last Christmas.

Nesby, saw his chance. On instinct, he forced the gun into Ferguson's stomach and squeezed the trigger. The silencer suppressed the explosion from the weapon.

The policeman instantly stiffened, his back arching away from his assailant, face twisted in agony.

'Marc!' shouted Antonucci, running towards them.

Nesby threw the policeman off him and rose quickly.

Ferguson lay on the floor, hands clutching at his stomach. Blood seeped out between his fingers. His mouth was wide open, ready to scream for help, but there was no sound and no help coming, except from Petra who knelt beside him, cradling his head.

'What have you done?' she screamed at Nesby, who was looking down at them both.

He raised the gun towards the young journalist.

Looking up at him, tears ran down her face. Not only was her lover dying in her arms, but she was going to die also.

Holding the gun still, Nesby pointed it directly at Antonucci's head...

And blinked.

The pain from the side of his body had now come back with a vengeance. Clutching his side, he realised he wasn't over the crash after all and that it was only the painkillers that had been keeping the pain at bay. He lowered the gun and sunk to the settee clutching his side.

Petra wiped away the tears. With every inward breath her stomach convulsed. She wanted to be sick. Not thirty minutes before she had been making love without a care in the world. Now, her lover lay in her arms, dying.

Stumbling over the words, she asked, 'Are you going to shoot me too?'

Nesby was pushing hard on his side, as if that would alleviate the pain. It didn't. Nick Mason would pay when he caught up with him.

'I should do.'

'But why?' she asked. 'Why did you do this?'

'It's my job,' he said simply.

She looked down at Ferguson and realised he had died in her arms. Tears streamed down her face as she lowered his head to the floor. She started to rise.

'Where are you going?' he asked raising the gun towards her again.

'To the chair.' She pointed towards the armchair facing him.

'Go on then. And don't make any sudden movements.'

'I'm not going to try anything,' she assured.

She sat on the chair and attempted to appear relaxed. She was anything but. Her stomach churned. Her head was full of questions. Her heart was breaking after seeing Marc killed.

'Can I ask you something?' he asked.

'You have the gun. You can ask me anything you want.'

He lent forward.

'Why did you bother with this scumbag? I mean, a bent cop. What could you possibly see in him?'

'He is a policeman. He's no scumbag,' she said.

'Correction. I'd say he's an *ex-policeman* now. Wouldn't you?'

The tears had begun to fall again. Petra was finding it hard to come to terms with what had just happened, and what was likely to happen.

'You've killed an innocent man, a policeman, how do you think you're going to get away with his murder? I've seen you. There'll be traces of you, fingerprints...' He held his gloved hands up. 'Okay. Not fingerprints, but still, something will give you away.'

'You've been watching too many cop shows. The cops around her are numb. They will never be able to pin this on me.'

'How do you know that?'

'It's not for you to worry about. I will make sure of it.'

She didn't know why, but she had to keep him talking. Maybe she could find a way out of this hell.

'So how are you going to dispose of Marc's body? It won't be easy.'

'I'm not going to.'

'What? You can't leave him here.'

'Just get me some water. And don't try anything silly, I can see you from where I am.'

Petra went to the kitchen and returned with a glass of water. Returning to the chair, she asked, 'So what's next?'

He downed two painkillers with a gulp of water and thought for a moment before answering.

'Well, I think it's your lucky day. I'm going to leave here without harming you.'

'How can you be sure I won't ring the police as soon as you go? I mean, they'd catch you in no time.'

'I'll be taking all your communication devices for a start. And for your own safety, I wouldn't contact the police too soon.'

'Why?' she asked.

'Because I can always come back and finish the job.'

'But how do I explain Marc's death to the police?'

'I don't know. I haven't thought of that.' He winced with the pain from his side. 'You could tell them that he caught a burglar in the night while you were asleep. When you woke up, you found him dead on the floor.'

'And you get away with it Scot-free?'

'Essentially, yes.'

Nesby rose from his chair and began to look around the apartment. Once he had collected Ferguson's and Antonucci's cell phones, computers and tablets he left. Dumping the bag into the boot of his car, he drove off punching a number into his own onscreen display.

'The ticket I asked you to get me for Dubrovnik.'

'Yes,' answered the airline operative on the other end of the line.

'I want them for your earliest flight tomorrow.'

'Okay. Be at the airport at 6am. I'll get you on the first flight out.'

Nesby killed the line and headed back to the hotel.

CHAPTER 30

Luka's spare bedroom contained a double bed, a wooden wardrobe, a low chest of drawers, a vanity desk and a matching chair. There were no ornaments, pictures or signs giving the previous incumbent's identity away. A single shaft of light from the window speared through the darkened room.

Mason woke on his back, looking up at the off-white ceiling. Sadie lay beside him with her leg and arm across him. Her breathing was even, noiseless. He needed to move but was reluctant, fearing he'd disturb Sadie. He wondered if her life would ever go back to a *normality* that she would recognise.

Deciding he'd have to take a chance on not disturbing her, he gently moved her arm off his chest and slid out from under the cover. Sitting up straight, Mason glanced at Sadie and assured himself that he hadn't woken her up, before standing and putting on his trousers and t-shirt. The wooden flooring was cold and fresh on his feet. He padded through into the hallway as quietly as he could.

There was no one in the kitchen. A warm, glass coffee pot sat on the heated stand on the counter. Cups stood in a row, soldier-like, alongside it. Mason picked a cup and poured a black coffee for himself. Stirring two sugars in, he sat down at the wooden dining table in the centre of the room. This was the point of no return. Mason had followed Lester to Croatia knowing that one of them would die.

He took a drink from the cup. The coffee was strong enough to wake the dead! You don't get coffee like this at home, he mused.

Luka came into the kitchen and broke the silence. 'Morning, my friend. How did you sleep?' he asked, throwing his dirty captain's cap on the table.

'Like a top.'

Luka looked confused.

'Like a… top? Sorry, I don't know this.'

'It means I slept well.'

'That's good. I was afraid that the memory of my mother-in-law would unsettle you. She spent many years in that room, and unfortunately ended her days there.'

'I'm sorry to hear that.'

Luka waved Mason's words away. He poured himself a coffee and sat opposite his guest. He offered Mason a cigarette, who accepted gratefully. Luka lit both cigarettes.

'What are your plans today, Nick?'

'I'm not certain yet. I will need to speak to Željko. He might be able to help.' Mason took a deep drag from the cigarette. 'At least I hope he can.'

Mason's cell, which was on the table between them, sparked into life. He recognised the number immediately. JP calling from England. He swiped the screen.

'Yes?'

'It's JP, Nick,' the mechanic started.

'What can I do for you?'

Mason could hear Shakin' Stevens playing in the background. His friend must have the Welshman's music on a loop as Mason had never heard any other music on the sound system in the garage.

'Nick, Tom Lester is headed to a place called Sarajevo.' He pronounced the j as you would for Jeeves and not as the traditional Serbo-Croat 'y'. 'I've no idea where that is, but I've heard he's doing some deal out there.'

'I know where it is, JP.' He emptied his cup and beckoned to Luka for a fresh drink. His host took the hint and poured Mason another. 'Have you any other information?'

'No. I thought that would be enough, Nick. Look, why don't you come home and lay low for a while.' JP suggested. 'I'm sure Lester will forget about you in time.'

'I can't do that, JP. We've got to a point where it's him or me, I'm afraid.'

'You're mad!'

'That may be the case, but I can't let this one go.' He took a pull on the cigarette. 'Look, when it's all over we'll have a drink over at your place.'

'Good idea. I'll dust off my coveted Japanese release of Shaky's Greatest Hits on vinyl for you to listen to.'

'Can't wait,' said Mason before killing the line.

'You look like you need a stronger drink than coffee, my friend.' Luka opened a bottle of brandy that stood in the middle of the table and poured a generous glug into Mason's coffee. 'That will pick you up, I'm sure.'

Mason took a drink and said, 'A bit early in the day, but that's good. Thanks.' He stubbed his cigarette out in the ashtray between them.

'What's bothering you, Nick?'

'It's Lester. He's in Sarajevo meeting someone. Do you know if it's Željko?'

Luka poured himself some brandy, too, but in a small shot glass.

'I've heard about the visit of some drug lord from England. He's a stranger, and tongues have started to chatter.'

'We know who he is though, don't we? It's Tom Lester and he's meeting Željko, for sure. If he's in Sarajevo that, at least, gives me some time.'

'Yes, but I have some more disturbing news for you, Nick.'

Mason stiffened, 'What else is there?'

Luka sipped his brandy.

'Lester meeting Željko is only part of the story.'

'What do you mean *part*?' Mason asked.

'Nick, there is talk in the town that this English drug lord isn't just here to meet Željko. He's here to meet Slaven Bogdanović too.'

'Who's Slaven Bogdanović? I've never heard of him.'

Luka stood up and refilled his coffee cup. He stood back and leaned on the kitchen counter. Before answering he inhaled deeply on his cigarette.

'Slaven Bogdanović is a man you don't want to meet. On the surface he is Željko's friend. They meet up every month at the Hotel Europe for dinner. But no one is fooled by this, what would you say, *cordiality*? They are competitors in the drugs market and businesses throughout the country.' Luka extinguished one cigarette and lit another up straight away. 'The question is, does Željko know Lester is due to meet Bogdanović too?'

Mason sat up straight. 'Shit! I thought my problem was Željko, but it could have been this Bogdanović all along. At least I know Željko.'

Luka pulled a chair out and sat at the table again.

'You may know Željko, Nick, but don't pretend he's your friend. He can be ruthless if crossed. Be careful.'

Sadie walked into the kitchen, 'Be careful about what?' she asked curiously. She was wearing jeans and a white t-shirt which was tucked in haphazardly. Her hair was dishevelled and uncombed. Her skin was pale from the night's sleep.

'Nothing really,' Mason answered evasively.

'Come on!' she ordered. 'We're in this together remember. 'If there's something I need to know, tell me.'

Both men looked at each other. They sucked on their cigarettes in unison.

Then Luka said, 'Your call my friend.' He stood up and poured a coffee for Sadie. 'Cream? Sugar?'

'No, I'm fine.' Sadie took the cup and sat at the head of the dining table. 'Well?'

Mason thought for a moment before answering.

'Okay. Lester is close by. He's in a town called Sarajevo, just over the border, in Bosnia. Željko is with him.'

'How far is it? Are we going?' she asked.

'No.' He took a drink and wished there was more brandy in his coffee. 'We're gonna sit tight and wait for him to come here.'

'Is that a good move?'

'It's the best chance we've got. I don't know Sarajevo like I do

Dubrovnik.'

Sadie sensed his evasion and asked him directly, 'There's something you're not telling me, Nick. You need to tell me everything.'

He looked over at Luka, who was leaning against the kitchen worktop in front of the window.

His friend shrugged.

'There's an added problem,' he started.

'And that is what exactly?' she cut in.

'There's another guy who we think might be involved with Lester... A competitor of Željko.'

'So, what's he got to do with us?'

'Well, if we annoy him, Lester might be the least of our problems.'

'Great! When you hit the shit, Nick, you know how to keep digging, don't you?

'It would seem so,' he said, taking a drag from the cigarette.

He stubbed the cigarette out in the ashtray and picked up his cell. He punched in a number and waited for an answer. It came in seconds.

'Yes?'

'Gunner, it's Mason?'

'What can I do for you?'

'I'm in Dubrovnik and I need a piece of equipment. Do you have that name for me?'

'Yes. I called ahead, as promised. His name is Zlatko Vlasić. Solid guy. Just don't mess with him, Nick. His services will be expensive, but it'll be worth it.'

'Where can I find him?'

'He's in the main café in the port of Gruž.'

'That's great, Gunner. I owe you one!'

'Bye!'

Mason looked up at Luka and asked, 'Can you drop us off at the main café in Gruž? I need to meet with a guy called Zlatko.'

'I can, Nick. But I know this man. He's not someone you should associate yourself with.'

'I've no option, unfortunately. I need a gun and this guy can get me one.'

'Zlatko is dangerous, Nick. Associating with him can get you into an awful lot of trouble.'

'Don't worry. I'll be fine.' He looked over at Sadie, 'Right! Let's get cleaned up and go meet this guy.'

*

Within the hour, Luka had dropped them at the corner of the market in Gruž. 'Be careful, my friend,' he warned as the got out of the vehicle.

'I will. We'll get a cab back to the apartment,' he said.

'As you wish. But if you need me in the meantime, I'll be on the boat across the harbour. I must do some repairs.'

'Cheers. See you later,' he said, shutting the door.

Luka headed off into the daytime traffic, a heavy mixture of tourists and locals.

Mason looked down the row of shops and cafés on their right. It was clear which one they were heading towards. It had a large sign above the window that ran its whole length that said 'Le Jardin'. It was red and white, square-backed, reminiscent of the Croatian flag, with 'Le Jardin' written in bold black lettering.

To their left, over the busy road, several cruise liners were docked. Thousands of people would have disembarked from these ships earlier in the day, Mason thought, thankful he wasn't in the Old Town today.

'Come on, it's over there.'

'Nick, wait!'

'What is it?'

Sadie stood looking at him, her hair moving with the gentle coastal breeze. Her face had reddened. She said, hesitantly, 'Do you really want to do this? I mean, we could be out of the country in a matter of hours. Before Lester even arrives. He won't even know you've been here.'

'I can't do that, Sadie.'

'Why?'

'I've told you. I'm not running away. It's not my style.'

'It wouldn't be running away. It would be saving your life.'

'Sadie, no matter where I go the spectre of Tom Lester will be hanging over me. I can't let this go.'

Without warning, a black SUV pulled up at the kerb next to them. The occupant, a young man in charcoal trousers and a pristine white t-shirt, opened the passenger door forcing Sadie and Mason to step back momentarily. He walked past them without a glance and entered Zlatko's café.

Sadie lowered her head and asked, 'So what happens if you get killed? Where does that leave me, Nick?'

People, a mixture of locals and tourists wearing shorts or beach hats, walked past without giving them a second thought. The very notion that at any moment these two people could be dead in the next few minutes wouldn't have crossed any passer-by's mind.

Mason reached out and gently lifted Sadie's chin up. Her eyes glistened in the mid-morning sun.

'Sadie, I can't promise anything. This is just something I have to do. Lester is responsible for the death of my father. You, yourself were nearly killed. Next time it will be me. I can't allow him to have a clear shot at me, or you.'

She reached up and put her arms around his shoulders, hugging him tightly.

'I know. I'm sorry. It's… it's just nerves. When I came here, I knew I wasn't coming to sit on the beach. It was my choice.' She kissed him gently on the lips. 'Just don't get killed. That's an order.' She smiled weakly.

'I won't,' he promised. It was a promise he intended to keep.

'You know, I know it's not the time, but we could just get on that floating city there that masquerades as a cruise liner, and sail off into the wide blue yonder?'

Mason looked over towards the ships docked in the harbour and said flatly, 'Maybe another day.' He took her hand and led her towards Zlatko's café.

CHAPTER 31

Mason opened the door for Sadie to enter the café. She thanked him but didn't go further than the entrance mat until he'd passed through.

'Drink?' he asked.

'Yes. A strong one!'

Sadie sat at a window table and watched Mason go to the counter. As she waited, she drummed her fingers anxiously on the table.

Mason returned from the bar without the drinks.

'And?' Sadie asked.

'The barman will bring the drinks over.'

'Not that, you imbecile!' she whispered. 'What about Zanko, or whatever his name is?'

Mason smiled. 'It's Zlatko, not Zanko.'

'Okay, So I'm showing my ignorance. All things foreign are not my strong point. I'm English.'

'Speak for yourself. Some of us English are okay with foreign.' Mason said, grinning.

The barman brought the drinks over and placed the glasses on the table. Once he had left, Sadie asked again, 'Zlatko?'

Mason took a drink of the large brandy. 'The barman asked why I wanted Zlatko. He said he was a very busy man.' He waved his arm dismissively. 'All the usual hoodlum stuff you see in the movies.'

'So…?' she coaxed.

'So, I mentioned my good friend Gunner Tudge back in England and that he had arranged a meeting.'

Sadie took a sip of her brandy.

'Nice drink, if a little large.'

'That's one of the things I like about living here. They're very liberal when they pour you the local stuff. You'd never get this amount in rainy England, not for this price.'

'Look, are we gonna meet up with this Zlatko, or are we just gonna have a nice little drink in his café?' she pressed.

'To be honest, I don't know. The barman just said he'd see what he could do.' He took a drink and said, 'Nice guy. He's from Paris. His name is Jules, as in Jules Verne, the writer.'

'I know who Jules Verne is. I'm not that much of a stupid Brit!'

'Keep your hair on,' Mason said, smiling. 'Came over here to work a few years ago. Never going home. Loves it out here.'

'It doesn't get us anywhere, you fraternising with the Europeans, does it?'

He took another sip from the brandy and said, 'You'd be amazed how much a little listening and flattery will get you. You should try it occasionally.'

'It hasn't got us anywhere yet, has it?'

'*Au contraire*, my dear Sadie. While we were talking, I noticed Jules tap away at a button just below his counter. I wouldn't be surprised if we were being watched at this very moment.'

'Watching us have a drink isn't getting us an interview, is it?'

'While they're watching us, I'm sure a quick call to Tudge will be made. Make sure we're not cops and that we match the description Tudge gives them.'

'You seem to know a lot about all this cloak and dagger stuff...'

'I do,' he confirmed, sinking the remainder of his drink. 'Wait there for a minute.'

'Why?'

'I need to have a little word with this nice young Frenchman. Get a few things straight.'

Mason got up and headed for the bar before Sadie could respond.

'Jules,' he said as he put his empty glass on the high counter between them, 'I'm getting a little irritated at all the time that this is taking. Either Zlatko will see us now, or he can foot the bill for this cheap brandy you're serving, and we'll be on our way.'

Jules momentarily glanced up at a camera high up behind Mason's head.

'I can get you another drink, certainly, while you wait.' Reflecting his nerves, the barman's English suddenly became more accented with a Parisian inflection. 'Please, sit down and I will bring you another drink.'

Before Mason turned away, he noticed the previously affable Jules repeatedly pushing a button under the counter.

'So, what's he said?' Sadie asked before Mason had the chance to sit back down.

'The drinks are on the house, and I suspect we'll be seeing Mr Vlasić very soon.'

'Good,' Sadie said, sinking her drink. She surveyed the empty café. 'Despite the smell of recently baked bread, which I love I'm starting to feel a little creeped out in here. It's almost lunch time. Why is it so dead?'

'No idea. It's in a perfect location, as far as I can tell. Prices are reasonable. It may be that Zlatko has a reputation.'

Jules, the barman, arrived with the fresh drinks. He put them down on the table and placed the used glasses on his tray.

'I have just received word that Zlatko has arrived back from an important meeting and will see you shortly. And, of course, the drinks are free while you wait.'

Before Jules turned away, Mason thanked him.

Sadie watched the barman retreat a fair distance before she spoke. 'Well, whatever you said worked. He's come back from 'wherever' to see you.'

'Don't be silly, Sadie. He's been here all along.'

'But he said he's just got back from a meeting.'

'Don't believe everything you hear from these people. Zlatko is making us sweat while he makes the call to Tudge, that's all. Classic hoodlum tactic: Be in control and keep the other man on the back foot. Simple.'

Sadie took a heavy gulp of brandy.

'This world is very weird to the normal person.'

'Yep!' he agreed.

Sadie refused a third refill, preferring an espresso.

Mason had only had a sip from the third brandy, when a young man approached. It was the same man from the sidewalk earlier. He came from the door adjacent to the bar. His jet-black hair was closely cropped, cut short on the top while being perfectly shaped with gel. He was thin and tall, towering over Mason who was still seated. The young man said, 'Mr Vlasić will see you now.'

'It's about time. My patience is running a little thin, even with the free drinks.' He started to get up, 'Come on Sadie.'

Before Sadie could move, the young man ordered, 'No! Just you.'

"Fraid not, sunny Jim! She stays with me.'

A slight crease appeared at the side of the young man's eyes as he began to worry out loud. 'But Mr Vlasić is a very private man. He sees very few people during business hours.'

'I have a feeling he won't mind. Just show us the way. What's your name?'

'My name?' Mason nodded. 'Neven.'

'Don't worry, Neven. You won't get into any trouble. I'll explain everything to Zlatko; if he should ask.'

'Then come this way.'

Neven led them through a door behind the counter and up a tight staircase. At the top, there was a heavy-looking door with a keypad at the side. He suddenly twirled around and asked them to turn towards the wall behind them and put their arms up.

Sadie hesitated.

Mason said, 'It's okay. This jackass hasn't worked out we've only come here to *get* a weapon, not bring one.' He had noticed a gun popping up over Neven's waistband as they had followed him upstairs. If the young Croat wanted to search them, he was free to do so. Mason wasn't going to argue.

Neven began patting Mason down from his shoulders downwards. Once he was satisfied he wasn't armed, he said, 'Okay. You can put your arms down.'

He began to do the same to Sadie. She felt he lingered a little too long in places that made her feel uncomfortable. It was a blessed relief when he said, 'Right, you too! Hands down.'

Their escort returned his attention to the door pad and punched a number in quickly. Mason thought he saw the numbers 1-9-6-3. If that was the case, he couldn't help but think that was the year of Zlatko's birth, or someone else's in his family. Code numbers tended to be easy to work out. You didn't need to be a computer genius to gather vital information about people.

They stepped through the door. It closed heavily behind them. Mason noted that it was thick enough to be bomb-proof. From there, Neven led them down a narrow, soulless corridor. There were no signs and on the two doors they passed, one on either side, there was no clue as to what those rooms were being used for. At the far end of the corridor, a door had been left ajar. Neven knocked on it.

The three of them stood waiting for an answer. After what seemed like an eternity to Sadie, she heard, 'Come,' in a heavy, deep accent. Neven pushed the door open and led them through.

The room was sparse. A few steps in stood a high pine table, the height of a lectern. A few yards beyond that, facing them, sat Zlatko Vlasić behind a low coffee table.

The room could be anywhere in the world. There were no signs or pictures on the bland-coloured walls to give its location away. The parquet floor was cold, clean, sterile and lifeless.

Neven stood next to his boss arms folded. Mason noticed for the first time that Neven had a gold necklace around his neck, so tight there was hardly any breathing space. Dangling from the neckless was a gold cross with Jesus nailed to it. Religion even gives hoodlums solace, Mason thought. Something it had never done for him.

A second door at Zlatko's end of the room opened and a young blonde woman entered. She wore heavy black trainers, black trousers, and a white t-shirt. The go-to uniform in these parts, Mason mused. A bullet belt crossed down from her right shoulder, between her chest, and settled around her hip area. A holster with a gun weighted the belt down into place. She walked over toward her boss, whispered into his ear and then stood, arms crossed, just like Neven.

Zlatko introduced his young employees, 'You've met Neven. This is Elana. Now, how can we help?'

'We've been sent here by a mutual friend, Gunner Tudge.'

Zlatko held a hand up, 'I doubt we have any mutual friends, Mr Mason. Business partners, maybe.' He waited for a moment, and then said, 'Please continue.'

Mason felt like leaning on the high table in front of him but didn't.

'I believe Gunner Tudge has been in contact with you suggesting a weapon I could purchase.'

'He has,' confirmed Zlatko.

Mason thought there was something theatrical about Zlatko. He was in control of every movement, his words deliberate, and thoughtful. He wore navy trousers with a crisp light blue shirt. A thin navy tie hung from the open collar. His mane of hair was swept back away from his thin face.

'Can you supply a weapon?' The Englishman asked.

'May I ask what you would want such a weapon for, Mr Mason? Croatia is a law-abiding nation. This isn't the Wild West, or England, you know? People don't go around with guns in their pockets.'

Mason looked at the three people in front of him. The young girl, Elana, had a weapon to hand. He had seen Neven's gun when they came up the stairs. Zlatko himself could easily have one hidden in his waistband, out of Mason's sight.

'Forgive me, Zlatko, but your young friend there has enough bullets across her chest to start a small war. This place doesn't appear that safe from where I'm standing.'

Zlatko glanced at the girl beside him, 'Forgive Elana. She feels the need to, how shall I put it, yes, she prefers to make a *bold statement* around visitors.'

'Well, I don't know if she speaks English, but tell her from me, she doesn't intimidate me.'

'I don't need to. She speaks perfect English.'

'I do,' confirmed the girl as she moved towards Mason. She was light on her feet, cat-like. Mason turned towards her as she came around the high table. She stood directly in front of him and casually looked him up and down. As her eyes lifted to his face, she effortlessly raised the gun from its holster and placed it gently under his chin.

Mason refused to flinch.

Sadie took a step back and quietly cried, 'Shit!'

The girl's eyes didn't move from Mason's. They were steady, piercing his thoughts. 'You're thinking *how can I get out of this*, aren't you Englishman? *How can I take control of this situation? She's small. I can take her any time I want.* But don't you worry your narrow-minded little British brain. You move one tiny muscle out of place in Zlatko's presence and I will personally end your insignificant little life.'

She looked over Mason's shoulder without moving the gun from its deadly position and said to Sadie, 'I will begin with his balls. You will have no use for him after that.'

Sadie's breathing was deep with fear. Her voice caught and no sound could come out of her mouth.

'Zlatko,' Mason said without turning his head towards the Croat, 'Do you want to call this Shih tzu off? She's giving me a headache with all her yapping.'

The corner of Elana's mouth suddenly twitched.

'I don't like foreigners coming here,' Elana whispered in Mason's ear. 'And nothing would give me greater pleasure than ending your life, right here, right now.'

'Elana, come here,' Zlatko ordered quietly. 'Your theatrics are not scaring him. Maybe another time.'

She pushed the gun a little harder into Mason's chin and then abruptly took it away and re-holstered it. She returned to her boss's side.

'Good,' said Zlatko. 'Maybe we can move on.'

Sadie placed her shaking hand in Mason's for reassurance. He looked down at her and said, 'Don't worry, it's okay.'

'Now, my time is precious so let's get down to business,' Zlatko said. 'I have a weapon here for you. It will be in the alley at the side of the building. Just behind the blue bin there are two loose bricks. Take it. Replace the bricks.' He leaned forward and took a sip from his cup. 'But before that, I need you to go back to your seats in the café. Jules will serve you some more drinks. When we are ready, he will bring you your check. This is in effect the price for the gun. I will pay for your drinks. A friendly gesture on my part. Go to the bar. Jules will give you an envelope. Put the money inside and return to your table. Once that has been checked, he will indicate for you to leave and go for the weapon. After this, I do not want to see or hear from you again, Mr Mason. Is that clear?'

'I think I've got that straight,' Mason said.

'And if we do meet again, Mr Mason,' Elana said tapping her holster, 'I will be more than happy to rid this country of your presence.'

'Thank you. I'll keep that in mind,' Mason said as he took Sadie's arm.

'Neven will take you back to the café. Goodbye, Mr Mason.'

CHAPTER 32

When Mason and Sadie arrived at the restaurant later, Željko was sat in his usual place at the back where he could survey his kingdom. Apart from him, there was only a couple sitting at a window table. They were young, Mason thought as he and Sadie passed their table, probably on their first foreign holiday together. He was very red, as if he'd stood in the sun and not moved all day. There's no accounting for an Englishman in the midday sun, as the old song went.

Mason had secreted the Makarov pistol he'd acquired from Zlatko down the back of his trousers, under his linen jacket. It was a jacket he didn't need in the sweltering heat, but it was a must if he was to hide the weapon.

As the pair approached Željko, the Croat lifted his head and smiled, as if surprised at seeing an old friend.

'Nick, you're back,' he said stubbing out a cigarette in the full ashtray before him. 'It's good to see you.'

Željko rose from his position behind the table and shook Mason's hand. He tipped his head in a bow towards Sadie, who smiled in his direction. The restaurant owner then approached Petar at the bar and ordered, 'A bottle of Remy Martin and three glasses for me and my guests', Petar.'

Petar looked suspiciously at Mason as if to say he didn't trust the Englishman. He placed his handgun onto the counter between them.

'Petar! Petar! That is no way to greet our friends. Put that filthy thing away,' Željko told the young barman, who did as he was instructed. 'You must forgive Petar. He takes my protection very seriously.' With that, he smiled, picked the bottle and glasses up, and said, 'Come! Sit at my table. Petar! Food for my friends.'

Sadie and Mason followed him back to the table and sat with their host. Once they were settled down, Željko poured three generous measures of brandy and beckoned them to drink.

'This has all the hallmarks of being a business meeting, my friend, and not a social call,' Željko said, wagging a playful finger at Mason. 'My bones tell me these things. Am I right?'

Mason replied simply, 'You are.'

'I can always tell. And you know, I don't normally like talking business with ladies present, Nick, but I think in this case I will have no option. No?'

Mason didn't reply.

'So, what can I do for you this time?' he asked taking a small drink from his glass and then replacing it on the table.

Mason picked the bottle up and perused the label. 'Are we celebrating? This is an expensive brandy.'

'Only the best for my friends, Nick. And with such a beautiful young lady, you deserve the best.'

'Flattery? That's been in short supply of late,' Sadie said, glancing at her companion.

'Surely Nick treats you well, my dear? If he doesn't, just let me know. I will have some serious words to speak with him.'

'I will, thank you,' agreed Sadie tipping her glass in Željko's direction.

'Have you two finished?' Mason asked a little irritably. When no answer came, he asked Željko, 'Where's Tom Lester now?'

'I have no idea!' Željko replied honestly.

Mason recalled his conversation with JP who had told him that the Croat and Lester were meeting in Sarajevo.

'But you've met with him recently?' Mason coaxed.

'I have Nick. But that was business. Business that is of no concern of yours.'

Sadie appeared to have drifted off from the conversation as she wasn't looking at either Mason or Željko. When Mason turned to her, she seemed to be more interested in Petar who was leaning on the desk seemingly intent on hearing every word being spoken at the table.

'You know, Nick, you seem to be putting yourself a little too close to my affairs. I have warned you before that nothing must get in the way of my business. I fear your vendetta with Tom Lester, a legitimate business associate of mine, is becoming an irritant.'

'Željko, I promised I wouldn't interfere, and I won't.' The younger man touched his heart and said, 'Please accept my assurances.'

Mason needed information. He couldn't afford to lose the trust and, more importantly, the help of the Croat. If Lester was near, he needed to know. And while his words of assurance were genuine, he couldn't help but think to himself that if Lester walked into the restaurant now, he would shoot him stone dead and accept any retribution that came his way.

'Željko, can I ask you...?'

'Ask me anything that doesn't lose me money,' Željko interrupted, 'and I will answer truthfully.'

'Of course.' Mason paused a beat before continuing, 'Slaven Bogdanović. Who is he? And should I be worried about him?'

Željko took a moment before answering. He had always found the less he told people about his business dealings and partners the better. But in this instance, he thought that he had little to lose. Mason would be dead or out of the picture soon, anyway. His deal with Lester was assured. In case it didn't work out, he had negotiated a backup plan to cut the Englishman out of the deal. He could tell Mason the truth. He savoured a mouthful of his brandy before starting. 'Slaven and I go back a long way. Today we are in many ways... competitors. It was not always this way. In the former Yugoslavia we were both accomplished men. He was a professor of literature. He taught and wrote books about Camus, Ivo Andric, and more. Whereas I was a manager at the Ministry of Transport. I did not write books,' he smiled briefly. 'We drank at the same bars occasionally. Ate at the same restaurants. We even socialised sometimes together. Then, unfortunately, the war interrupted our comfortable lives.

I say *comfortable* because, in the old Yugoslavia, we had freedom and a good life. We wanted for nothing and didn't need a dinar more than we had in our pocket. We soon adapted, like so many others, to the new realities on the ground. Slaven's work as a professor at Sarajevo's university had given him a phonebook full of people. And I was in contact with many people who could move things around, legally, or otherwise.

'You must understand that we were Yugoslavs, not Croatians or Bosnians. Even today, with all my riches, and Slaven would tell you the same, I would rather we were back there, in Yugoslavia.

'And so, with our common heritage, we helped anyone. We weren't warmongers. We were just two people accepting the new reality. With our knowledge and ability, we could get food, water, and other supplies to the people in Sarajevo when no one else could. What we found was that our humanitarian gestures morphed, I think this is your word, into a business capable of working within the law and outside of it too!' He paused in contemplation for a beat and then continued. 'And without intending it, we became very rich, but as you might say, on different sides of the street. Two competing empires were built. Two competing entities.'

'But don't you meet up with him? You're still friends?' Mason asked.

'We are. If there is no conflict in our work, all is fine.' He lit a cigarette and offered the pack to Mason, who took a cigarette and lit it. Sadie declined. 'We meet up once a month at the Europa Hotel in Sarajevo. Slaven likes it there. I would prefer Dženita, a nice little Kafana around the corner. They make the best cevapi. We discuss ongoing business issues and ensure there are no hiccups.'

'Is Lester a hiccup?'

'He could be,' the Croat answered honestly.

Mason sunk the last of his brandy. He didn't wait for his host to offer him another, he just poured himself another three fingers.

'How?'

'In many ways. For instance, he could jump into bed with Slaven.'

'And if he did?'

'That would make me very angry,' Željko spat the words out.

Mason noticed a tobacco strain land just near his glass. Suddenly, Željko realised that Petar hadn't brought the food. He turned to the barman. 'Petar! Food for my guests' he ordered angrily.

The younger man jumped at the order from his boss and went through the door beyond the bar.

'Sometimes I wonder if that boy's mind is on the job at all,' Željko admitted.

'Just looks nosey to me,' observed Sadie, casually.

'Maybe,' Željko pondered.

Mason thought for a moment and wondered whether to tell Željko what he knew. Inhaling deeply from the cigarette, he decided to go for broke. He had little to lose. 'I've been told that Lester was meeting with Bogdanović too. Do you think your old friend is trying to scupper your deal with Lester?'

Željko took a large mouthful of brandy as Petar returned with the food. The barman placed a large plate of cheese, meats, olives, vine tomatoes and biscuits on the table between the three of them. He returned with three small plates, knives, forks and napkins and returned to his position at the bar.

The Croat waited for Petar to return to the bar, out of earshot, before starting to speak. Then, he said, 'There is no way Bogdanović or Lester can do business without me. They have no idea how the deal has been put together. I have never discussed the origin or transport arrangements involved. Lester only knows when and where the first shipment will be delivered. Bogdanović only knows that I have a deal with a foreigner. Unless...' He paused.

'Unless what?' Mason asked.

Željko pondered before speaking again. 'Unless my organisation upstream has been compromised.' He paused for a beat, then said, 'Look! Let's eat and be merry. We have this wonderful food and drink. Today is not a day for worrying. I have guests. I have food. I have health. What more could a man want?'

Sadie reached over for a piece of meat, 'Beats me! This looks gorgeous!'

'It is, for sure,' Željko agreed. 'Petar! Give that young couple over there a bottle of wine. On the house. I'm feeling generous.'

Petar reached for a bottle of Plavac and two glasses, put them all on a tray, and took them over to the young couple at the window table. When the waiter had explained that the wine was a gift from Željko, the young man mouthed 'thank you' in their hosts' direction.

Željko smiled back, refilled his glass and said quietly to Mason, 'Nick, you are a man I can trust, and I have several people I know who would lay down their lives for me, if need be, but I feel now that it would be better if we keep all our discussions private. For all I know, even that young couple over there are working for my friend Slaven.'

CHAPTER 33

The lounge in Luka's apartment was open and airy with a clean, bright parquet floor. The two large windows were open. A slight breeze weaved its way around the room. Luka had told Mason and Sadie to relax and use the apartment as their own, before he had left with Manuela for the local Konzum supermarket to pick up some household supplies.

Mason and Sadie had taken their host at his word. They rested on a two-seater settee with a low wooden coffee table in front of them. A wood-carved cigarette box, the like of which is often seen in old black and white movies, took pride of place on the table, with two freshly brewed cups of coffee, one on either end. One of Mason's Burner phones sat idle beside his cup. A small television stood in the corner. The screen was dead.

Sadie had bought an English copy of Hello magazine on her way back from Željko's and was leafing through it. The mixture of celebrity and royalty fascinated her. Perhaps there wasn't a real difference between the two? Maybe the royals were just hereditary celebrities just with a few bows and curtsies thrown in for good measure.

'Do you think this princess gives two hoots about people like you and me?'

Mason removed a cigarette from his mouth, blew the smoke clear, glanced at the picture and said, 'Wouldn't think so. They live in a different world to us.'

Mason rose from the settee and said, 'I shouldn't, but I feel like a stronger drink. Brandy?'

'I'm fine with this coffee, thanks.'

He stubbed his cigarette out in the ashtray and went and got a drink for himself, returning to his seat just in time to hear Luka and Manuela arrive back.

Luka entered the lounge and asked, 'Everything okay?'

'Yes, thanks. Did you get everything you needed?' Mason enquired.

'Everything and more. We went for a bag of groceries and ended up with a suitcase full!'

Manuela came into the room and noticed Sadie with her magazine. 'Could I read that after you please, Sadie?'

'Of course. There are lots of interesting articles in it.'

'Do you want to join me in the kitchen? I'm preparing dinner.'

'Yes, that would be good,' Sadie said, following Manuela out of the lounge.

Luka poured himself a brandy and sat opposite Mason. He threw a packet of cigarettes and a lighter onto the table.

'So, what are your plans, Nick?'

Before answering, Mason touched the cigarette packet and glanced at Luka as if asking for permission. Luka nodded. Mason took a cigarette out of the pack and offered it to Luka, who also took one. Mason held the flame under Luka's cigarette before lighting his own.

The Englishman sat back and rested his arm on the side of the settee.

'To be honest, I'm not a hundred per cent sure. This is a shitstorm and I'm right in the middle of it.'

'Tell me. What did you expect when you came here?' Luka asked. 'Did you think it would be easy? That Tom Lester would just walk up to you and let him kill you?'

Mason took a deep drag from the cigarette as if it would aid his thoughts.

'I suppose I just had revenge on my mind. Lester was responsible for my father's death, and others too.' He should pay for what he's done.' Mason's words were laced with vengeance.

Luka drank from his glass before speaking. 'Nick, these people you're dealing with now are bad men. Very bad men. I don't know much about your past, but I imagine you were on the edge of this world. These people will stop at nothing. Death is part of their world. Whether people live or die means nothing to them.' He took a drag from the cigarette, 'They order assassinations and kill with a clear conscience. They are not concerned with a higher authority that may judge them later, and they also accept that when death comes to them, it's an inevitability.'

Mason stood and turned towards the window, Luka at his back. After a few moments of thought, he said, 'If Tom Lester accepts death will eventually catch up with him, then he understands the clock is ticking.'

'You won't need to explain that to him, Nick.' Luka stood and poured some more brandy into their glasses. 'Here, have another drink. It will help you settle.'

Mason turned back towards his host and sat down again on the settee. He stubbed out the remainder of his cigarette and took a short drink.

Mason's phone sprang into life. He looked at Luka as if asking for permission to answer it. His host nodded and then got up and left the room. He stabbed the green button and said, 'Mason.'

'Nick it's JP. How are you doing my friend?'

'As well as can be expected, I suppose. At least I'm not dead yet,' he added.

'Don't joke like that,' JP rebuked.

'I don't really feel like I'm in a jokey mood, to be honest, JP. The closer I get to Lester the more the reality of the situation is sinking in. I've got a weapon, so I'm prepared for him.'

'You sound like you have doubts, Nick. If you're not sure, you can always pull away. There's time. No harm will be done if you walk away now.'

'Tempting, but no. I can't back down now.'

'You could be dead tomorrow, Nick. Are you prepared for that?'

Mason hesitated before answering, 'I am.'

'Then all is good because I have news.'

'Hit me with it.'

'Okay! I've just learned that Lester is heading for Dubrovnik from Sarajevo. He's travelling with a gangster who goes by the name Slaven Bogdanović'. He pronounced Slaven as Slay-van which should have been said as Sla-van. 'He sounds like a nasty fellah; someone you shouldn't be getting mixed up with.'

'That probably goes for all the people I'm mixing with here, JP. I don't seem to meet many normal people.'

'Perhaps you're in the wrong business, Nick. Get yourself a job and meet some normal people.'

'If only I could.' He paused for a beat before continuing. 'I do know of this guy already. He's some sort of acquaintance of Željko's. Have you got anything else for me?'

'Anyone normal would have thought that would be enough. I'm warning you of impending peril. This old house of yours is gonna come tumbling down, Nick. These are bad people. You need to be prepared.'

'Stop with the Shakey references. I can still hear it in the background, you know.'

'Arrr, one of my favourites,' the mechanic confirmed.

'Glad to know I can share in your favourite pastimes, JP,' Mason sarcastically said down the phoneline back to the UK.'

'The CD's about to finish, but before we end the call, I have some more important information for you.'

'I'm all ears,' Mason said.

'Something's come up and I think you should be concerned.'

'I'm concerned with everything out here, JP. What is it now?'

'It would seem there's a snake in the grass. Or rather a blade of grass amongst the snakes.'

'What are you talking about?'

'I've had a whisper from a source that someone within Željko's organisation is passing information about you to Bogdanović and Tom Lester.'

'What?'

'Lester knows where you've been for a while.'

'But how?'

'Word gets around, Nick. You must remember, information is money. Which reminds me that you never pay me anything.'

'I'll buy you a pint when I get back.' Mason thought for a

moment, before adding, 'Could it be Željko?'

'No. It's someone inside his organisation, I know that much. If you can think of anyone who you've pissed off over there, it's probably him.'

'But I don't know anyone over here, other than Željko and a few of his cronies.'

'Then I suggest you think long and hard and be very careful who you trust.'

'Okay, JP. Thanks for the tip. I'll get back to you as soon as I'm back in England.'

'And don't you forget, you've promised to bring that new lady of yours to my place for a meal and an evening of Shaky. By the way, can you hear the track in the background?' Mason could hear, as he always did when JP was on the line. The mechanic didn't wait for him to answer. 'That's a track called Last Man Alive, you probably don't know it, but you're a limited man where music is concerned. Anyway, I'd just like to say, make sure when all this shit is over, that you're the last man standing. If not for me, then for that beautiful friend of yours.'

'Hand on heart, I promise. Oh, and by the way, Sadie is more into Pink than Shakey, so show a little respect when we come over and play some decent music for the girl.'

'I don't possess any of Pink's music, but I'm sure I can stream some for Sadie. Goodbye, Nick, and be careful.'

'I will. Bye JP.'

Mason cut the line just as Luka returned.

'Was the news bad?' Luka asked.

'Why'd you ask?'

'Nick, you're as white as one of Manuela's best Sunday blouses.'

Mason finished the last of his brandy slowly, 'I've just found out that Tom Lester has someone out here informing him of my movements.'

'I see...' Luka let his words trail for a second. 'And you think this person may be me?'

'It could be,' Mason agreed there was a possibility.

Luka finished the last of the brandy he had left on the table.

'Well?'

'But it isn't. I'm sure of that.'

'Thank the Lord for that. Not that I *believe,* you understand? But I'd hate to think I'm going to share my expensive rakija with someone who thinks I'm a traitor.'

'For what it is worth Luka, I think you're a straight-up guy. Even though there are some shades at the sides, you're an honest man who wouldn't harm someone for no reason.'

'Thank you for that endorsement, Nick.' He smiled. 'I wish I had a drink to celebrate.'

'My pleasure. But I wish we knew who this bastard is. If I wasn't looking over my shoulder before, I certainly will be now. It could be anybody.'

'It could be, Nick. But for now, please try and enjoy your meal. Manuela has prepared something special for you and Sadie. It's Sarma...'

'What's that?'

'It's sour cabbage leaves stuffed with a mixture of diced beef, garlic, and onions, on a bed of rice. There is plenty of salad, olives, and wine, too. But of course, we'll start with the rakija.'

'Sounds good to me, Luka.'

CHAPTER 34

Petar Babić sat anxiously in the subdued lighting of the private room at the back of Slaven Bogdanović's cafe. Stubbing his cigarette out, he instantly lit another with twitching fingers.

The young Croat sat at a small, well-stocked bar. Islands of gaming tables scattered the room. A small stage was next to the bar where Slaven's private dancers performed whenever he had clients in town. Petar had been there once before and had witnessed a couple of drunken Russians throwing money at the dancers before losing millions of roubles on the tables.

Petar's nervousness had been accelerated since Željko's recent drug agreement with the Englishman, Lester. Before, passing information to Slaven about Željko had been easy, and routine, but with this deal, it had suddenly become far more complicated.

Petar only worked at Željko's bar to earn money for a dream move to Florida, in the United States. He had heard that life on the USA's southeast coast was good from a grammar school friend of his. Jobs were plenty and renting an apartment was easy.

His life had been uncomplicated until Slaven approached him one afternoon. In exchange for information about Željko's whereabouts and meetings, Bogdanović would double his earnings, in cash. There would be little or no risk to Petar. It would be low-level information he would pass on. Željko would never know his competitor had someone at the heart of his organisation.

And Slaven was right. Petar had passed on the information Bogdanović required for a couple of years without a hint of trouble. No one suspected a thing. But then the Englishman came on the scene...

Tom Lester had met Slaven at a gathering in Montenegro and wanted information about Željko, his organisation and trustworthiness. Petar knew this because he was in Kotor, Montenegro, at the same time. He had taken a few days off from the cafe saying he wanted to meet a girl there. Željko, his boss, had suspected nothing.

Petar had been enlisted to gather information there which may help Lester in his dealings with Željko. His remuneration would be increased again, and his dream relocation to Florida would become a reality sooner rather than later. He had been given Lester's number and was told to speak directly to him. When he passed information to Slaven, he would also add the new intelligence to his report.

Everything had been moving along smoothly... and then there'd been a death. Lester had requested the killing of an associate from England, a man called Bevan. Željko had fulfilled the commission willingly. When Petar asked Slaven about the Englishman's murder and Lester's part in it, he had been told to keep his mouth shut and carry on doing the job he was paid to do. 'If' he did that, he had nothing to worry about.

Petar had thought about collecting his money and travelling to Florida there and then. But he was just shy of the amount he had hoped to take and so had stayed to see the job through.

It seemed to Petar that all Englishman were trouble. His limited dealings with Lester convinced him that the Englishman had a sense of entitlement. It was as if he thought the English were better than anyone else and that every other person should bow and scrape to him. Petar knew that in the circumstances he had no choice but to meet up and answer any questions Lester put to him. After all, the Englishman and Slaven were his paymasters.

As he stubbed out his cigarette, the door opened and Slaven and Lester entered the room. The door was closed behind them by someone unseen.

Petar rose from his seat.

Slaven stopped him, 'No. Stay. We'll sit here.' And, looking at Lester, 'Tom, sit at the bar with Petar. I'll get us a drink.' The foreigner sat at the bar, leaving a stool between himself and the young Croat. Slaven reached for three glasses from the shelf and poured generous helpings of Badel into them.

As Slaven put the glasses in front of his guests, he noticed Petar's nervousness. The young man's hands were visibly shaking.

'It's okay, Petar. There's nothing to worry about here. We're just gathering information. That's all. Have a drink, relax.'

Petar picked his glass up and took a sip. He couldn't shake off the feeling that the Englishman wasn't here on a friendly errand, he was here for business.

Lester picked his glass up and said, 'Right! What have we got? What's Željko up to?' After a heavy slurp, he put the glass down and withdrew a large cigar from his inside jacket pocket. Slaven reached for Petar's lighter on the bar and held it under the cigar until Lester was satisfied it was lit.

Slaven looked at Petar, 'Now Petar, I need you to tell Mr Lester exactly what's been happening over at the restaurant.'

'Yes, of course,' Petar replied.

'This better be important,' the Englishman said.

'I think you'll find it is, Mr Lester,' Bogdanović assured.

'Go on, then,' Lester ordered Petar.

"Err, yes,' Petar started, 'it's this deal you have with Željko. I'm convinced he's going to renege on it.'

'Why do you think that?' demanded Lester.

'I don't think it,' Petar hesitated for a second. 'I know it. He has told Mason that once the deal is completed, and he knows everyone that is involved in the shipments to England, the Englishman can do as he pleases with you.'

'What?' Lester shouted! He jumped to his feet and started to pace the room. 'This is war, Slaven! You know that don't you?'

'It would seem to be,' Slaven agreed coolly.

'You assured me Željko was an honourable man. What

happened?' he asked, pointing the smouldering cigar towards Slaven.

'What can I say?' Slaven said holding his hands up in mock surrender. 'I've never known him to double-cross anyone.'

Lester looked at Petar.

'What does he know? Am I in imminent danger from him?'

'I don't think he knows too much. He just wants to ensure the pipeline is clear for him to move in before Mason does anything to harm you.'

'Good. Then we still have time before this buffoon tries anything he'll regret.' He refilled his glass from the bottle his host had left on the bar. 'Now, Slaven, where is he getting his merchandise from? Do we at least know that?'

'His usual suppliers use a route through Republika Srpska, Bosnia and then into Croatia. There's probably some Russian influence in the chain before that. I've had some friends asking questions, but as yet they've found little to confirm he's using his favoured people. I would go so far as to say he's using someone completely new. An untried and tested supplier. If he is, he's getting sloppy!'

Lester sat back down. 'You need to re-double your efforts. If he is about to shaft me on this deal, we need to know where we can get hold of the merchandise ourselves. And at a good price! I've made promises and paid good money on the strength of this deal. If I get fucked over on this one, someone is going to pay!'

'Don't worry, Tom,' Slaven assured. 'All will be fine. I can give you my guarantee on this. The worst that can happen is that the flow of merchandise will be a little behind schedule. Once Željko's partners find out his side of the deal is dead they'll come running to me. They will have no other option. And once that happens, me and you, Tom, have a deal. You will become the richest importer of drugs into the United Kingdom, and maybe into western Europe. Because if you pull this off, there's scope to increase your influence without question.'

'You'd better be right, Slaven!' Lester warned. 'I lose my patience when I'm threatened. And your friend, Željko, is testing my resolve here.'

Petar took a drink of brandy, realising he was completely out of his depth sat in this room with Lester and Slaven. This was a world where he didn't belong. But what could he do? Nothing yet, for sure. But as soon as he could, he would leave the country and take his chance in the USA. He had just enough money to get started there. His friend would help him find work and once he was on his feet financially, he would be fine out there.

'Tom, leave it with me. I'll keep digging for information. Petar here will inform us of any movements Željko makes. Won't you, Petar?' Slaven smiled at his informant.

'Yes, of course.'

'Good. Then there's no need to worry. We can deal with Željko and Mason when the time comes.' Looking back towards Petar, he said, 'Now if you could leave us. We have some other business to attend to.'

'Certainly, Slaven.' Petar agreed sinking the last of his drink and leaving without further comment.

CHAPTER 35

Nesby's flight to Dubrovnik that morning had been uneventful. He'd packed light and got through customs after being questioned about his reasons for travel and his intentions while in Croatia. He'd had limited experience of foreign travel, but it did strike Nesby how disinterested the Border Guards were.

He'd hailed a cab from the Airport Terminal and given the address to the driver that Lester had sent him via Whatsapp before he'd left England. He was dropped off forty minutes later at the front of a restaurant and told by the driver to ask inside.

He resisted the temptation to eat something and went straight up to the apartment after being given his room key. He was thankful for the air conditioning, it was hot outside.

Nesby was nervous. He knew he was only in Dubrovnik to do one job: kill Nick Mason. He'd spent the whole of his adult life having just one job to do, kill someone. And while he didn't mind the actual killing, he could do with a break. With some luck, Lester would give him some time off when this assignment was completed. He'd spent the whole drive from the airport marvelling at the scenery. Maybe, with the money he'd get paid, he could hire a vehicle and explore the coast.

His carry-on bag contained enough items for the few days he expected to be in Croatia. He could purchase anything else he might need later. Once Lester had been in contact, he'd get the job done quickly and hopefully move on.

'Thank heaven for Spotify,' he thought after clicking through the TV channels and finding no English-speaking stations apart from CNN and BBC World News. The news was not something he wanted to watch. Instead, he found a smooth jazz playlist on the music app and punched the play button.

He'd unpacked the few clothes he had brought and stowed his bag away in the small wardrobe. After an uneventful meal he'd gone to bed early and slept fitfully.

The injuries he'd sustained in the crash while chasing Mason were still giving him trouble, many days after. Whilst the bruises had started to recede from his torso, the occasional spasm of pain checked his movement and reminded him to move more gingerly. He was sure there would be no such spasms if he could just move a little more slowly.

After a light breakfast in the restaurant below, he returned to his room. His breathing was starting to even itself out in the warmer temperature of Dubrovnik. Sitting in the chair next to his bed, Spotify on a loop, his eyes were ready to close, but then his cell phone cut the music dead and the ringtone sprang into life.

Nesby jumped up into a sitting position, wincing slightly at the twinge of pain in his side. Damn!

'Yes,' he said into the mouthpiece.

It was Lester. He said he'd be round shortly and to 'stay put'.

Nesby pondered whether to ask him to pick up some cigarettes on his way in but thought better of it.

Just as he'd finished freshening up, a knock sounded on the door. He opened it.

Lester came in without a word. He was dressed in salmon-coloured trousers, sandals, and an open-necked check shirt. He had a manbag over his shoulder. Even though the temperature was high, Lester gave no impression of being uncomfortable. He took his sunglasses off and hung them from his shirt pocket.

'I'm sorry I can't offer you a drink, Tom,' Nesby apologised. 'There's no minibar in the fridge.'

Lester brushed it aside saying, 'No matter,' and went out onto the balcony. 'Nice view,' he said without turning around.

'Yes. It's a good room, Tom. Thanks for sorting it out for me.'

'It's the least I could do.'

Both Nesby and Lester sat on the plastic chairs at either end of the balcony. Nesby couldn't help but enjoy the smell given off from the trees nearby. He couldn't put a name to the trees, it wasn't his thing, but they gave off a pleasant aroma.

'So? What's the score, Tom?'

'First, tell me about Ferguson.'

Nesby shuffled a little in his seat before answering his boss, 'He gave me a bit of trouble, but it's done. He's dead. There will be no further problems from him.'

'What do you mean, he gave you a *bit of trouble*?' Lester asked, concerned.

'Before I had the chance to kill him, he put up a bit of a struggle. That's all. Left me a little bruised.'

'Did you cover all the bases? You didn't leave any traces behind?'

'Ferguson is dead.' He pondered whether to tell Lester about Antonucci, the journalist, still being alive but decided to wait a moment. He only needed to answer the question at hand. 'What more bases do you want covering?'

'Witnesses?' Lester said dully.

Nesby paused for a second before admitting there was a witness to Ferguson's murder who was still alive.

'Well?'

'Ferguson's mistress, Petra Antonucci. I killed him at her apartment, and she was there.'

Lester bristled.

'And you let her live?'

'She was innocent boss. She has no way of connecting you with me. She doesn't even know why I killed him. Just that I did.'

'I find your stupidity bewildering sometimes.' Lester rose from his seat and leaned on the balcony barrier, surveying the marina in front of the hotel. 'Every loose end you leave creates a trail. And that trail will always be picked up by some savvy copper or journalist hoping to get a promotion or a scoop!'

'Tom, I left no clues. Honestly. There's nothing. I even disposed of their computers, memory sticks and cell phones. If there was anything he had stored on you, there's no trace of it now.'

Lester turned towards Nesby and ordered, 'Leave that for now. There's nothing we can do about it. There are things to do here that are more pressing.'

'Like Mason?' Nesby asked.

'Yes, like Mason. We've also hit a few stumbling blocks regarding the deal.'

Lester turned back towards the marina. 'It's nothing you can do anything about at the moment.'

'So, what do you want me to do?'

Lester glanced back and looked into Nesby's eyes coldly, 'You have a simple task while you're here. Find Mason and kill him.' He reached into his bag and lifted a pistol from it. 'Here,' he said handing it to Nesby, who took it. Lester dug into the bag again and withdrew a box. He went back into the room and flung it onto the bed. 'Bullets. If you need any more, let me know.'

'Yes, Tom.'

'Oh, and one other thing.'

'Yes?' Nesby asked.

'If he has the girl with him, kill her too!'

'It will be my pleasure, Tom.'

'Once you've completed that simple task, you can take some time off.'

'Thanks, Tom. I'd appreciate that.'

'I'd suggest resting for the rest of today and beginning your search tomorrow. It shouldn't take you too long to locate them.'

'Will do, Tom,' Nesby agreed. 'I could do with a little rest.'

Lester left the room adding nothing more and shut the door behind him.

CHAPTER 36

The café at the apex of the inlet at Lapad was sparsely populated when Sadie and Mason arrived the following day.

The heat of the day was now climbing, and a rising number of customers started to arrive, sheltering under the extended canopy from the direct sun.

Mason and Sadie had walked down from Luka's apartment earlier in the day. Sadie wanted a forage around the market at Gruž, so they'd skirted the inlet to the market and returned once she'd perused the many stalls.

Mason had been looking over his shoulder throughout, constantly checking for anyone watching them and had satisfied himself that none of Lester's men had traced their steps from Luka's place.

Sadie was eyeing her new fridge magnet, a representation of the Old Town, when the waiter arrived with their drinks. He placed their Gin & Tonics with ice and lemon down on the table and slid the bill under the ashtray. Mason thanked him as he walked away.

'Do you think I could start a collection of these magnets?' Sadie asked. 'They seem to be very popular.'

'You could.' And then he added, 'If you wanted to follow the predictable crowd.'

'Hey, Buster! Stop with the smart-alek remarks!'

She put the magnet back in its little brown paper bag and returned it to her small shoulder bag that lay on the spare chair.

Mason sat back and lit a cigarette. He smiled to himself as he looked out over the harbour. The sky was a vivid blue. The boats swayed with the choppy water across the road that separated the café from the harbour. The light breeze was warm and salty and gave no real respite from the heat beyond the canopy they sat under.

'I think I could live here permanently,' Sadie declared, taking a sip of her drink. 'What about you?'

Mason turned to face her, 'I was living here quite comfortably until Lester came and spoiled the party.'

'O yes. I forgot.' She thought for a moment, before adding, 'Perhaps when all this is over you could go back to normal.'

'Maybe,' he replied, 'but let's get through this first, shall we?'

They sat in silence, Mason surveying the area for Lester's men and Sadie relaxing in the warmth of a country she'd never dreamed of visiting before.

Mason was checking all the new customers for tell-tale signs: over-interest in them, a person deliberately avoiding eye contact, someone never touching the drink they had ordered. All dead giveaways!

Sadie broke the silence, 'What shall we do?'

'We could have a light lunch and tomorrow, I was thinking we might go to the Old Town, and I'd treat you to a decent meal,' Mason revealed. 'They have some fantastic restaurants up there.'

'That would be nice, but is it wise?'

'We can't run forever, can we? We can't hide from Lester in Luka's apartment all the time. It's good of them to put us up, but they need space to live their own lives.'

'At the expense of yours?' she asked directly.

He paused for a beat. Then, 'Maybe...'

'You're one crazy frog!'

'Yep,' he said stubbing his cigarette out in the ashtray.

After a period of quiet, Sadie asked, 'What about a beach day?'

Mason didn't answer. His attention had been stirred by a customer who had just arrived. The man hadn't ordered a drink and didn't appear to be looking for a waiter, either. In this heat, the least you'd want would be a glass of chilled water.

Mason's attention stayed on the newcomer, a very white, fit, muscley guy with close-cropped hair. Whenever Mason saw such a severe haircut, he immediately thought 'ex-army'.

He'd had enough. After five minutes, this guy still had no drink and had not even taken a cursory look at the menu.

Mason leaned to his side and slowly brought Sadie towards him, their lips almost touching. Sadie smiled nervously. Mason had never been this demonstrative in public with her. He kissed her gently and then nuzzled into her ear and began to say the words she'd been hoping never to hear, 'One of Lester's men is sitting at the other end of the café.'

Sadie jerked at the revelation. He held her still. 'I need you to go to the bathroom. Take your time. There's no rush.' She began to disengage from him. He pulled her back and kissed her on the mouth again, before continuing to give further instructions. 'When you come out, I'll have gone. Go back to Luka's apartment and stay there until I come and get you. If I don't come back, go to Željko. He'll make sure you're safe. Do you understand?'

She brought her face towards his. The tears in her eyes hadn't yet escaped, but he could see they would imminently.

'Yes, I understand. But listen to me, Nick Mason. Don't you dare think of not coming back for me.'

'Don't worry,' he calmed. 'I'll be back.' He paused a beat, kissed her, and said, 'Now, go!'

Sadie rose from her seat, grabbed her bag, kissed him once more, and headed for the bathroom inside.

Mason threw some Euro notes on the table, leaving a generous tip, and got up himself. He walked down the steps to the path and faced the inlet, hoping this was not the last thing he would ever see, but was content if it was. The old galleon tourist boat was moored up not far away.

Just as Mason was about to move forward, he felt a hand on his left shoulder. He glanced at the hand. A spider's web was clearly painted between the thumb and finger. He didn't respond to the instruction whispered into his left ear, 'Walk slowly, you douche-bag. I'd like to have a private word with you!'

As they walked, Mason got the whiff of an awful aftershave that emanated from the guy holding onto his shoulder. Far too citrusy.

Speaking from behind, Lester's man said, 'Tom sent me. I'm Nesby and I'm to kill you. Just like I did your father.'

Mason stiffened. He would have to do something, and quickly. He didn't want Sadie coming out before he had dealt with Lester's man.

He turned with a sharpness that the man behind him had no chance of responding to, swiping the arm off his shoulder as he turned. He punched Nesby to the floor and kicked him in the midriff. While his enemy cramped up on the floor in pain, Mason turned and ran in the direction of the cruise liners moored up in Gruž. He had to get Lester's man well away from Sadie. Then he would deal with his father's killer.

At the end of the gangplank of the old galleon tour boat, a sports motorcycle was leaning on its stand. Mason noticed the key deep in its slot. He turned briefly and saw his assailant staggering to his feet. Taking a split-second decision, he mounted the bike, swiped the stand, and turned the key. The engine roared into life as he turned the throttle. Within seconds, he was racing down the path, away from the boat and towards Gruž on the bike.

Nesby, now some distance behind, saw the chances of getting Mason slip away as the motorbike got further away. He had to do something, and fast. Lester would be furious if he let Mason escape again. He looked around for suitable transport. He had to catch Mason. Then, coming swiftly around the corner, a young man on a motorbike stopped and dismounted. Taking his helmet off, the young Croatian waved at his friends in the café and called out, *'Dobar dan'* – Good day.

Nesby took his chance. He pushed the motorcyclist out of his way and jumped on the motorbike. Before the young man knew what was happening Nesby was in hot pursuit of his prey on the stolen bike.

Mason had tracked the path next to the moored boats until he had reached the extended concrete jetty that was home to the ferry for Bari, in Italy. He had ridden this way and that around the pedestrians as they sauntered in the mid-day heat marvelling at the views. He dragged the bike around to a stop, the rear tyre screeching as it arced. He saw Lester's man racing towards him on what looked like a high-powered bike. Pedestrians were jumping out of his way, screaming frantically.

Mason had to do something, and quick!

Turning towards the market that he and Sadie had visited earlier, he decided to take a chance. If he could create mayhem in there, maybe he could lose his pursuer.

He revved the engine and set off with the front wheel bucking like a stallion. Holding the handlebar, he eased the front of the bike down onto the tarmac and headed across the road, leaning left and right through the gaps in the heavy traffic.

Nesby saw Mason up in front crossing the road. He deviated onto the road himself and headed up towards the market through the centre of the vehicles, their horns blaring as he passed.

Onlookers stopped and looked at the two motorbikes, wondering if they were in the middle of a movie scene.

Lester's man saw Mason turn towards the market entrance. Nesby had gained on him now to the point that if he turned off the road, he would have a clear view as to where Mason was heading.

Nesby reached the market turn mere seconds behind. He turned across the traffic to his right to follow. As he crossed ahead of a small car, the vehicle clipped the rear wheel of the bike. It momentarily knocked him off course, taking his breath away briefly, but he managed to regain control of the bike and continued his pursuit.

Running the bike through the middle of the market, Mason didn't look back at his pursuer. He was still hoping that he could lose him.

Market-goers were jumping out of his way, some falling into the stalls, spilling products onto the floor.

Behind, Nesby, with sweat pouring from his forehead, was gaining. He was close enough to take Mason out with one shot, but alas, couldn't. He wished the accelerator was on the other bar as he was right-handed and couldn't shoot with his left.

Mason turned sharply out of the market area, rear wheel skidding, back out onto the busy coastal road. He was now approaching Le Jardin. Cruise liners lined up facing it, their occupants visiting the Old Town.

Mason rode straight across the road, heading for the boats, taking no notice of the cars screaming to a halt with screeching horns blaring all around. It was either him or the man on the bike behind. He was going to make damn sure it wasn't him.

Nesby meandered through the cars, just behind Mason. Nesby had scouted this area earlier, he knew they were heading into a dead-end.

Mason ploughed on into the coach park that serviced the cruise liners. It offered no escape route, walled in by mesh fencing. Straight ahead there was a massive white cruise liner moored up. He could turn back and face his pursuer or, maybe, he had one chance.

He determined to go for it!

He rotated the accelerator to full and the bike almost took off! He headed for the big white boat at speed.

Nesby did likewise, laughing to himself. What was this crazy man trying to do? *'You're cornered, you fool!'*

At the last moment, Mason turned the bike onto its side, kicking it from underneath him as it fell. He rolled clear of the bike, which crashed into the boat and slid down the small gap, and into the water below.

Nesby saw what Mason had done only when it was too late. He didn't have a chance to question his prey's actions. Before he knew it, his bike had headed straight into the boat with a crash! The gap between the boat and the concrete shoreline was just enough for the mangled bike to drop through, but as Nesby hit the boat a fraction of a second later the vessel had started to move back with the tide towards the concrete shoreline. Before his whole body disappeared down into the water as the bike had done, the boat crushed into his back, pinning him to the dock.

As his arms clung to the side, he couldn't scream. His eyes were wide with the horror and realisation of what was happening. Tons of metal fractured every bone in his body. And then, at last, blood spurted from his mouth as the last of the breath was crushed out of his lungs.

Mason, from his prone position, just had time to see Nesby being crushed to death by the ship. He turned away as Nesby's body slipped down into the water when the boat moved away from the side again. Nesby's death had been horrible. He felt like throwing up.

Out of the blue, he felt a tap on his shoulder. Not again! He turned around, thinking the worst. Thankfully, it was Neven, Zlatko's man.

'Come! Get away from here. You can't be seen around here when the police come.'

Neven helped Mason up onto his feet and led him to the café for a drink.

He sat at the bar and drank eagerly from the glass that Neven had given him.

Already, there were blue flashing lights and sirens blaring noisily at the port.

'You need to stay here for a while,' Neven advised. 'The police won't disturb you here. When it is quiet you can go.'

'Thanks.'

'My pleasure,' Neven said standing at the door, watching the commotion on the dock facing the café.

Exhausted by the episode, Mason was happy. He'd killed the man that had murdered his father.

CHAPTER 37

Rising earlier that day, Petar Babić had made a final decision. He was getting out of Dubrovnik, and fast! Things had been getting difficult. He sensed that Željko knew something. Maybe he was aware of his arrangement with Slaven Bogdanović and by default, the Englishman, Lester? Increasingly, he got the feeling that Željko didn't trust him. It wasn't anything tangible, more a gut feeling. Occasionally he had felt a wary look here, or a concerned glance there. Had he been sent on minor errands that wouldn't have been his concern before? Petar just couldn't put his finger on one single thing that confirmed his suspicions. Yet his stomach had begun to turn somersaults at the very thought that Željko knew how he had been earning extra money from his competitor, Slaven Bogdanović.

Petar showered and dressed in his regulation uniform of white shirt, black trousers and shiny black laced shoes. He'd struggled to get a little bread and cheese down for breakfast.

Logging into his online bank account, he determined that he had just enough money to acquire a one-way ticket to Florida and survive for a few months there. It was time to leave. His friend in the US would find him a job before his money ran out, he was sure of that.

He would go to work as normal and during his lunchbreak he would book a flight out to the US as soon as practicable.

Picking his cell phone and keys up as he was leaving, he realised he had only a couple of cigarettes remaining in the pack. He decided to call in at Nermin's Tabak kiosk on his way to the restaurant. It stood on the corner only two blocks down.

He stood at the kerb, checking the passing traffic outside his apartment block and waited for a gap in the busy traffic before trotting across the road. He reached the kiosk in minutes. It was no bigger than a garden shed. Rows of newspapers, local and foreign, lined the forward-facing counter. Doors, open at the side, housed magazines, mainly of the celebrity type. Behind Nermin the Kiosk owner, rows upon rows of cigarettes and cigars stood like battalions of soldiers waiting to go into battle.

Nermin was a lot older than Petar and remembered the old days of Yugoslavia. Occasionally, both Nermin and Petar drank together at a local café, their common bond being 'Hajduk Split'. Nermin remembered the 1970's when Hajduk won all Yugoslavia's soccer competitions, including the league four times.

The younger man waited for a customer to complete his transaction and stepped up to the counter. 'Nermin, how are those old bones of yours?'

Nermin threw some coins into the money tray before him, 'Young enough to beat the crap out of you, young man!'

'Promises. Promises,' Petar smiled. 'My usual brand, please. Make it two packs.'

Nermin stroked his beard which grew into a greying point a few inches from his chin. 'You know, you're my most loyal customer. And I must tell you, these Jadran cigarettes will kill you one day.'

'We all have to die of something, Nermin,' he said while pocketing the two packs, and then added, 'But you seem to defy all the odds.'

'Pay up and get lost, you cheeky bastard!' Nermin said playfully.

'Are you up for a drink later?' Petar asked while passing the money for the cigarettes over.

'Yes, I will be there when I shut up later.'

'Good, I'll see you there,' the younger man said waving as he turned away.

He travelled a couple of blocks down and turned right into a small connecting street. Petar took no notice of the cars and a large black van parked up as he sucked on a cigarette. He should have!

As he passed the van the back doors were flung open. Two men jumped out and took hold of both their target's hands. He attempted to free himself. A third man in a black suit got out of the passenger seat door calmly and raised a gun towards Petar's face.

'Get in the back, now!' ordered the man in the suit.

The young Croat did as he was told, shaking with fear. Who were these men? Who did they work for? Željko? Slaven? Maybe Lester?

He was pushed to the floor of the van, while his two assailants sat above him on benches that ran down the inside of the vehicle. Petar heard the front door slam shut just as the vehicle pulled away from the kerb.

*

The stone walkways that skirted high above the Old Town were narrow. On the inside the wall looked over the town. On the outside the wall towered over the rocks and sea below. In one area the walkway opened up and a café occupied the space. Several tables with umbrellas shielding patrons from the sun.

After leaving Le Jardin at Gruž, Mason had immediately gone to Željko. The Croat had promised he would keep him safe.

Later in the afternoon, they both sat at the café on the Wall. Their view was limited, with the umbrella above them and the walkways, left and right, revealing only a few steps either way.

Željko took a deep drag from the cigarette, allowing the noxious smoke to ruminate in his lungs, before releasing it into the Croatian air. He had matters to consider, serious matters. The mole had been located. It was now time to punish the traitor.

Mason on the chair beside him, knew nothing of the reason behind their being at the cafe. Željko had told him simply that they were to meet Luka.

A waiter came and asked them if they wanted a fresh drink.

'Slivovitce for me.' Željko ordered. 'Another drink, Nick?'

'A small beer, please,' Mason requested.

It was proving to be the hottest day of the year. The heat was bearing down on the town, evidenced by the scant clothes worn by the tourists passing by the café. The locals, however, seemed to be taking it in their stride.

'Why are we here, Željko?' asked Mason emptying the dregs of his drink.

The Croatian tapped his cigarette on the ashtray, 'Just a little bit of business.'

Mason was concerned. Lester had been in town for days now and must have met with Željko. The last thing he wanted was to bump into Lester by chance. He wanted to be prepared, to have the advantage.

'This business doesn't happen to have anything to do with Tom Lester does it, Željko?'

The waiter approached, put their fresh drinks on the table, picked their empty glasses up and retreated to the café entrance, out of earshot.

Željko took a sip, 'It does, and it doesn't. But you've no need to worry. I have no plans to meet Tom Lester today.'

Mason relaxed back into his chair, 'Thank God for that. The last thing I need right now is to meet up with Lester. For one thing, I must make sure Sadie is safe.'

'Yes, your new friend,' Željko interrupted. 'Is she someone special, Nick?'

Mason lit a cigarette and offered the box to Željko who took one and lit the fresh cigarette with the dying one from his mouth.

'She's becoming so,' admitted Mason.

'You should be careful, Nick. Does she know of your life, the things you have done, you are willing to do? It takes a strong woman, a special woman, to accept a criminal lifestyle like yours, my friend.'

Mason's mouth was dry, so he took a gulp of beer before answering. 'She knows a little. I've left the gory details for a more opportune moment.'

Željko advised, 'It may be better to leave those so-called gory details where they are. Do not take them home to your woman, Nick. My wife knows nothing of my other life, this life. All she knows about is the businesses I run legitimately. It's safer for them that way.'

'Yes, of course,' agreed Mason.

Mason had noticed that over the last few minutes or so no tourist had passed the café. He thought that strange. The Old Town must be one of the most visited places in Europe and he knew for a fact that there were cruise ships in town. Normally the human cargo would head straight down here.

He wasn't complaining as such. The umbrella he sat under protected him from the sun, and the cool coastal breeze was a slight respite.

Mason heard footsteps coming towards the café. So the tourists were here after all.

Željko clicked his fingers towards the waiter who immediately brought a glass of iced water. 'Uđi u kafić i zatvori vrata!' – Go inside the café and shut the door,' he ordered.

'U redu.' – Of course.

Mason watched him retreat inside the café, closing the door as instructed.

A man in a suit came into view from Mason's right-hand side. His jacket was open and as he moved closer to Mason and Željko, the Englishman noticed a gun clipped to his belt.

Immediately after he got to their table, Petar Babić, the young barman, was dragged into view by two heavies that Mason had never seen before.

Mason sensed danger for the young man. It wasn't just the heat of the day that was causing Petar to sweat.

'For the benefit of our English guest, we will speak in English. Sit.' Željko said without any emotion. 'There's water for you. It's warm out. Enjoy.'

Petar did as he was told. His hand shook as he picked the glass up. Hardly able to swallow, he put the glass down and asked,

'Why am I here, boss? I have work to do in the restaurant.'

'Not today, Petar. Not today.' Željko took a beat before adding, 'I'm terminating your employment as of now.'

'But why?' the younger man pleaded. 'I'm a good worker. I've done everything you've asked of me.'

Željko was quiet, unmoving.

Petar was breathing heavily. He undid the top button of his shirt. It didn't look to Mason as if it changed anything, his chest was still heaving.

'Željko, I can't afford to lose my job. I can't pay my rent without work. I have commitments.'

Petar shrunk back into his chair as Željko leant forward and pointed a finger. 'It has recently come to my attention that you've been working for two masters, young man. That I am not your sole employer.'

'No! No! That's not true.' pleaded Petar.

'But I have your bank statements here.' Željko took a sheaf of papers from his inside pocket and threw them on the table. 'These tell me everything about your financial situation. There is far too much money in there for a person like you. You would have to work many years for me and spend nothing to save that much money. What do you say, Petar? Do you have some other means of employment? Or do you like to gamble? Is that it?'

Petar's eyes were flitting here and there, not settling anywhere. He desperately needed an explanation. But he didn't have one. There was nothing he could say that would make this easier.

'I… I…' he stumbled.

'Don't trouble yourself,' Željko stopped him holding a hand up. 'You cannot simply explain this away, young man.' He looked up at the suited man who had abducted Petar. 'The picture.' The man handed his boss a picture of Petar and Slaven Bogdanović. 'Look at this Petar.'

Petar leaned forward and did as he was told. What little colour he had drained from his face.

'But Željko, I can explain.'

'Please don't.' And with that, he nodded.

The three men who had brought Petar grabbed him. He fought back, kicking the chair he'd been sitting on, catching one of the men in the knee. But it was to no avail. They lifted him off his feet. He was shouting, pleading with his boss.

'Željko, please! No! No!' he shouted.

Mason could see the terror in the young man's eyes as he forlornly scrambled to get away from the men.

Željko didn't respond. He lit a new cigarette and took a large drag, not even looking in Petar's direction.

Petar was lifted higher as he battled his assailants. Nothing he did made a difference. They were too strong for him.

Instead of turning down the pathway away from the café they carried him to the wall and, without any emotion, threw him over it.

There was a blood-curdling scream as Petar plummeted to his fate, death on the rocks far below the walled city. The Englishman heard a dull thud as Petar's body smacked into the rocks.

Željko stood, and said, 'That's done. Let's go.'

Mason was speechless at the Croatian's cold-bloodedness. What he had seen was quite possibly the most horrific thing he had ever witnessed. Petar was nothing more than a kid. Did he really deserve to be killed for what he had done? If he didn't know before, he now knew that Željko was one ruthless bastard!

He got up in unison with Željko. Before continuing down the walkway, behind the Croat, Mason made a move to look over the wall, to make Petar's death a reality instead of something imaginary. A heavy hand on his shoulder stopped him in his tracks, pushing him towards the Croatian and down the stone passage. With Željko in front, and three killers behind, Mason had no option but to follow.

CHAPTER 38

Mason sat facing Sadie at the dining table in the kitchen of Luka's apartment. He took a deep gulp from the glass of brandy in front of him.

Disregarding Željko's advice to keep Sadie away from the details of his criminal activities, he'd recounted in detail what had happened earlier, first to the man at the café and then his meeting with Željko later in the Old Town. She'd listened carefully and poured him more brandy while he spoke. When he got to the point where Petar was thrown over the wall, she poured herself a large drink and sunk a mouthful of the brandy, too.

When he had stopped speaking, she asked, 'So what happened afterwards? I mean, what did Željko do?'

Mason knocked the ash from the end of his cigarette and said, 'He just walked away.'

'What do you mean he just walked away?' she pressed.

'Just that,' Mason answered flatly. 'He led me and his men back down from the wall and onto the car without even a backward glance. He spoke to the men in Croatian, which I couldn't understand, and then took me to the restaurant. He said nothing about Petar, or what had happened. It was as if the incident had never taken place.'

'This guy sounds like the ultimate 'cold fish',' she said, taking another drink.

They sat in silence for what seemed like an eternity, then Sadie asked, 'What about the police? Did they do anything?'

'Not that I could see. Two policemen were at the fountain talking to some young girls when we passed, but they didn't appear to be doing anything regarding Petar's death. I've seen those policemen before. They just patrol the Stradun through the day. There's a bigger police presence in the evening.' He took a sip of brandy. 'Tourists were passing us on the steps as we left, as if they'd opened the wall again for the public.'

'Željko must have some serious clout if he can close the Old Town walls at will.'

'For sure,' he agreed. 'Anyway, afterwards, we sat at his restaurant, at his usual table, and had some rakija. There was a brief attempt at conversation, then he made his apologies and left. Said he had business elsewhere. I finished my drink and came straight here.'

'Jeez! You know how to spend a day out in the sun, don't you?'

'It's not exactly a choice, all this, you know?' he said, lighting up a new cigarette.

Sadie got up, took her empty glass to the sink, and rinsed it. 'It hasn't exactly been a bed of roses for me either,' she revealed, tucking her hair behind her ear. 'When you unceremoniously left me at the café this morning, I had no idea you'd return with multiple-tales of death and destruction. I mean when you rang me and said you'd killed the guy from the café, and once you'd seen Željko you'd come back for me, in my wildest dreams I never thought you'd be telling me about yet another murder. It's like the Gunfight at the OK Corral out there when you lot get together.'

She took a plate of cheese and bread that Manuela had prepared earlier to the dining table, placing it in front of Mason. He pushed it away as she sat back down.

'You know, it's incredible! No matter what I do I can't get myself out of this situation. Ever since I could walk my dad used me wherever he could in his criminal exploits, and it's influenced everything in my life.' He paused, peering into his glass as he turned it around slowly. 'You know, he used to have me running around town with cash for bets when I should have been at school learning maths? And as for English, I gained more from reading a few books because I was never in school long enough to learn. Do you know, I have got no idea what it's like to have a real job. Or a normal life, for that matter!'

She reached over and held his hand, 'It's not all it's cracked up to be, you know? For a start, the taxman likes to reduce all your wages to subsistence levels. Being a freelance hitman releases you from any form of debilitating tax bills, I suppose.' She smiled weakly.

'Never paid a tax bill in my life. I wouldn't know how to.'

'Bit like Del Boy then from Only Fools?'

He took a drag from his cigarette and said, 'A bit, but without the humour, I suppose.'

Mason pondered his situation, something he had found himself doing more and more recently. Before Bevan visited Dubrovnik everything had been going fine. Here on the Adriatic coast he had finally found something akin to peace. That was until Bevan had been murdered on Tom Lester's orders. Since then, the deaths had been mounting and each one brought Lester closer to Mason. Inevitably it had come down to it being Lester or Mason who survived. One of them needed to die to end all this mayhem. He was hoping against all hope that it would be he who survived.

Sadie cut into his thoughts, 'There's a lot to be said for normality, you know. I was quite content.'

'Was?' he raised an eyebrow.

'Well, yes. Everything was pretty stable for me. I worked, paid my dues, and did a few things with my meagre earnings.' She smiled. 'And then you came along... and ripped it all up!'

'I'm sorry,' he said earnestly. 'If I could turn back the clock and save you from all this I would, for sure.'

She gave a half smile, 'Don't be sorry. To be honest, life was getting a little stale.'

'Well, it's certainly livened up then.'

'It has. If there's one thing you've done for me, it's inject a little, what should I call it?' She paused for a beat. Then, 'Yes, you've injected a little bit of *unpredictability* into life.'

'I'd say, that's putting it mildly.' He stubbed his cigarette out in the ashtray. 'Look, when all this is over, we'll go somewhere special, I promise. Some place far away from all the danger. Somewhere as far away from the likes of Tom Lester and Željko Kovačić as is humanly possible.'

'It better be where the sun shines, Bozo! I've become accustomed to the sun shining from morning till night. With a breath of sea air blowing through my hair.' She reached over and lifted his chin so she could see his face. 'A girl gets used to this weather pretty quickly, my friend.'

Mason looked at her with moist eyes. What had he done? Bringing her into this world, his world. One of uncertainty, crime, unscrupulous characters, and even death. She didn't deserve any of this. He promised himself that even if he couldn't get himself away from this madness, he would get her out.

CHAPTER 39

Early the next evening in Dubrovnik's Old Town it was warm. Hemmed in by the high walls, there was little in the way of a breeze. The Stradun, or Main Street, was busy with the early evening tourists, adding to the clammy claustrophobic feel.

'Well, I promised I'd bring you for a meal,' Mason said as he and Sadie stood at the Onofrio water fountain, near the Pile Gate. He smeared the film of sweat from his forehead with a brush of his hand.

Sadie had borrowed a summer dress from Manuela for the occasion. Its colourful flowers with white background complemented her newly tanned skin. She'd also borrowed sandals and a small handbag from her host. A silver locket hung from her neck with a favourite picture of herself and her sister inside.

Mason was dressed in jeans, a white shirt, trainers, and a jacket that was a little too heavy for the conditions.

'You did, and it better be a good one, pal! I don't want some fast-food crap I can get on the high street at home.'

He turned a water fountain tap on, leaned down under it, and drank some refreshingly cold water. He then wiped away the excess water from his mouth with the back of his hand.

'I'm not sure you'll find better food anywhere. I've been to this restaurant a few times. It towers over the harbour at the other end of the Stradun. It has a great view of Lokrum, an island just off the coast.' He pointed up the main street. 'There's some great fish on the menu, but they do a good steak, too.'

'Great!' she enthused. 'I'm ravenous.'

'Good,' he said putting his arm around her waist and bringing her closer to him. She reached up and kissed him, smiling as she drew away.

'I was thinking we could call in at a bar first, have an aperitif, and then move on to the restaurant. What do you say?'

'Sounds good to me. Lead on gallant knight…'

Mason took Sadie by the hand and led her slowly down the Stradun. For a fleeting moment, he let his predicament fade from his mind. He was happy to be with Sadie walking in the early evening in the most beautiful of cities.

As they passed the ice cream parlour a large queue had formed. Sadie said she might want to call in after their meal if it wasn't too late.

'If you think you can eat anything after the meal, you're quite welcome to an ice cream,' Mason said. 'For me, this shop sells the world's best ice cream.'

Mason pointed to a bar further down the Stradun, 'That's the bar we're heading for. It's good for sitting at and watching the world go by.'

'People watching, you mean?'

'Yes,' Mason confirmed with a smile.

'Excellent! I like to people watch. It's just my thing on a warm summer's evening.'

Mason's cell rang, disturbing their conversation. He swiped the screen to answer. 'Mason.'

'Nick,' it was Luka. 'I have some important news for you.'

Mason stopped suddenly.

'Who is…' Sadie began but was interrupted by Mason holding up his hand.

'Go for it,' Mason said into the cell's mouthpiece.

There was a slight pause on the other end of the line before Luka began speaking again. 'Nick, it's bad news.'

'Go on.'

There was a further beat, then Luka said, 'I've just found out that Tom Lester is definitely in Dubrovnik. He's rented a penthouse in the Old Town.'

Mason wasn't surprised.

'It was bound to happen, Luka.' He scanned the higher apartments along the Stradun. Any one of them could be Lester's. 'Do you know anything specific?'

Sadie was motioning for Mason to let her in on the conversation.

He put his hand over the mouthpiece and mouthed, '*Lester's in town.*'

'Great! If anything's going to put me off my food, it's having that slimeball on the next table.'

'It'll be fine,' Mason assured her without any real conviction. 'Luka, sorry go on.'

'From what I can gather, he's been here for a day or so. Probably wanting to meet with Bogdanović, or maybe Željko.'

'I think Željko would have mentioned it yesterday when I was with him. The man who attacked me at the café was one of Lester's men, so it's no surprise he's in town.'

Mason had only had a brief conversation with Luka about the deaths the previous day. He had not wanted to discuss what had happened in front of Manuela. The less she knew, the better. It was bad enough that Sadie had to know.

'Nick,' Luka faltered slightly. 'I have more disturbing news.'

Mason brought the cell closer to his ear. 'Go on.' The concerned look on his face wasn't lost on Sadie. She put her arm around his waist and brought him closer to her.

'News on the street is that Željko and Bogdanović have cut Lester out of their drug deal. The talk is that they've decided he's surplus to requirements.'

'Shit! He is going to be pissed.'

'I'd say so,' agreed Luka. 'Look, Nick, it's none of my business, but if I were you, I'd get out of town as fast as I could.'

'Thanks for the advice, my friend, but that's not an option. This thing, whatever it is, needs sorting out once and for all. I'll be in touch. Keep well.' Mason swiped the cell phone dead.

'So what's happening?' Sadie asked urgently.

Mason said casually, 'Nothing now. We're going to have that drink and go about our business.'

Sadie wasn't convinced Mason was telling her everything but followed anyway.

They reached the bar and waited for someone to come and seat them.

'But what about Tom Lester?' she asked. 'He's one dangerous individual.'

'Yeah! He certainly is, and I think he just got a reason to be a whole lot more dangerous.'

A young waitress sauntered up to the dais in front of them. She had black hair that matched her uniform and a small cross dangling from her left ear. A warm summer had turned her skin a healthy colour. 'Would you like a seat?' she asked.

'Yes, please,' Mason confirmed.

'We're just having a drink,' Sadie added.

'Just one moment,' said the waitress, and turned away. Just as she did so, a bullet crashed through the top of the dais spraying splintered wood everywhere. Mason immediately shielded Sadie, pushing her low behind a table. 'Keep your head down!' He shouted. He surveyed the area with screams ringing out around the café.

People were running away in panic as if a bomb had gone off.

The waitress was on the floor clutching her arm, blood seeping through her fingers as she squeezed tightly. Her face had turned white with shock. As Mason crawled over to her a bullet flew over his head and smashed through the window of the bar behind him. A scream rang out from somewhere inside. He was able to reach a cotton napkin from the table and wrap it around the young waitress' arm above the wound.

'You'll be fine,' he assured. 'Stay down until someone comes to help.'

It crossed his mind that it was the first time he'd been on the Stradun and not seen a policeman. That's typical, he thought. Whenever you needed one, they're never around!

The girl whimpered, tears running down her cheeks. She couldn't find any words. Mason looked around and saw a young couple cowering behind a table beneath the gaping window.

'Come here,' he beckoned to the man.

The young man was obviously into fitness. His muscles stretched the fabric of his England football t-shirt. He held his partner's hand and they both inched towards Mason, keeping below the level of the tables. Immediately, the couple began to attend to the young waitress.

'My wife's a nursing assistant,' the man assured Mason. 'She knows what she's doing.'

'Good,' Mason said. 'Take care of her.'

Mason moved back to Sadie who had been watching from behind a table. Sitting beside her, he took his cell phone from his inside pocket and handed to her.

'Take this! I need to draw Lester away from here.'

'How do you know it's Lester?' she asked.

'Who else can it be? I don't know Bogdanović, and Željko has no reason to shoot the city up over me. No, it's got to be Lester! If I could just find out where he is.'

'What are you going to do?'

'Once I've located him, I can draw him away. I need you to get yourself back to Luka's. You'll be safe there.'

'Nick, that will be dangerous. Can't you just wait for the police to come and deal with it? He's shooting up a historic town full of tourists. They've got every reason to jail him.'

'I'm afraid, not.' He took the handgun from his waistband and asked, 'Have you ever seen the movie High Noon?'

'No,' she answered.

'Well, it's just struck noon and it's time to face the bad guys.'

'Except it's not noon, Nick. And you don't need to face up to anybody.' She wrapped her arms around him and hugged him tightly. 'We can get out of here, Nick. We just have to get out the back. We can easily escape. There's no need to put yourself in danger.'

Mason held her shoulders and pushed her back a little. He could feel her breath on his lips as he said, 'No, Sadie. It's time. Please do as I ask.'

She burst into tears.

'Please don't leave me here,' she begged.

'If there was any other way, I'd take it. But there isn't. Lester will always be after me, forever hovering over my shoulder. I must face him now.'

Sadie's breathing was heavy, and the tears streamed down her face. She realised that she couldn't talk Mason out of facing Lester. She could see in his face he was immoveable.

'What do you want me to do?' she asked resignedly.

'Go into the café and wait. Try and get out before the police arrive. You don't need to answer any silly questions from them. I'm going to distract Lester, get him away from here. Once I've dealt with him, I'll meet you at Luka's. I promise.'

She looked at the cell phone he had given her.

'Okay. What do I need this for?'

'So, I can contact you. To check you're safe.' He paused a beat and then asked, 'Are we clear?'

She looked him in the eye, the tears still evident on her face, 'Just to be clear, I think you're mad, but I'll do what you say.'

'Good! Now let's get you into the building.'

Inch by inch, they crawled into the café. A dead man lay on the café floor, blood spreading from a chest wound. Others cowered behind tables. Mason made sure Sadie was safe behind a wall at the back of the room before he left her.

When he got back to the café door that opened onto the Stradun a shot punctured the door casing above his head, wood splintering in all directions. Fortunately, none hit Mason or the other people cowering down behind the tables.

The English couple were still tending to the waitress who was crying into the chest of the nurse.

Mason eased himself out just enough so he could locate where Lester was firing from. He was pointing his gun, arm raised, from one of the side streets that they had passed earlier. Mason had to find a way to get him out into the open.

His luck was in. Suddenly, Lester was shunted out onto the Stradun surrounded by a bunch of men. He almost fell to the ground in the melee. They were shouting at each other in a foreign language, Mason guessed German as he recognised some of the words.

Lester turned to them grimacing and fired a shot into the group. One of the men dropped to the floor, dead in an instant. The other men ran back up the street, disappearing from Mason's view.

This gave Mason a chance. He lifted his gun and fired in Lester's direction. The bullet embedded itself in the corner of the wall next to Lester, fragmenting the centuries old stone. He ducked instinctively, looking in Mason's direction. He let off a couple of quick shots and ran off towards the fountain and the Pile Gate where Mason and Sadie had entered the Old Town.

CHAPTER 40

In Lester's wake, ducking in and out of confused tourists, Mason ran towards the fountain at the Pile Gate, gun in hand. As he arrived, a woman saw him with the handgun held in front of him and let out a scream. He stopped, immediately hiding the gun in the back of his waistband. It didn't stop the woman running behind the fountain away from Mason in a state of panic, dragging her two crying children with her. Others scattered in all directions in an effort to get away from the gunman.

Realising he was now out in the open with innocent tourists running for cover, Mason dashed over to the fountain and crouched down beside it, hoping the centuries old stone structure would give him some protection.

He was sure Lester had escaped from the Old Town. By now, he could be anywhere. A large taxi rank was situated just across the road from the Pile Gate. Alternatively, one of his drivers could have whisked him away. It was all guesswork for Mason. He just knew he had to find Lester, and quickly.

Mason rose slowly and inched his way to the inner gateway, finally reaching the gated opening. This was divided in two by a divider rope, one side for incoming visitors, the other for exiting ones. Judging by appearances, more were entering the Old Town than were leaving. Dusk always saw an influx of people coming into the historic area for their evening meals and entertainment, sometimes held in *Pred Dvoram* further up the Stradun.

A break in the people coming in afforded Mason an opportunity to exit without putting bystanders in danger. If Lester had picked a vantage point somewhere outside the Town, he could easily pick Mason off. He would have to be vigilant.

Standing at this first exit, he stayed close to the wall with the Pile Gate just in front. Steps rose between him and the Gate. A ramp rose to the right and back left, finally reaching the top of the stairs in front of him. He didn't know if this was a modern innovation allowing disabled people easier access, or whether it had always been there.

He opted to trace the ramp, staying close to the wall as he took one slow step after another. At the top on the right lay a small door. It appeared locked, old, and hardly used. As Mason approached, he gave it little attention and moved closer. Standing with his back in the doorway, he surveyed the scene from a safe vantage point. A trickle of people entered the Old Town from the Pile Gate, phones held up, taking photos.

It was at this point that, without hearing anything, Mason felt a hand grab his shirt collar from behind. He couldn't co-ordinate his movements with the force and strength of the person pulling at him and was dragged violently into a dark room. It took all his strength not to fall as he was slung into the dank space.

He was flung unceremoniously backward onto a chair. The chair would have fallen over under Mason's weight, but it was too close to the wall behind it. Mason hit his head on the rough stone and immediately regretted his amateurish pursuit of Lester. He should have been more observant. Just because the door looked unused didn't mean it was. If he survived, he swore an oath to himself that he'd be more observant in the future.

Suddenly, the room flooded with light causing Mason to shield his eyes. This was a mistake. Lester smacked his arms down with the butt of his handgun.

'Put your hands down! Keep them where I can see them,' he ordered.

Mason sat with his eyes struggling to adjust to the sudden burst of light, looking at the silhouette of the man who had been ultimately responsible for the killing of his father. The time had come. It was him or Lester!

'Sit back properly, with your hands on your head,' Lester

ordered.

As Mason settled as comfortably as he could on the wooden chair, he felt the gun dig uncomfortably into the small of his back.

Lester walked slowly towards him. 'Stay still, or I'll shoot you dead where you sit.'

'I'm all yours, as they say, Tom.'

Lester stood to one side of Mason and searched under the left side of his jacket and his pockets. Then moved to the other and did the same. Once he was satisfied Mason was unarmed, he stepped back and brought a chair closer, always keeping the gun pointing in Mason's direction. He sat down and stared at his captive for a moment.

Then, 'I know we've had a checkered relationship, Nick, but to be honest, you've really pissed me off this time.'

'Yeah?'

'Yeah,' Lester mimicked. He took a cigar out of his inside pocket and lit it. 'Forgive me for not sharing.'

'Apology accepted. I wouldn't want to deprive you. I know you like your Cubans.'

Lester took a deep drag from the cigar and, after a beat, asked, 'Where did all this go wrong, Nick? I mean, I gave you one simple job. Granted, I didn't know that job would entail you killing your long-lost sister. How could I know?'

'You're forgetting. You set your rottweiler, Kosinski, on me,' Mason reminded his former employer.

Insincerity cloaked Lester's response. 'I did. Sorry and all that. But how could I let you get away with all my money? I'd have been a laughing-stock. No, I couldn't let you take what was mine, Nick.'

Lester tipped some ash onto the blackened floor before continuing, 'And you'd have got away with it, wouldn't you? Unless Bevan hadn't come out here to do some work for me with my former mate, Željko.'

Mason knew that Željko had reneged on the deal with Lester but didn't want to say so, so he asked, 'What do you mean "former mate.'"

Lester took a deep drag from the cigar and contemplated his answer. Eventually, he said, 'Former mate because he has dumped me for Bogdanović. The two of them have united behind my back and made a deal. They've cut me out!' He spat the words out. 'The idiots think they can get the merchandise from here to the UK and onto the market without my involvement. Don't they know I'm the man who makes the deals? Both of them. They're seriously deluded!'

Mason could hear voices outside the door. People were passing by, completely unaware that he was being held at gunpoint only feet away. If he could just get to the door, he could make a run for it.

'You know crooks, Tom? They're not to be trusted.'

'That's true, Nick. Even Bevan who I thought was close.'

'Why did you have him killed Tom?'

'Simple.' Lester spat on the floor. 'Treachery. Can't abide it. I've had my suspicions for a while. But then he was seen with you. For all I knew, you two were plotting to bring me down, while all along he should have been paving the way for my deal with Željko.'

Lester had yet to tie Mason up or restrain him in any way. Either that was a mistake by his captor or a simple intention by him to shoot Mason dead where he sat.

'Do you mind if I have a smoke, Tom. It's stressful with you pointing that thing at me,' Mason said looking down the barrel of the gun.

'Go ahead. But, as they say in the movies, don't make any sudden moves.'

'I won't.'

Mason carefully took a pack of cigarettes out of his inside jacket pocket. He felt another twinge from the gun lodged in the back of his trousers but was careful not to give anything away. He couldn't believe Lester had been so lax in his search for weapons.' He gestured to Lester to give him a light. Lester reached over and lit Mason's cigarette.

'So, how do you know Bevan wasn't simply trying to bring me in?'

'I don't. But he was seen with you. You see, I've had a mole in Željko's organisation for a while.'

'Petar?'

'Yes, Petar. He reported that you and Bevan had been together and not informed Željko of this development. I knew he hadn't contacted me. If he had been intending to bring you in it was an unusual way of doing it. He had all the help he needed right here in Dubrovnik. My conclusions were simple, something was wrong. Besides, like I said, I'd had suspicions about him for a while. His heart didn't seem to be in the job anymore. It was easier to dispose of him and come out here myself.

There was a beat before Mason asked, 'So, what's your plan now?'

Lester inhaled deeply and then blew out a thick cloud of the smoke.

'I'm not sure you need to know, but I'll tell you anyway.' He paused for a moment, before continuing, 'I'm going to block all entry points Bogdanović and Željko plan to use. I know every detail of the British coast. Where and when people and contraband can be smuggled into the country. If I can't interrupt the arrival of their drugs, I'll make sure the border force has the information to do so.'

'Forgive me, Tom, but I don't know whether you watch the news, but the border force can't stop anyone coming into the country. They're both underfunded and useless, everybody knows it.'

'You've no need to worry your little head over such things, Nick. I know my way around. I have the politicians and police wrapped around my little finger. When I say I want something happening, it happens.' Lester allowed a little smile to cut across his face.

Mason knew that he had to think of something fast. He could still hear people passing the door through to the Old Town. If only he could take advantage of that in some way? But for now, he had to keep Lester talking.

After a lull, Mason confirmed, 'I killed your man at the harbour?'

'Retribution, was it?' Lester asked, unconcerned about Nesby's death.

'Retribution? Until he tried to kill me, I'd never met him.'

'Retribution for the death of your father.'

'Yes...'

The room's stench was seeping into Mason's pores and getting into his nose.

Lester held his hand up to stop Mason continuing.

'Nesby, the man you disposed of, had no specific instruction to kill your father. I certainly didn't order it, Nick. I'm being honest, here. I told Nesby to scare your father so that you'd return. Nothing more. Nothing less. He took that decision himself.'

'But if you hadn't sent this Nesby, my father would still be alive.'

'Spilt milk, Nick. Spilt milk. Your father would have died soon enough anyway. Did you see how ill he was?'

Mason threw his cigarette to the ground. He couldn't smoke anymore with the intense rage he felt rising in his chest. His heart was pumping hard, his temples pulsating with the fury inside him. And then, suddenly, an opportunity presented itself. The door was pushed in. A security guard began to speak but was stopped by a bullet from Lester's gun. It travelled clean through the guard's chest and lodged itself into the wall behind. He dropped lifeless to the floor.

Mason jumped from his seat and threw all his body weight into Lester who had stood and turned to shoot at the intruder. Both men crashed to the floor in a heap, the weapon dropping to the floor. Mason was instantly on top of Lester punching him as hard as he could, but without landing a debilitating blow.

Lester was able to throw Mason off with a combination of his feet and hands. Mason fell to the side, burning his hand on the cigar that now lay on the floor.

Lester took the opportunity to stretch for his gun, but before he could Mason had regained his composure and was hurling himself back towards his captor. They rolled on the floor, each trying to gain the ascendancy.

No one else had come round the door since the guard had been shot. If Mason could get to the door safely, he could then make his escape. He got hold of Lester, who was still trying to reach the weapon. Mason knew that if he let go his fate would be the same as that of the guard.

Lester, with all his energy managed to break free of Mason and get to his feet. Without turning towards Mason on the floor, he took a step and picked his weapon up.

Mason knew the game was up. Lester had got to his gun. Death was imminent. Then, he suddenly realised, his own gun was still in his waistband. Before his assailant could turn towards him, Mason had grabbed his gun and lifted it. As Lester turned, Nick fired. The bullet whistled passed Lester, who turned and ran out before Mason could let off a second round.

Mason got to his feet, pointing the gun towards the door. He crouched over the guard touching his neck, checking for signs of life. There were none.

He stood in the doorway, looking for Lester, but he wasn't there. Without delay, he ran to the Pile Gate exit. People were still streaming in for the evening's entertainment. The guard must have come independently. Perhaps he'd been doing his routine checks for the evening.

When Mason reached the road, through the tourists, he saw Lester violently dragging a taxi driver out of his car. The Englishman dumped the elderly Croatian driver unceremoniously on the floor and jumped into the driving seat, leaving the man on the pavement with other cab drivers crowding around. Lester made his exit at speed, a squeal of tyres marking his departure.

Mason ran to the taxi rank, bypassing the drivers who had come to the aid of their colleague and jumped into a still running Skoda Superb. It's availability light still flickered on and off as he sped off in pursuit.

Travelling up *Ul. Branitelja Dubrovnika* Mason could see Lester in the stolen white Mercedes. Weaving in and out of a succession of buses, Lester's car passed the Hilton Imperial a fraction of a second before Mason's. They continued travelling at pace, horns blaring all around.

Up in front, Lester pulled out from behind the single-decker Babin Kuk bus only to be confronted by another one coming in the opposite direction. The two bus drivers slammed their brakes down hard, just leaving enough space for Lester to slice through. Mason followed almost immediately, clipping the back end of his vehicle on the oncoming bus.

Lester made a hard right onto *Splitski put* taking little notice of the lights. Horns sounded all around. Mason had no choice but to do the same, experiencing the same reaction from the local traffic not used to two British drivers acting like lunatics on the road.

A T-junction greeted them at the lights and Lester took another right onto *Ul. Vladimira Nazora*, then a lean left onto *Ul. Pera Bakića*.

Mason wondered where Lester was heading. He can't have known the city that well, he'd only been here a short time. He checked his fuel gauge. Good. The cab driver must have filled up recently.

Up ahead, Lester took a left and got onto the *Magistrala*, heading north towards Split.

Mason, in his eagerness, put his foot on the pedal too hard and the back end of the Skoda slipped. He corrected the slip immediately and continued the chase. He picked up his speed and was now right behind Lester. He floored the accelerator, bumping into the rear of the Mercedes. He was close enough to see the driver in front jump in his seat on impact, clinging on to the steering wheel. This was possibly the first chase Lester had ever been involved in. Mason had to make sure it was his last.

The *Magistrala* was high above the coastline and below to his left Mason could see the cruise liners that had docked in that day below.

The highway was clear of most traffic. If Mason could overtake Lester, he'd have a chance of stopping him.

Just before they reached the Franjo Tuđman Suspension Bridge, Mason put his foot down again and pulled out onto the oncoming carriageway. Just as he was coming up side-by-side with Lester, a car that had come from Mason's blind side, up from the *Jadranska cesta*, clipped Lester's Mercedes pushing it into the chasing Skoda. Neither Mason nor Lester could stop their cars from spinning out of control. The cars circled and buffeted around until settling across the highway, almost blocking the whole road.

Lester was first out of his car. He began to run over the high bridge.

Mason found his door jammed shut. He couldn't get it open, no matter what he tried, pushing and kicking as hard as he could. He decided to give up and climbed over to the passenger side. With some extra force, the door opened. When he staggered out of the vehicle, the innocent driver from the other vehicle began remonstrating with him in Croatian. Mason held his hands up.

'Sorry. Sorry!'

The man was unconvinced and made a move towards Mason, grabbing him by the shoulders. Unable to shake him off, Mason pulled out his gun and pointed it up in the air. The man immediately cowered down and ran behind his own vehicle.

Mason looked along the bridge. Lester was already halfway across. He tucked the gun back into his waistband and gave chase, lungs burning. He hadn't been exercising much recently, just eating and drinking. If he survived this, he had to get back to the gym.

Lester was running in the middle of the road with cars screaming past him.

Mason caught him up at the northern side of the bridge. He reached out, almost grabbing Lester's jacket, but he was easily shrugged off. The second time, Lester was closer to the iron fence that protected cars from plunging into the Adriatic below, and Mason managed to get a grip. He pulled Lester back as hard as he could.

Lester swung out with his fist as he turned and caught Mason on the chin momentarily stunning his pursuer. Mason staggered back. Lester charged and ducked into Mason's stomach. They both crashed to the floor with Lester on top hitting out, Mason below striving to repel the onslaught.

Mason pushed the heel of his hand into Lester's face, forcing his head back, stretching his neck muscles close to breaking point. Lester's face screamed with the pain, still trying to punch at Mason. Eventually, he couldn't take the pain any longer. He grappled with Mason's hand, to force him away.

Lester's attention was now on defence instead of attack. It gave Mason a chance to throw him to the side. Lester rolled away.

Mason's body ached all over from the buffeting it had been put under. His lower back in agony from having the handgun pressed hard against the concrete floor. Using the fence, he managed to get up a fraction of a second behind Lester, who had already started his escape. As Lester began to run, Mason flung a leg out and caught Lester's trailing foot.

Lester spun around, losing his balance.

Mason watched on as Lester rotated like an out-of-control puppet, crashing into the barrier, and tumbling over. Mason quickly moved to the fence, stretching a hand out to the man who had spared no expense in trying to kill him.

Lester was holding on to a banister for his life. He knew what was below, the ocean. Almost two-hundred feet below. Realising Mason was looking down at him, he called out, 'Help me! Grab my hand.'

Lester's legs were swinging, trying to find a purchase on something. With one big heave, he let go of the rail with his right hand and reached for Mason's hand.

Mason refused to reach down further.

Lester grabbed back onto the banister.

'Get hold of me, you bastard! I'm going to fall.'

Instead of the fear that should have been visible on Lester's face, there was anger. Anger that he was not being obeyed.

Mason was leaning over the fence watching him. He mulled over whether he should save Lester or let him die. The man now begging for help had his father killed. He had killed Bevan, the man who had helped him and Ashley escape. He was responsible for all the deaths at the old people's home. He had tried to kill Sadie. He had probably contributed to the deaths of many more through his drug dealing. In all consciousness, Mason didn't care whether Lester lived or died.

Until Lester shouted, 'I've got money in my hotel room. You can have it all. Just help me up and it's a deal.'

Clarity washed over Mason. He could not deal with the devil himself. Reaching behind his back he lifted the gun from his waistband. The gun that Lester hadn't found during his cursory search. Pointing it at Lester, he saw the drug baron flinch.

'What the fuck! Stop playing games, Nick. Put that away! You have to help me!'

'I have to do what?'

'Help. You must help.' Lester was starting to lose his grip on the rail. 'I'm going to fall,' he said looking up at the gun.

Mason said, 'This from the man who had my father killed.'

'That wasn't me!' he pleaded. 'It was Nesby.'

'It was on your orders. You're looking at payback.'

'No! Please!' Lester begged.

'I think we've got a situation here, Tom,' Mason said matter of factly. 'You hanging there. Me holding the gun. Someone might call it, an invitation for revenge.'

Mason stared coldly looking into Lester's terror-filled eyes. He then squeezed the trigger.

The bullet created a red hole in the middle of Lester's forehead at the front, while shredding his skull at the rear. His body twitched violently, for a fraction of a second maintaining his grip on the railing, before releasing and twisting backwards like a rag doll.

To Nick, the fall happened in slow motion. He did not move his gaze until Lester's dead body hit the water, some two hundred feet below.

Mason peered down at the sea. Once he was happy Lester wasn't coming back to the surface alive, he replaced the gun in his waistband and turned away. His job was done.

Postscript

The restaurant was empty except for its owner, Željko Kovačić, who sat at his usual table at the back of the dining area. That morning's newspaper lay open in front of him, but his attention was elsewhere.

The solitude he was so fond of was broken by the new waitress. She was whistling as she came in from the kitchen, placing a tray of clean glasses onto the counter and beginning to shelve them.

Željko noted the difference between her and the previous incumbent, Petar. The boy always had an agenda, his mind always elsewhere. It was a trait which had ultimately cost him his life. But that was all water under the bridge, the restaurant owner thought. The new waitress had a different outlook. She was bright, able, outgoing. Plus, being in a foreign country was not a problem for her. His menu had an English translation and most of his customers spoke the language, anyway. In fact, Željko was glad he'd employed her.

'This bar needs music, Željko,' she told him as she finished putting the final two glasses onto the shelf.

The owner had no real reason to argue. He had always kept the restaurant quiet. It gave him the time and space to think. Much of his business empire was run from the very table he sat at. That empire had now developed into a multi-national drug import and export business. Thanks to the groundwork done by the Englishman, Lester, and his own hook-up with Slaven Bogdanović, he had become a major player in the importation of drugs into the United Kingdom. He congratulated himself with a slug of brandy.

'Bring the radio in from my office and play it, would you? But not too loud, please. I don't want to frighten the customers away.'

'What customers?' Her tone mocking, as she left to fetch the radio.

At that moment, Željko's attention was caught by the first customer of the day coming into the restaurant. Dressed in a heavy suit and plain tie, Željko guessed the customer was English. The big, clean-shaven man took his jacket off and sat down at a window table. He paid no attention to Željko as he perused the menu.

The waitress returned with the radio. Noticing the customer, she placed it on the counter and approached him, notebook in hand.

'Can I help you, sir? Or would you like a little more time?' she asked, taking a pencil from behind her ear.

'I'd like a local beer, please.'

'Bottle or draught?'

'A bottle.'

'Of course.'

The waitress retreated to get the drink for the patron. She couldn't help thinking that he looked familiar.

Željko hadn't taken his eyes from the man. On many occasions he had people coming into his place asking awkward questions, or simply attempting to intimidate him. He could smell a hoodlum or a policeman, they were both the same, within a hundred metres. This was the latter, he was sure. He rose and approached the customer.

'Welcome! Welcome,' he said to the customer with a slight bow. 'I am the owner of this restaurant. My name is Željko. I think this may be your first visit to my humble establishment?'

'It is. In fact, it's my first visit to Dubrovnik.'

'I hope you like our city. I would suggest a visit to *Stari Grad*, the Old Town, it's beautiful.'

'I may just do that.'

The waitress returned with the customer's drink. Before she had chance to retreat, the Englishman introduced himself.

'My name's Phil Grimes.'

AN INVITATION FOR REVENGE

'It's good to meet you Mr Grimes. We are glad to have you as our guest. Our waitress, here, will be happy to help as much as she can.'

'I'd like that.' He stared straight at the waitress and asked, 'Would it be possible for me to speak to her for a moment? I could buy you both a drink.'

The waitress warily backed off a step. Where did she know him from?

Realising her discomfort, Željko sat opposite the visitor and asked, 'And why would you want to do that?'

The Englishman took a drink from the bottle and wiped his mouth with the back of his hand, the sweat mark under his arm evident to the Croat. He then reached into his jacket pocket and slid his police identity card onto the table for both to see.

'Because I think she's Sadie Kellerman. A person of interest in the investigation of multiple murders at a care home back in England.'

That's it! Sadie remembered seeing him on Mason's cell phone when they were coming out to Dubrovnik.

'You intrigue me,' Željko said, rubbing his chin. 'When were these murders committed, if I might ask?'

'A few weeks ago,' Grimes answered, taking a pull from his e-cig.

'Oh, that's a shame! I was hoping to hear lots of details.' The Croat looked up at the waitress, smiling. 'Alas, we can't help you. Maria has been here for the last six months. I employed her as a favour to a very good friend of mine.'

'Is it possible for "Maria" to sit with us? The drinks would be on me.'

'What do you say, Maria? Shall we sit with this nice Englishman? He's offering free drinks. It's up to you...'

The waitress reluctantly nodded. She turned and said, 'I'll get the drinks.'

'Please get a fresh bottle for our guest as well, please,' Željko said. 'He looks like he needs the refreshment.'

Grimes wiped his brow with a stained handkerchief.

When the waitress had placed the drinks down and seated herself, Željko urged Grimes to begin.

The policeman took a drink from the bottle and, wood creaking, leaned back in his chair. He then began to outline what had happened at the Lynne Residential Home and to another resident who was killed at a local park. He gave a brief description of the investigation he had led into both murders.

'If I may interrupt for one moment, Mr Grimes?' Željko asked.

Grimes nodded, taking a hit from his e-cig.

'What has all this got to do with Maria here?'

Grimes wiped the sweat from his brow once more. The waitress winced as she caught a whiff of sweat coming from his direction.

'I think Sadie here…' Grimes began to answer but Željko cut him off.

'Maria! You see,' he pointed at a name tag on the waitress's chest. 'Her name is Maria.'

'As you say, Maria.' Grimes paused for a beat before continuing. 'I think she was there when the killing took place in the park. I also suspect she has some sort of connection with Tom Lester, a gang leader killed here in Dubrovnik recently.'

The waitress tucked her hair behind her ear and then sunk a large swallow of the brandy she had poured herself. It took all her strength to stop her hands from quivering. How the hell had this man found her?

'You provide no proof, Mr Grimes. Whereas I can supply all the documents I need to confirm that this is, in fact, Maria, a young lady who has been on my payroll for months. And your connections? It is simple to connect someone with anyone.' He waved his arm as if wafting a fly away, 'If you have a desire to do so.'

'Try this…' Grimes took a drink before beginning. 'Sadie, sorry *Maria*, worked at the Lynne Residential Home. She was caring for William Mason when he was killed in the park, but somehow escaped. I think with Mason's son, Nick. Nick Mason, we know had worked for Tom Lester at various times. We also know that he was out here, as was Lester.'

'All of this sounds very interesting. But you haven't confirmed that this Sadie is wanted for anything. Only that she is a, what did you call her? A 'person of interest'.'

'Yes. That's it. But if I can talk to her, I'm sure she would be able to fill in a few gaps we have in the investigation.'

'Gaps?' Željko asked.

'Yes, gaps. For instance, we still don't know who or why the killings took place. In fact, one of my colleagues, Marc Ferguson, was murdered during the investigation. We think Ferguson may have had some dealings with Tom Lester. That's still being investigated by a separate team.'

'It seems to me that you don't know very much Mr Grimes. This trip, I'm afraid, appears to be somewhat of a fool's errand for you. We have no information that might be of any help.'

Grimes hesitated, fidgeting with his e-cig, before imploring, 'Look! I need help. I was the SIO in charge. That's the Senior Investigating Officer. When my investigations drew a blank, I was ditched. In fact, they're pensioning me off. If I could confirm a few things with Maria, I will get up and walk out of here and you'll never hear from me again.' The Croat and the waitress glanced at each other. He paused a beat. 'OK, I'm going to take a leak. It will give you two time to decide whether you want to help me to solve this crime or not. I promise that whatever you say, I will not give any information up that might lead to you.'

Grimes drained his bottle of beer and went to the bathroom.

When he was safely out of ear-shot, Sadie exclaimed, 'Shit! Željko, what do I do? If *he* can find me, anyone can.'

'Sadie, it sounds like they have most of this worked out. We just have to keep you safe and protect my business.'

'I told you I wanted no part of your dodgy business dealings.'

'Sadie. I made a promise that you will be clean; and you will be. I think that you can answer some questions without any fear from this man. I wasn't joking when I said I could provide evidence to protect you. What do you say? Answer the questions and get him off your back, or maybe have someone else coming to look for you?'

'Are you really sure this is what I should do?'

'Just keep it simple. In fact, I'll do the talking.' The Croat turned and saw the policeman returning.

Grimes sat down enquiringly. 'So, what's your answer?'

'You have a couple of questions.' Željko confirmed. 'Maria will nod or shake her head. When she has had enough, she will return to her duties behind the bar. Is that satisfactory?'

Grimes thought for a moment, then nodded. 'It is.' He looked straight at the girl who called herself Maria. 'Is your real name Sadie Kellerman?'

Sadie nodded hesitantly.

'Good. We're getting somewhere.' He took a drink from the new bottle, then asked, 'Do you know Tom Lester?'

Sadie shook her head.

'Do you know Nick Mason?'

Sadie looked at Željko before responding, and then nodded confirmation.

'Did Lester have anything to do with the Lynne deaths?'

She nodded again, clearly feeling the heat. She answered for the first time.

'Nick told me Lester's men killed everyone at the Home.'

Grimes nodded.

'What about Mason? Did he have anything to do with the murders?'

Sadie stood up and stiffened, the chair tumbling over behind her.

'Nick had nothing to do with those murders!' she blurted out, fighting back tears, before turning away and rushing into the back room.

'I think you have the information you need, Mr Grimes.' Željko said. 'But I warn you. If Maria is dragged into any investigation related to Nick Mason or this Tom Lester character, I will hold you personally responsible. And you need to be aware, my reach is far and wide.'

Grimes took a drink. 'I have no intention of pursuing Sadie

Kellerman. As I said, I'm off the case. She is safe from all areas of the investigation. I just wanted to dot a few 'i's and cross a couple of 't's. She has nothing to fear from the police.'

'I'll drink to that,' Željko said, raising his brandy and taking a drink.

Grimes put his coat on, dropped his e-cig into a pocket, and left without another word.

Sadie returned to the table and sat next to Željko.

'So, am I safe?' she asked.

'Yes. Just keep your head down and do your job.'

'I can't reach Nick on his cell. I'd like to know he is safe too.'

'He'll be in touch when he wants to be. But be assured. He is safe. Now, I have something for you. Come with me.' He led Sadie to the bar and opened the draw underneath. Lifting a small box out, he passed it to Sadie. 'This is for you, from Nick.'

Sadie tentatively opened the box. She lifted Mason Senior's pipe out.

'Would he have left this for you if he had no intention of coming back?' Željko asked.

Fighting back tears, Sadie said, 'No.'

'Of course not.' He lifted Sadie's chin and looked her straight in the eye. 'Now take the day off. Go see Manuela. Go out and have a drink. Eat. Relax. Enjoy the beautiful city of Dubrovnik.'

The End

Thank you for reading this book. Please take a moment to comment and rate this book on Amazon.

Printed in Great Britain
by Amazon